Praise for *Not Yours to Kee*

"One missing baby. A missing woma turns. In this heartfelt and heart-pounding domestic suspense, I found myself racing to the breathtaking conclusion. A sensational debut."

—Rea Frey, #1 bestselling author of *Don't Forget Me* and *The Other Year*

"A thought-provoking look at the secrets that lie beneath the surface of seemingly perfect lives, *Not Yours To Keep* is a slow-burn that pays off with a thrilling end. Ideal for readers, like me, who enjoy a peek inside the heads of morally gray characters who find themselves in 'what would you do' moments."

—Jen Craven, author of *The Baby Left Behind*

"With high-stakes emotion and pulse-pounding suspense, *Not Yours To Keep* will have you turning pages well past your bedtime... In her debut novel, Zelly Ruskin writes full-throttle drama with a tender touch."

—Katie Sise, best-selling author of *Open House* and *We Were Mothers*

"Electric and haunting. A taut, perfectly paced thriller that will surprise and satisfy. Ruskin is a writer to watch."

—Taylor Larsen, author of *Stranger, Father, Beloved*

"Zelly Ruskin's ability to combine her career and personal experience with fertility issues and adoption procedures into the fictional mystery *Not Yours to Keep* makes for a compelling read. This debut novel will both rivet and educate couples facing such life-changing dilemmas and decisions."

—IndieReader

NOT YOURS TO KEEP

A Novel

Zelly Ruskin

She Writes Press

Published 2024
Printed in the United States of America
Print ISBN: 978-1-64742-724-5
E-ISBN: 978-1-64742-725-2
Library of Congress Control Number: 2024909007
For information, address:
She Writes Press
1569 Solano Ave #546
Berkeley, CA 94707

Interior Design by Kiran Spees

She Writes Press is a division of SparkPoint Studio, LLC.

To my children

You are my strength, courage, and heart.

Author's Note/Content Warning:

While I have strived to create a story that resonates and engages, as you would expect with any domestic suspense, certain elements within the narrative might evoke strong emotions that could be triggering for some readers. As you immerse yourself in this suspenseful journey, please be aware that it references fertility, miscarriage, childbirth, teen sex, child sexual abuse, addiction, and mental health issues. If the themes raised in the book affect you or someone you know, please reach out to someone you trust for support, or a trust-worthy support group/organization.

ONE
Billie

The at-home stick Billie grabbed at CVS yesterday was about to determine whether she'd be a mom or confirm her fate to be an infertile adoption specialist with painful personal insight into her clients' plight. She'd made herself wait the whole night to try it because the results were most accurate first thing in the morning. As night faded and a hazy sepia tone spread over Boston's little suburb of Millpoint, Billie could see outlines of the unlit houses nearby. Besides the neighbor's tabby cat crossing her backyard, she seemed to be the only one awake at five in the morning.

She'd been reorganizing the spare room since three. She pushed the reading lamp another inch to the right on the eucalyptus-colored nightstand, then fluffed the winter-mint-and-peach-patterned shams and accent pillows. About eighteen months ago, she had decorated the room with the painted blush walls to highlight the centerpiece hanging between the windows: a floating glass frame with pressed pink roses, peach orchids, Queen Anne's lace, and eucalyptus leaves. Her bridal bouquet. Billie gently touched the smooth frame. Her mother created the piece of art, concealing her signature and the date, June 2010, under a flower petal.

After two years, Billie still found new shapes and textures when she looked at it. Made bittersweet by the loss of her mother, she cherished the wedding memories, especially the image of her, Tyler, her mother, and her in-laws laughing in front of the Parker House, unable to oblige the photographer's quest for a serious-looking family portrait. Billie had known she wanted Tyler's babies as soon as they started dating. She'd fallen in love with the nurturing, jovial way he interacted with the young patients at the children's hospital where they'd volunteered. She'd adored the way the kids, no matter how sick, lit up when he arrived. And later, after they got engaged and were looking to buy a house, he was the one who made sure there were enough rooms for their future children. There'd been no doubt in her mind that Tyler was going to be an amazing father.

Now, with sixty seconds before the result of the pregnancy test would be clear, Billie worried that, at thirty-two, she'd already waited too long. The couples she worked with often blamed age for their fertility issues. Because of her work, she dealt with the impact of infertility every day. The longer they'd tried, the harder she hoped it wouldn't be her and Tyler's fate.

Billie remembered the shared anticipation one year ago, as she and Tyler sat on the edge of the bed holding hands, waiting for the minutes to tick by. Then he'd counted to three, so they'd look at the results together. They'd both laughed and cried when they saw the plus sign and then made love. In the six hours they'd waited for a nurse appointment at the gynecologist's office, they'd dared to turn their dreams into plans. Each soared with confidence as Tyler went to work and she went for an official pregnancy test. Billie's gynecologist, who she'd referred to for the first time as her OB, had confirmed the pregnancy.

The cramping and bleeding began within twenty-four hours. With it came the loss and grief that eased over time but hadn't been forgotten. The fear that it would happen again was still tangible.

Although their spontaneous newlywed sex life had remained intact, there'd been a collective holding of the breath every twenty-eight to thirty days. The disappointment of not being pregnant had become more difficult to shrug off every month.

When the timer went off, Billie slowly opened the guest bathroom door, looked at the little indicator window on the pregnancy dipstick, and rushed down the hallway.

TWO
Anne

Anne set an old plastic saucer filled with water under her building's fire escape stairs and waited. In a few short minutes, Thing 1 and Thing 2, the twin black-and-brown tabby cats she'd befriended, poked their heads around the corner. Thing 1 looked wary, but Thing 2, the bolder feline, paid her no mind as the duo gracefully crept to the bowl. Boston was experiencing a May drought, and the cats appreciated the fresh, cool liquid. Thing 2 licked his paws while Thing 1 took his turn to lap at the water. Then, when they'd had their fill, the cats sauntered back to the alley, their tails raised high.

Animals had always seemed comfortable around her, and she preferred them to most humans. When she was in high school, Mama Sue said she was a natural with their goat and chicks and encouraged her to study to become a vet technician after graduation. It wasn't Mama Sue's fault her dream never came true. Mama Sue was like a fairy godmother. She'd sheltered Anne and her mother when they needed a place to live. She'd always put Anne's needs first.

Before the fall semester began at the community college, Anne had worked as a day camp counselor. Though she'd enjoyed it, the little girls in her group had told their mothers she stared at them and hugged them too long. The mothers had complained to the camp director, who, in turn, had several talks with her. She'd tried to rein in her compulsion to understand what it would be like to be one of their mothers, to know how it felt to hold a four-year-old. It took a lot of energy to stop gazing at them, imagining one of them was really hers. After she got fired, she waitressed, but it didn't last long. Whenever she waited on tables with little girls, she would drop trays and knock into customers as she looked for the port-wine birthmark that would identify her baby.

Anne walked a couple of steps to her apartment, then went back for the cat bowl. She'd forgotten to take it in a few times, and her landlord threatened to evict her if she continued to feed "them vulgar strays." She added the saucer to the pile of dishes in the sink and heated the teapot on the stove.

Despite losing her jobs that summer fifteen years ago, she'd begun taking college animal science classes in the fall. She'd liked them and believed she'd succeed in a career working with animals until the afternoon she and Mama Sue went to buy groceries. She'd followed a sweet little voice's rendition of "The Itsy Bitsy Spider" to aisle three. A beautiful toddler with creamy, dimpled cheeks was sitting in a shopping cart between the shelves of cereals on the left and baking goods on the right. The little girl's smile broadened, and her eyes seemed to dance when she saw Anne looking at her. She understood, now, that the child had been too young to be her baby, but at the time she hadn't slowed down to think. The pull was relentless. She felt a connection. The child's mother yelled for security when Anne pushed up the little girl's sleeve to check for the special birthmark.

She'd sprinted out of the supermarket, and Mama Sue chased after her, as best her pudgy body allowed. She pushed Anne into the car and sped them away, turning into an empty lot when she thought they were out of danger. Anne could still feel her fairy godmother's warm body embracing her and hear her soothing shushing.

"It isn't good for you here," Mama Sue had said. "The community is too small, and even after five years, it's got too many triggers for you."

"I only wanted to look at her arm. I really thought it might be her. I won't do it again, Mama. I swear."

"You don't mean to, I know. But you're not strong enough yet. We must make some changes. You need to get out of this town. It'll be better for you, you'll see."

When the kettle whistled, Anne poured the boiling water into a teacup, adding one of the generic tea bags she'd pocketed from some convenience store's condiment station. Sitting on the olive-colored love seat she'd rescued from a dumpster years ago, she steeped the bag in a mindless rhythm while Willow the Weatherwoman pointed to different areas of storm clouds on the map behind her.

"This just in." It was obvious from the way the announcer paused and shifted his eyes that he was listening to someone in an earpiece. The screen switched to a live shot on the steps of a downtown Boston courthouse. A smartly dressed legal team was making a statement about a high-profile case they'd won.

Anne reached for the clicker, but before she hit mute, the camera lens zoomed in on one lawyer standing behind the podium, and she froze. An icy wave washed through her, and she paused the screen. Standing now, she looked hard at the chin and then the eyes, which looked right back at her. The shock pressed upon her. The teacup's narrow ear slipped from her grip. Kneeling in front of the TV screen, she outlined the shape of his face with her finger. With each stroke, images and thoughts she'd never wanted to resurface swirled around her. She knew that face.

THREE
Tyler

Tyler's parents had insisted he and Billie spend their second anniversary weekend at the family's vacation house at Lake Sunapee. They'd left after dinner to avoid summer traffic, but even on a Thursday it still took almost three hours to get there from Millpoint. Billie had slept most of the drive and woke when the interior lights came on. Tyler smoothed her hair. "You were conked out."

"This growing a human thing is tiring, and we've only just started," she said.

It had only been a week since Billie jumped on top of him while he was sleeping and shouted, "It's positive, it's positive!"

Tyler popped the trunk and pulled out their suitcases, expecting Billie would remove the bags of groceries she'd packed for the weekend. Instead, she dug through the items until she found a bag of cherry Twizzlers and tossed a handful into her mouth.

"You like licorice now?"

Billie raised her hands. "Impulse buy."

"What else is going to change?" Tyler took the crumpling brown paper bags from the trunk. "Are you going to turn into one of those alien pregnant people who demand pickles with peanut butter and whipped cream in the middle of the night?"

"Oh geez, that sounds nasty. Promise you'll hold me hostage if I get cravings like that."

"It's going to be some kind of fun these next eight months," Tyler said, and laughed.

Early on their second day at the lake, Tyler woke Billie to watch the sunrise together. Afterward, she slipped into the shower with him and snuggled against his back.

"Hiya, handsome."

Morning showers had always been their thing, though bathing was rarely part of the equation. Hot water cascaded over his head, splashing her as he turned to kiss her.

"Best two years of my life." He kissed her again.

"Mine too," she said.

He held her hips and lifted her as she wrapped her legs around him, but he quickly put her back down.

"I swear, your anniversary gift should've been a notarized doctor's note permitting you to make love to me." She soaped up a loofah and handed it to him. "Do my back?"

Tyler was scrubbing shampoo into a thick lather while she rinsed off. She had an impish twinkle in her eye when she opened the shower door to get out and reached for the shower faucet.

"Don't even think about it." He held a handful of suds, prepped to retaliate if she flipped the water temperature to cold.

"Lucky for you, I need food. I'll make us breakfast."

"How about western omelets?" Billie was slicing green and red peppers when Tyler joined her after his shower. He sat on an island stool, admiring her ease around the kitchen, finding everything she needed like she cooked there every day. She'd always been comfortable here, and with his rowdy relatives, who usually joined them.

His grandparents originally owned the land and built the house. They'd passed it down to his mother and aunt, fifty-fifty. Tyler remembered the smell of sawdust and the toy construction helmets he and his cousin Charlie wore when their families remodeled the place and created an addition to make space for them all. The kids' rooms were on the main floor. He and Charlie had artfully used the Jack and Jill bathroom to torture Charlie's sisters by hiding behind the shower curtain, booby-trapping the door, and often sneaking into their bedroom to scare them while they slept.

Billie passed him his eggs and a bottle of Tabasco. "What are you thinking about?"

"That I owe my mother an apology and a thank-you for putting up with me as a kid."

"She's told me many stories about you," Billie said with a laugh. "Don't worry, there'll be fair payback when our mini-you comes along."

Her words struck him. *How can someone like me be responsible for teaching, influencing, and protecting a new human?*

"You know, your mom believes this is a baby-making weekend," Billie said. "I've never known anyone more tenacious about having grandchildren than your parents. Your mother asked when the babies are coming the minute we said 'I do.' And your father never fails to mention you'll be the end of the family line if we don't have a son soon."

"Maybe we shouldn't jinx anything. Let's not tell them, or anyone else, until after the first trimester."

"Damn pragmatist. I don't trust myself not to give us away. Especially to your mom."

"My mother is probably a direct Boston town crier descendant. The news will travel across the state in seconds. They can't know."

Tyler shook the hot sauce onto his omelet a little too hard, questioning if he should be allowed to be a father. After all these years, he still didn't feel he deserved it.

Tyler dragged the kayaks from the water onto their small private beach while Billie carried the paddles. They'd spent the morning paddling to the smallest of the three islands in the middle of the lake and back. He squinted as he looked directly into the sun. It was in the noon position.

"We stayed out longer than I intended." He checked if Billie showed signs of discomfort. "I shouldn't have let you do something so strenuous."

"I'd have quit and made you rescue me if I'd needed to. Stop being such a worrywart and come rest with me on the dock."

After Tyler rubbed sunscreen on her back, Billie lay on the towel, looking like she was lying on a soft downy bed rather than rough wood boards. It felt hard and uncomfortable to him, but he closed his eyes and listened to the water lapping at the dock piling. The overall stillness around them made him miss the usual chaos and noise when his relatives were together at the house.

He watched puffy white clouds move across the light blue sky, sometimes colliding and reforming. "My cousins and I used to lie here when we were young. On nice days like this, if you stayed still and stared up at one spot, the clouds' motion created the illusion you were lying on a drifting boat."

Tyler looked over at the tree-bordered yard above the strip of sand. It had a handful of Adirondack chairs, some facing the water and some around the firepit he and his father had built. He thought about all the nights the fire crackled while the family sat around it playing charades. It had never been the same since Charlie died. His lupus diagnosis seventeen years ago had changed the family forever. Tyler sat up and let his feet dangle over the dock's edge. But then, if it hadn't been for Charlie's illness, he might never have met Billie.

He'd always told himself he volunteered with the kids Dr. Pearse treated to honor Charlie by making patients like him feel better. But did he volunteer to lessen his guilt for not saving his cousin?

"The night we met at the charity dinner for Dr. Pearse's foundation . . . It doesn't seem fair that I'm only here with you because I failed him," Tyler said.

Billie sat up and rubbed his back. "His body rejected the kidney. You must know there wasn't anything more you could do. None of it's your fault, Ty. You couldn't give him your kidney. No one can blame you for it."

"I know. For a long time, I resented his parents for not saving him, not protecting him. I get it was childish. But I was sixteen, and that's how it felt. Sometimes it bubbles back up, only now it's even worse because I know everything possible was done, but it wasn't enough."

Billie moved so close beside him he could feel her thigh's sun-baked skin stick to his own. He finally looked directly at her.

"What if I can't protect our child either?"

"I'll tell you what I always tell my clients. If you're worried about being a good parent, you already are one." She kissed his cheek and laid her head against his shoulder.

This should have made him feel better, but Billie wouldn't have said it if she knew the truth about him.

"What if the baby gets something genetic, like lupus?" It was the only valid reason he could come up with for reconsidering having the baby—besides that he wasn't the man Billie thought he was.

"You can't think like that. We both want this child, and we'll love him or her no matter what. Won't we?" She looked at him with wide, questioning eyes and Tyler regretted scaring her. If he were a better person, he'd tell her everything right now. But he didn't know if he could cope with seeing her looks of love transform into disgust.

"Of course we will," he said, unconvinced. He stood, wiped some dirt off his shorts, and then pulled Billie up next to him. "This is getting too morose for a romantic weekend. What d'ya say we drive into town for lunch and then homemade ice cream, with or without pickle sprinkles on top?"

"Stop saying pickles. Although bacon would be tasty." Her hair caught in the wind as she beamed at him, and Tyler soaked in his wife's carefree beauty.

FOUR
Billie

Before they left Lake Sunapee, Billie and Tyler walked the road around the lake. She stopped as their property came into view. "Can we stand here a minute? I feel like I'm in a peaceful painting with the lake and mountains behind the cedar beach house." She leaned against Tyler, sighing when he put his arms around her and clasped his hands over her abdomen. She had everything she'd ever wished for.

The sun was bright, and birds she couldn't see were harmonizing the morning after their trip. Billie took a breakfast bar to eat in the car on her way to the florist. She usually bought white carnations to show her love and affection, but this time she'd asked for blue irises, for hope and faith.

A few miles down the road from the flower shop, Billie turned into the entrance of the Greenbriar Cemetery. Despite the well-tended landscape, designed with a similar ambiance to the Boston Common, she always felt a sorrowful chill as she drove in. Ahead of her was a tangle of narrow roads and walking paths woven through rows of old gray gravestones and modern marbled ones. A visitor could lose themselves for days in there if they weren't careful.

Billie parked by a red granite headstone with a matching built-in bench and walked up the gravel path until she came to an old elm tree at the base of a hill. There she knelt before the modest headstone and brushed loose dirt and grass clippings off her parents' grave markers. Her father had died in a car accident when she was fifteen, so his marker was tarnished, while her mother's still held its polished brass finish.

"You're going to be grandparents." Billie arranged the bouquets in the in-ground flower holders. "*Grand-mère et Grand-père*," she said in French. "I'm sure you'd have liked those names. The doctor thinks I'm about six weeks." She'd felt shortchanged when Dr. Zambor insisted on waiting two more weeks to do an ultrasound. Zambor was old-fashioned, but her explanation was sensible—they'd see more and get better information at eight weeks. Billie touched her abdomen and continued speaking to her parents' graves. "Once we get past thirteen weeks, I'll relax, but it's different from last time. I can tell."

This time she'd have the joyful discomfort of her belly expanding until she couldn't see her swollen ankles, she'd waddle when she walked, and, this time, she'd feel the quickening—the baby's earliest movements—and later she'd sing to him or her when they kicked.

Sitting quietly for a while, she took in the gentle rustling of branches in the breeze and the far-off sounds of shovels striking stones to prepare for a new grave. She traced the letters and dates on her parents' markers, then blew a kiss before walking away.

There was never a steady stream of new clients in the adoption world, especially birth mothers, so it was a slow day at the office. Billie took advantage of the current ebb of appointments to work on the adoption unit's policy manual her supervisor had asked her to update. Her coworker, Paige, came into her office carrying a bag from the deli down the block.

"One turkey, Muenster, lettuce, tomato, onions, and Russian on a spinach wrap." Paige placed it on a napkin on Billie's desk, and then she pulled out a small bag with flames pictured on it. "And one bag of barbeque chips." She held it up and looked at Billie with one arched eyebrow thick with questions.

"Why are you looking at me like that?"

"Are we stress eating?" Paige took her own sandwich from the deli bag and curled into one of the client chairs. "Other than an occasional salad, I can't think of a single time you've had real lunch, if you bothered to stop for lunch at all." She pushed her powder-pink glasses higher on the bridge of her nose. "I can give you fifty minutes of therapy, free of charge."

It had been hard for Billie not to tell her secret, especially last week, when Paige had asked about her anniversary weekend. The warm, trusting yet unlikely friendship the duo had developed amused Billie. Where she was department store chic in her fitted pantsuits, dresses, and pumps, Paige was bohemian thrift in long, gauzy skirts and Birkenstocks. She'd been raised by die-hard hippies.

"Thanks. What's happening with the wedding?" Billie asked. She finished her meal as Paige described the plans for the small free-spirited July gathering at her parent's incense-infused backyard. Nothing at all like Tyler and Billie's conservative Parker House event.

"Did you come to an agreement about changing your name?"

"Still debating. I could take his, but professionally I think it makes sense to keep my maiden name like you did. I might hyphenate. We've also talked combining."

"Making you what, Paige Rellertinger?"

"You see my dilemma? Shoot, it's twelve forty. Are you coming?"

"I want to finish the paragraph I'm working on first. I still have time."

"Very daring. Must be the chips," Paige said. "I'll save a seat for you."

"Your restroom humor seems to have stalled."

"Ha! Good one." Paige tossed her food wrappers in the trash and stood in the doorway. "Don't wait much longer. The bathroom troll arrives at one."

"I just found out her name is Rosa, and she works downstairs in home health care."

"There's a functioning ladies' room on the second floor. Why does she always use ours?"

"I have no clue."

"Got to go. No pun intended," Paige said. "Troll time."

It was the ultimate hypocrisy for social workers, people whose duty it is to be objective while supporting and assisting families, and treating their clients' mental and emotional health, to refer to someone as "the troll." But against this righteous thought, Billie had to agree that the woman, Rosa, was unpleasant to be around.

Rosa was a giant-sized woman you could smell before you saw her. Her short black-gray hair was matted and speckled with crumbs of dandruff. Large acne-scarred cheeks and hairy moles accentuated her round face. The stained short-sleeved blue shirt she wore every day insufficiently covered a bulging, rubbery belly that hung over her tight polyester plaid pants. Until a few days ago, no one on the third floor knew her name or even her job. They only knew never ever to get trapped in the elevator with her and, above all, to stay away from the bathroom at ten and one. Rosa had an astonishingly regular constitution. Every morning and every afternoon, she thudded down the hall, pushed her way into the ladies' room, and slammed herself into a stall. And there she would sit, and grunt, and wheeze, and sit. Unsuspecting women would come flying out of the bathroom, gasping for air.

It was ten to one when Billie looked at the desk clock. The chair snagged on the carpet as she pushed it back to dash to the bathroom. She only had minutes to get there before the bathroom troll arrived. *Rosa*, she reminded herself.

She checked both stalls, then moved into the furthest one. She took a quick pee and wiped herself in a hurry, but then she noticed a blood spot on the toilet paper square. *Shit*, she thought, *I have my period. I can't have my period, I'm pregnant!* Billie wiped again, to be sure. "Don't do this," she said aloud. Feeling like she was sinking into the darkest, suffocating depths of nothingness, she sat back on the bowl for support.

Grunt, sniff, wheeze, SLAM! The walls of the stalls shook. *Are you fucking kidding me right now?* Billie felt a rush of heat wash over her body as perspiration formed on her neck. She rolled an enormous wad of toilet paper into her underwear and took a second wad to cover her nose and mouth before escaping into the hall. At her desk, she grabbed the phone. She started telling the doctor's receptionist her plight before realizing the woman had said, "Please hold," when she answered.

Billie assured the doctor she felt well enough to drive there on her own. There was no way she was taking an ambulance if she wasn't gushing, but she was also afraid of what could happen while getting to her car. A cab was the smartest move, and it was faster than waiting for Tyler. *Tyler!*

She used her calmest voice when she called him. "Honey, I don't want to alarm you, but there's a little bit of bleeding." Billie choked on the words.

"Oh . . . kay."

The uncertainty in his voice was difficult to bear. "I'm going to Dr. Zambor's office now."

"I'll meet you there."

There was no time to feel or react. The only thing on her mind was her blueberry-sized baby who, against her better judgment, she'd already imagined naming Ryan if it was a boy or Casey if it was a girl. Billie grabbed her tote bag, then stopped at her supervisor's door. Her boss, Jay, looked at her over the papers he was reading.

"My God, you're paler than a pearl." He jumped up and tried to lead her to a chair, but she refused. "What's wrong?"

"I, I have to go . . . to the doctor. I'm pregnant. It's early. We haven't told anyone yet. But something's wrong. I'm probably losing it."

"Do you want me to drive you? You shouldn't go alone." He rifled through drawers and patted his pockets until he found his keys.

"I'll handle it." *Like I did before.* "The doctor says bleeding is common in the first trimester." Billie's voice cracked as she spoke. "She wants to check me, to be sure."

Paige appeared in the doorway and said, "She says yes to the ride. Sorry, I overheard you as I was walking by. I've got things covered here if need be." She looked at Billie. "Just let me know how you are."

She was already lying on the exam table when Dr. Zambor came in. In what seemed like one fluid motion, the doctor pulled a pair of sterile gloves from a box and sat on the stool by Billie's feet while holding her gloved hands in the air. Her wiry gray hair made her look like a scattered professor with no time for such frivolous things as conditioner. Her lab coat barely concealed a full, rounded physique, probably from a combination of age and inactivity.

"Let's see what we have here." The doctor placed one hand inside Billie's nether region while pressing on her pelvis.

She was conscious of her OB's hand exploring one particular spot. Zambor's compassionate expression stayed fixed while she tactfully watched for signs of pain. And Billie was keenly aware the one area the doctor had found, around where her right-side ovaries were, was indeed tender. She kept her eyes on the poster the doctor kept attached to the ceiling as a calming focal point. This one was a puppy. She preferred the baby pandas in Zambor's other exam room.

The doctor mumbled to the nurse standing by the counter. The assistant rolled a machine next to Dr. Zambor, who had regloved. She held a sizable vibrator-shaped tool and was unrolling a condom-like sleeve onto it.

"We're just going to get a better look. Nothing to worry about."

Billie looked at the adorable cream-colored Labrador on the ceiling again. *Please, baby, we'll get you a puppy. Just be okay.* Then, like Dr. Zambor, she watched the screen, waiting to see the baby's miniscule image.

When the doctor finished the exam, she looked up, her face framed between Billie's bare legs, still in the stirrups.

"Have I miscarried?"

"No," the doctor said.

"But there was no image. Am I actually pregnant?"

"You are pregnant, but we do have an issue. Sit up and I'll explain."

Billie swung her legs over the side of the cushioned table, gripping the edge with both fists.

Dr. Zambor washed her hands and was toweling off when she turned to Billie. "Sometimes, when a fertilized egg sets off to implant in the uterus, it doesn't make it the whole way."

"It gets stuck in the fallopian tube and plants itself there," Billie said. "I know about ectopic pregnancy. Is that what you're telling me? It's a tubal pregnancy?"

"Yes."

"But a fertilized egg can't . . . The tube could rupture." The faces of all of Billie's clients who'd told this story came to her mind. "Which means it's dangerous for me to continue with the pregnancy?"

"I'm afraid so," Dr. Zambor said. "We'll know more soon. But first, I want to get you admitted. I want to check the labs and consult with a high-risk obstetrician. If she agrees with my assessment that the risk of complications is low enough, I'd like to give you a dose of methotrexate, and if it succeeds, we can avoid surgery. But if it doesn't, we'll have to do the procedure immediately."

"So, my choices come down to losing my baby to an induced miscarriage, or by surgery, possibly involving removal of my tube or tubes."

The nurse walked in with a wheelchair. *When did she even leave the exam room?* Billie wondered as she wiped her palms on the creped exam table paper.

"They have a bed for her," the nurse said. She set the chair next to the table, and the locks snapped into place beneath her foot. "Get dressed and I'll be back for you in a minute." The undisguised pity in her voice sent Billie's heartbeat to her very dry throat.

"I'll see you over there." The OB squeezed Billie's arm before walking out.

The nurse wheeled her through the waiting area to the breezeway connecting to the hospital, where Tyler was speaking to the doctor. When he saw her, he came to her side with frantic energy. Billie clutched his belt loop as he walked in step with the wheelchair until they arrived at her hospital room, which was insultingly located on the maternity ward.

Tyler sat next to her on the hospital bed when they were temporarily left alone. His eyes were so full of fear and sympathy, Billie shut hers. "I don't understand what's going on. Why is this happening?"

"It will all be okay," he said. "You will be okay."

"How can you say that? It's my body refusing to let our baby survive." Billie heard her hollow sobs and felt the tightness in her chest and throat, yet she felt empty.

"Sometimes things aren't meant to be."

"That's great. I'm subjected to all the medical and physical intrusions while you get off clean and just serve up platitudes. Guess what? You don't have to wonder if we're doing the right thing having a baby anymore. You're welcome."

Tyler winced.

"I didn't mean it—can you forgive me?" Billie detested herself for the unnatural cruelty she'd unleased.

FIVE
Anne

Based on the heavy smell of ash, beer, and sex, Anne assumed she was in a motel room before opening her eyes. She'd slogged through the motions of her life in the five weeks since she'd seen the face of the lawyer with the distinctive eyes on TV. Her thoughts remained fixed on him as she frequently hung out at Duke's Pub, minimizing the emptiness of time spent in her apartment. For years she'd yearned to hear his laughter and feel the secure way he'd held her hand in his. Life had forced her to leave him, but she'd never stopped believing they would reunite one day. Love would prevail.

Anne rolled onto her back, looked at the filthy overhead light, and then reached for her cigarettes and lighter on the small bedside table. She viewed the tattered wallpaper and the heavy red curtain covering the one window by the door, certain she'd never been to this motel before. She put the cigarette between her lips, sat up, and flicked her Bic. A man standing at the foot of the bed was zipping his fly.

"What time is it?" The lousy lighting made it hard to see him well, but she could tell his hair was receding and fitness was a thing of the past. He looked to be in his fifties.

"One in the morn, darlin'."

"You're leaving?"

"Sure am." He held up his left hand and wiggled his ring finger. "But thanks for the early fireworks."

Ah, she remembered. She'd gone to the company's Fourth of July picnic. Instead of a cookout, they'd hired food trucks. He was the taco guy, and the more beer she'd consumed, the more interesting he'd seemed. They'd stashed a case of Molson under his truck until the event ended, and then they'd had their own party. When they'd come to the motel was unclear. So was his name, but that wasn't important.

"See ya, bud," she said.

"Yeah, probably not."

She tapped her cigarette ash on the bedside carpet as the door shut behind him. Anne had always jumped from man to man, never staying too long in a relationship. She'd never married, never even come close. Stanley, her psychiatrist, had pointed out the men she got involved with were never looking for anything but an emotionless good time for themselves. He'd wondered if it was because she usually met the guys at late-night bars when she was, as Mama Sue would have phrased it, stewed thicker than beef in a Crock-Pot.

Since the motel room was already paid up, she slept until an early morning fight in the room next door grew too loud. The used 1999 silver Toyota Corolla she'd traded for her beloved Mustang was easy to locate. There were just a few cars in the lot, and hers was the only one with its front end parked on the sidewalk.

Two days later, Anne sat at her desk staring at the words "Rudy's Plumbing" printed on her coffee mug. The stem of the letter *g* was a blue-and-white pipe. Its tackiness was a fair representation of her boss, Rudy, a beefy man with thinning hair gelled over his balding scalp.

Soon after Anne dropped out of college, Mama Sue had helped her move to her apartment in Graham, a town close to Hopkinton and not too far from home. She'd also taken her to Stanley, the psychiatrist, who gave her all kinds of pills. The meds had made her feel like she was walking through sludge all the time. The mental numbness had made it hard to stay employed for long periods. Anne had worked as a warehouse packer, on the assembly line of a bread factory, and at a phone company's call center before scoring the scheduler job at Rudy's Plumbing seven years ago. It wasn't the job she wanted; it was the one that had stuck.

Rudy often stood over her, pretending to look at the installation and service schedule she was responsible for. She'd learned to ignore the itchy skin on her arms and neck when he came too close. She would hold her breath, begging the phone to ring until he darted away. She had thought of him as "the Gnat" since her second week working there.

"Any other outgoing?" The young receptionist reached inside the mail bin beside Anne.

"All good." Anne stared at the girl's flawless ivory forearm.

"Hey." Two of the installers approached her desk to get their schedules. One asked, "Would you snag us some tacos for lunch?"

"What are you talking about?"

Then the other replied, "Well, it's Taco Tuesday. We thought you'd get some." The two of them looked at each other and broke out laughing. "Cause you had sex with the taco guy?"

"Classic morons." Anne lifted two piles of stapled papers. "Hey, don't forget your schedules."

Tuesday! She'd forgotten her morning appointment with Stanley. She thought he'd be pissed, which upset her more. *He's not your father.*

His feelings don't matter. This was a lesson she believed Stanley had wanted her to learn, yet she'd always had a difficult time absorbing it.

Before she dialed Stanley's number, Anne tugged at the top of her ear, thinking of an excuse for why she'd missed it. She worried about not being able to get more pills, but she'd been skipping them anyway. At first, she forgot to take them some days; then she tested out not taking them more days in a row. As far as she could tell, she was fine now, so she was going to quit altogether. She decided she didn't owe him an explanation; the session was her time to do with as she pleased. He'd get his money either way. Yet Anne still felt like she was about to be punished. She ached to leave for Duke's Pub, but the end of the day was an unbearable six hours away.

SIX
Tyler

Tyler and Billie stood by the hotel's roof railing, waiting for the formation of fighter jets to kick off the Boston Pops Fourth of July Fireworks Spectacular. The law firm held this elite annual affair only for partners and those on the trajectory to become a partner.

"Another drink, sir?" A young server sidled up next to him as he drained his glass. Tyler needed to make a good impression and hoped no one else saw him almost knock over the waiter's tray as he took the fresh glass.

"For you?" the server asked Billie.

"Club soda," she said. "Thank you."

The doctor had advised no alcohol when Billie got the methotrexate injection five weeks ago, and she was still cautious. She'd stayed one night in the hospital for observation and returned for a multitude of outpatient sonograms and blood tests for three weeks.

"Are you very nervous or something, Ty?" she asked.

"What do you mean?"

"Two in a row?" She pointed at his glass.

He looked over his shoulder. "The big boys' club over there gets offended if their guests aren't having"—he made air quotes—"a good time."

She was right, though. He was worried. After they discovered the tubal pregnancy, his mother often came over to check on Billie and fill their fridge with homemade meals and every sugary dessert she could bake. But he'd still worn himself out trying to take care of his wife and keep up at work. Tyler had made sure she stayed hydrated and fed, even when she had no interest in any of it. He'd held her when she needed comfort and suffered through as many chick flicks and tearjerkers as she wanted.

She'd gone back to work after the first week, but he continued to put all his energy into keeping her physically and emotionally healthy. He could tell she wasn't herself, because normally she would have noticed the strain he was under. He was having to stuff his briefcase with papers to work on after she fell asleep at night, averaging only three to four hours of sleep. But he couldn't keep up. Some of his clients noticed his decreased focus and complained to the higher-ups, who, in turn, hinted that Tyler risked losing his spot on the legal team for a prominent case. And he was not about to let his weakness stand in the way of his success.

Someone turned up the volume on the enormous outdoor speakers, flooding the rooftop guests with the national anthem playing for the packed crowd below on the Esplanade. The fighter jets appeared, then swiftly vanished in the distance, leaving a stream of white lines across the sky.

"You're a trooper for coming with me to this pretentious shindig," Tyler said.

"I'll smile and be polite to whomever you need me to. Besides, I owe you for taking great care of me this past month. You're a good man, Mr. Scott."

Am I? The miscarriage had confirmed his pessimism about being a father. The best way to never let his children down, Tyler had determined long ago, was never to have any. But he recognized his wife had the same insistent drive to be a mother as he had to be a partner. Billie always assumed he wanted kids because he liked them, and he'd never corrected her.

Tyler looked around at the firm's select group of Independence Day invitees—the lawyers vying to be named partner. Most huddled around the partners playing kiss-ass. He'd earned the firm's respect and deserved it. But he didn't just want to be a partner; he needed it. Particularly the salary and bonus package that came with it. The mortgage for the cozy house they lived in was over their allotted budget. He'd rationalized it as a smart investment when they'd bought it. But the unexpected medical and hospital bills were rolling in and depleting their savings. Not wanting to add another burden to all she was going through, Tyler made sure Billie was unaware of all this. She was coping with the loss by continuing to put her hopes into fertility treatments or adoption to make their family, which, if he couldn't talk her out of it, would be a substantial financial hit.

The firm's senior partner turned away from the group he was with and nodded at Tyler before he excused himself and walked over.

"Billie, you remember Michael Huck."

"Of course she does." His top boss kissed Billie's cheek. "She might just be the reason we keep you around." Huck placed his hand on Tyler's back. "I hope you don't mind my borrowing your husband for a few minutes, young lady?" Then he moved himself and Tyler a few feet aside.

"You know I've always been a fan, Tyler, right?"

"Yes, and I appreciate it. I've always tried to live up . . ."

"Said from the minute we took you on as an intern, that boy's got something special. Didn't I?"

"You did." Was Huck signaling he'd clinched the partnership or hadn't?

"But there's talk you've been slipping."

"I understand, sir. It's just Billie and I—" Tyler stopped mid-sentence. "I'm not going to make excuses. It won't happen again. This firm is my top priority, and that will never change. You have my word."

"That's all I needed to hear." Huck walked Tyler back to his wife. "You both enjoy the fireworks this evening."

When the concert performances started, he and Billie circulated the party, catching up with the colleagues and spouses whose company they knew they'd enjoy, politely acknowledging others they didn't know as well. They made sure to chat with Prachett and Lindeman, the other two named partners who would have a hand in deciding Tyler's future.

Everyone moved to the north side of the roof when the orchestra's rendition of Tchaikovsky's *1812 Overture* began on the broadcast. The first flare shot into the sky, erupting into bursts of brilliant white chrysanthemums, followed by red-and-blue palms. Tyler watched his wife's childlike glee, relieved she seemed more like her relaxed, contented self. Billie leaned against him and rested her head against his neck. His hands automatically clasped around her. He loved her so profoundly it caught him off guard sometimes. But she was all he needed.

SEVEN
Billie

When the methotrexate proved to have stopped the pregnancy, and Billie had somehow made it through with both fallopian tubes, her obstetrician recommended she and Tyler see a fertility specialist. Billie had only wanted Dr. Fischman. He had treated many of her clients, and while they were only her clients because they had not ultimately sustained pregnancy, they still praised him, and his success rate was, in fact, unusually high. High enough to have kept her composure while waiting four weeks for an appointment.

Now, sitting in the fertility specialist's dreary office, Billie gazed at the snapshots of roly-poly babies, tiny swaddled ones, newborns with their hands protectively capped to avoid scratches on their delicate faces. The wisteria-colored fabric board had one bare spot, one unused pushpin.

"Do you think we'll ever have one up there?" She gestured toward the collage.

Tyler arranged himself in his chair until he faced her and touched her forearm. "Of course we will, sweetie, of course."

The office air-conditioning was working double time to counter Boston's July heat. Billie clutched her cardigan closer. She'd been in the adoption field and spoken on the topic for half a dozen years. Until their first miscarriage, it had never occurred to her the conversation would someday feature her and Tyler.

After a quick knock on the door, Dr. Fischman, a harried-looking man, whisked into the office, already opening her file as he went to his desk. He pulled a few forms out, turning them over, going back to old ones. A cold sweat overcame Billie, yet she felt feverish.

"Birth year is 1980, uh-huh, I see . . ."

Before they'd begun trying, Billie had always thought of thirty-two as young, but now it seemed the chances of a natural pregnancy were diminishing with each passing year. Her clients averaged from thirty-five to forty when they began the adoption process. Most of them had already been through lengthy, grueling fertility treatments before coming to her.

Billie subtly placed a hand on Tyler's knee to stop his restless leg from bouncing. In return, he covered her hand with his own and drew it against his hip, which calmed her too.

"Ah, let's see, yep, okay." The doctor still hadn't looked up. "One, uh-huh." This time, he looked at Billie.

"You've had one miscarriage?" He went back to flipping pages. "And then the ectopic two months ago." Dr. Fischman folded his hands on top of her file. "I think the referral to me was smart. No point making you keep trying with false hope."

Billie felt sucker punched, as much from the doctor's words as from Tyler releasing her hand.

"I'm wondering, Billie, how much of your mother's medical history are you aware of?"

The question threw her. "My mother." She swallowed hard. "Died last year. Breast cancer."

"I'm sorry to hear that." Dr. Fischman's features transformed from a fact-seeking doctor into what Billie interpreted as a kind-hearted man who shared the pain of losing a parent.

"Thank you, Dr. Fischman. I coordinated her care and was her liaison with the medical team. What kind of history are you looking for?"

"Your uterus is slightly misshapen, which sometimes occurs with what's informally known as DES babies. It was a hormone given to pregnant women to prevent miscarriages."

Long ago, in one of her college psychology or sociology classes, Billie remembered, there'd been a brief chapter on the effects of DES. But it wasn't a common occurrence anymore, and it had never come up with any of her clients. Her ob-gyn had been so full of optimism, always telling her, "Let's wait and see," and "It's bound to happen," so she'd never asked Billie details like this.

"Although I'm slightly perplexed," the doctor continued. "The drug wasn't in use after 1971, so I'm not sure your mother would have received such treatment."

"I was born near Orsay, France. My father was a research scientist there. I know my mother had a few miscarriages before me. At the time, my parents were young and broke, so a friend took my mother to a small village doctor somewhere. She once told me he gave her some unknown medicine when she got pregnant with me. They moved back to Massachusetts when I was a baby."

"That would explain everything," the doctor said.

"Can we slow down for a second?" Tyler asked. "I think I get it, but what's DES?"

"It was a synthetic form of estrogen given to women with a history of miscarriages or premature deliveries. It was believed that increased female hormones would solve the problem. Unfortunately, it turned out to be harmful to women and their unborn children. Like Billie's mother, many women developed breast cancer."

Billie rubbed and turned her wedding ring. It infuriated her that medical incompetence had caused her mother to suffer and die. That she'd lost her mother and her own possible children to ignorance was inexcusable. It wasn't fair to blame her mother, yet part of her did. That one bad decision had caused both of their bodies to fail them.

"What might we expect? What treatment is there? What are the typical outcomes?" Tyler asked.

Billie half smiled at her husband, grateful he'd asked the questions she was afraid to. The potential that she'd be genetically predisposed to breast cancer was something she'd understood. But having fertility issues, and maybe other types of cancers, because of her mother's medical history was too much to reconcile. An acute pang nested in her heart—she might never make the babies Tyler wanted.

"There are several known health problems in DES daughters. In rare cases, there's been vaginal or cervical cancer, but you would have seen signs already." The doctor looked at Billie's chart. "For the most part, your Pap smears have been clear, no dysplasia or other abnormal cells noted. Some women with this unusual shape of the uterus have carried to term. Many, however, have experienced difficulty becoming pregnant, and there are potential complications."

"Like what?" Tyler asked.

"There's an increased chance of preeclampsia and, as you've experienced, miscarriages and ectopic pregnancy."

They both sat there, stunned.

"That's a lot to take in," Tyler said.

Billie saw the creases in his forehead as he looked at her. The doctor was watching her too. There was a long, expectant pause.

"What can we do?" Somewhere in the data bank inside Billie's brain, she knew the answers. There were few fertility stories and treatments she wasn't familiar with. But the words, aimed at her and her own malfunctioning body, sounded foreign.

"Here's what I'd recommend. We're going to run some blood tests." The doctor hastily checked off boxes on a lab form. "And we'll schedule some additional diagnostics, which I'll assess and discuss with you. But we can't start anything for a while."

"What do you mean? Why not?" Billie asked.

"We have to wait three months after the methotrexate to be sure it's out of your system before you get pregnant again." Doctor Fischman looked in her file, then used his pen to tick off days on a small flip calendar on his desk. "That brings us to September. Some testing can begin mid-August, just a few weeks away. Once we have all the preliminary diagnostic results, sometime around the end of September, I'll likely start you on some medication that will stimulate ovulation. It will probably take a few courses, so we'll check in about three months. If there is a successful pregnancy, we will watch you closely, monitor your progress, and do everything we can to bring you to term." He paused. "Look," Dr. Fischman added, "there are many treatments and options I can provide, but I'm not going to fluff this: your chances of conceiving naturally and carrying to term are extremely low."

"But there's IVF." Billie leaned forward in her chair. "We'd still be candidates for that, wouldn't we?"

"I'm not ruling anything out until my diagnostic analysis, but frankly speaking, I'm not hopeful. Let's start with the tests. Then we can talk again."

Tyler said thank you, got up, and held the door open. Billie stood, mumbled her thanks, then went past the bulletin board and back through the outer office. She felt as though she were stuck in a windstorm, deafened to all voices and sounds as she followed Tyler to their car.

EIGHT
Anne

Anne lifted herself off the couch cautiously, unsure if she trusted her legs to carry her the short distance to the sugary coffee she needed. Tipping fresh grinds in the used filter, she tapped her finger in rhythm with the archaic thrift store coffee maker's slow drip. She rummaged through her kitchenette for something edible. She shook a box of Honey Smacks into a bowl but scored only a few puffed morsels. A slab of dried peanut butter wedged to the bottom of a Skippy jar.

Despite herself, she glanced at the magnetic 2012 calendar on the fridge door. The July heading was printed in a frilly raspberry script as if it were a cheerful month to look forward to. She'd marked the preceding days with bold *X*'s, up until this day, Saturday, July 14. A blood-red circle with the words "TWENTY YEARS" in all caps highlighted the date. She suddenly wanted to smash her mug on the counter but didn't have the energy to do it. Anne gave up on the brew, deciding instead to hide in bed. The coffee maker gurgled with unfulfilled steam when she yanked the plug from the wall.

In bed, Anne lay on her side staring at a spider-shaped crack in the wall she'd named Damien. Her head vibrated with a dull hum, her awareness decreasing. It was much like the moment before anesthesia began erasing consciousness. Panic came fast. The walls seemed to twirl, and she felt like she was floating within them. She gripped the bed frame, and in a low, moaning whisper, she begged it to stop. But the lifelike imagery arrived anyway.

She's in a barbed-wired prison yard. Walking toward her is an inmate, her father. He turns his face toward her.

"Hello, princess," he says.

Panic seizes her chest.

"You looking for this?" He lifts a baby above his head.

"Give her back!" she shouts as she grabs the infant from him. But when she looks down, her arms are empty. "Where is she?" she cries.

Her father, ugly and smug, stands before her. She is as weak and powerless as her breath. Then she feels a gun's smooth metal in her hand. She pulls the trigger, pulls it again, pulls it again.

The sound of a ringing phone brought her out of it. Anne staggered across the room. As if someone had knocked the wind out of her, she couldn't get enough air to form the word "hello."

"Anne?" A pause. "Are you there?" her mother asked. "Are you okay?"

"I shot him."

"Repeat what you just said. What's happening?"

"I shot him."

"Shot who?"

"My father."

"Okay, honey, okay. Tell me everything, slowly," her mother said.

Anne described the vision. She was tugging and rubbing the top of her ear between her thumb and forefinger when her mother responded with a soft, patient voice. "It was a dream, honey. You know your father is gone. He can't hurt you."

"But he was right in front of me." Rubbing her eyes didn't clear her confusion. "He found her. The baby. He—it was so real."

"That would never happen. You're safe. You have to believe me."

After the call, Anne lay on the couch, but the images her mind had concocted had been too vivid. Usually, when she tucked herself under the knitted throw blanket her mother had made, she became calm, but today it wasn't enough. She wouldn't have withstood it without the pills and alcohol to numb reality. With a snarl, she kicked at the blanket until it landed on the floor.

Anne kept the television on and waited for news confirming her father's death for the rest of the weekend. The ordeal had left her so shaken a bottle of cabernet each night couldn't soothe her. She'd been dozing on the couch, but each time she closed her eyes, her father found her in her dreams, towing his personal belongings into her home. Anxiety spawned insomnia that left her glazed and sluggish in the daylight.

The hysteria and wine hadn't mixed well, and apparently the toilet had had enough. Early Monday morning, Anne watched the trickling stream of water with a plunger in her hand. Jiggling the handle settled the plumbing, but not her stomach. She sucked on a cracker, eager to calm it, but every time she thought about her father's imagined release, her guts revolted. She stuck her head out the paint-chipped window, hoping a summer breeze would help. Instead, the brilliant oranges, reds, and yellows of the emerging sun offended her.

Anne set a kettle on the stove to make tea to help her nerves. When she heard her neighbor whistling, she clenched her teeth, waiting for the rattle and thud when he tossed his trash into the dumpster, followed by the expected slam of his apartment door. He irritated her in this way every morning, but his precise routine was her cue to leave for work. She looked around for her car keys, finding them in the microwave under the neck of an empty wine bottle she'd managed to wedge inside.

"Impressive," she said.

Anne turned to blow a kiss to the urn on the console next to the television. "Have a good day, Mama Sue."

For the first time in weeks, Anne somehow got to work on time, although she hadn't been able to concentrate since she'd sat at her desk. When the office emptied at lunchtime, she stayed behind, removing the tinfoil from her cheese and mustard sandwich. She found the sweet and mildly spicy flavor satisfying. Anne opened her *Boston Globe*. She was the only one in the office who continued to read the newsprint version instead of going online. She liked the feeling of the thin paper in her hands, its familiar, dull musk. When you read the paper, no one spied on you. But the newspaper's black-and-white words were meaningless to her; they had been since that face had looked at her through the television. She had always been afraid to contact him, but now, with her mother's promise that her father couldn't hurt anyone, it was time.

Anne minimized the customer list on her computer screen. She typed "Tyler Scott attorney" into the search engine, then scrolled through pages of results. She clicked link after link and found mentions that could not be her Tyler. He was elusive and clever with his personal Internet presence. He didn't even have a Facebook page. At least they had that in common. Anne didn't have anyone to keep in touch with. She'd never stayed in contact with the kids from high school, she'd barely gone to college, and she didn't socialize with anyone from work. In her opinion, there was no point in having Facebook if there wasn't anyone to friend.

Except for a dashing LinkedIn profile image, her search only turned up articles and websites related to the law firm. The link to the company's website gave a sterile bio: when he joined the firm, his experience and education. He'd gone to Boston University, which didn't surprise her. She remembered his parents had big expectations for him and encouraged him to do well. When he didn't, they were kind and understanding, never cruel or disappointed. He'd been a lucky kid. The website bio continued with a list of awards and noteworthy affiliations. The personal details she sought were never included.

Anne dialed his office number a handful of times, hanging up whenever someone answered. Then, instead of confirming Rudy's customer appointments, she researched estate planning, Tyler's specialty. She spent the next few sleepless nights rehearsing what she'd say until she felt prepared enough to go through with a call to Lindeman, Prachett, and Huck.

She sounded pleasant when she asked for Tyler Scott.

"Your name?" his secretary asked.

"Suzanne Neuman."

"What is this regarding?"

"I would like Mr. Scott's assistance with estate planning and creating a will." The lie slid out as smooth as custard.

Her stomach felt tingly during the brief silence while the call transferred through to his office. Maybe she'd waited too long to contact him. What if he didn't remember her? She reminded herself that he was her destiny, the love of her life. She thought of their soon-to-be magical reunion.

"Tyler Scott," he answered.

The sound of his deep adult voice, no longer cracking with the onset of puberty, overcame her. The softness of his cheeks and the feel of the hairless skin on his chest came back to her, as though he were next to her once again. Aware he could hear her rapid breathing,

Anne disconnected the call. Like a schoolgirl who'd embarrassed herself in front of her crush, she raced to the office bathroom, berating herself as she locked the door.

Rudy asked Anne into his office before the next Monday morning staff meeting. Flushometers, valves, and gadgets left by sales guys littered his desk. He fidgeted with a logo'd measuring tape while he spoke to her.

"This is serious, Anne," he said. "Over the last few weeks, you've sent crews to the wrong address, mangled the schedule, and hung up on clients. These aren't acceptable mistakes."

"I haven't been feeling well and I'm seeing a doctor tomorrow," she lied. "I won't be in."

A doctor's office was the last place she intended to be. Anne pressed on her ear, sore now from pulling it too hard while she gathered the nerve to call Tyler's office again. She only spoke with his secretary this time, which helped. By sheer luck, he had an opening tomorrow.

Finding a parking spot about a block down from the tall city building, Anne was giddy. She filled the meter with a fistful of nickels and quarters from the floor of her car. She trembled when she got close to the entrance and fled to a bench across the street, behind a hot dog vendor's cart. The low-hanging elm branch above gave her a direct view of the office building without being too visible herself.

Anne pulled her phone from underneath the junk in her handbag and dialed Tyler's office number. When the secretary answered, she attempted to make her voice haughty and used language she thought sounded refined.

"I do hope you'll pardon me, but there's been a delay, and I'm afraid I won't make this morning's appointment. I shall have to reschedule."

Anne cringed as she heard the pseudo-garbage coming out of her mouth. *You sounded like a fucking idiot,* she scolded herself as she threw her phone back in her bag. But at least she'd been able to make another appointment for Friday, August 10. She assured herself she could wait another week. For Tyler, it would be worth it. For now, watching from the bench, being near where he worked, would have to suffice.

The warm smells of the fatty sandwiches and grilled rolls wafted around her. Unwilling to risk losing her seat and the direct view of the building's doors, she refused to succumb to her hunger as the lunch hour approached. She pulled a pack of Salems from her pocketbook and tapped it on her fist until one peeked out far enough to extract. The lighter clicked and flamed. The cigarette smoldered with Anne's deep inhale. A bitter, burning, minty taste singed her tongue, and the smoke clung to her lungs before she breathed it out in a cool stream.

"One dog, mustard, relish, and a Coke," the man at the front of the food line ordered. He pulled a wallet from his back pocket, then waited while they prepped his lunch.

He rolled the paper shell back and was already taking a bite when he stepped to the side. Anne gasped when the man's blue eyes glanced in her direction. His skin had a golden tan, and he looked sophisticated in a charcoal pin-striped suit. He was taller than she imagined he'd be. If not for his thick reddish hair, she might have mistaken him for his father. Anne watched Tyler cross the street, toss his soda can into a garbage, and walk through the building's revolving doors.

It was humid the sixth day Anne situated herself on the green bench slats. The tank and loose skirt she'd worn were ineffective against the

Boston heat wave. Sweat pooled on her stomach. Her already burnt, fair-skinned shoulders stung from the brutal sun overhead. Still, she waited.

When Tyler came out of the building, he waved at a woman walking up the block. She had maple syrup–colored hair and an eager gait as she moved toward him. They embraced then walked together, engrossed in their conversation. While they ate lunch at a little restaurant around the corner, Anne leaned on a lamppost. Her mouth watered, hungering to be in that seat instead of the pretty woman he doted on. She felt on the verge of a childlike tantrum and pried herself away. Lighting another cigarette, she sat on her car's fender and let the smoke linger in her chest until it became unbearable. She waited until the cigarette was a mere stub before leaving.

The next time, Anne walked a few paces behind him when he exited the building. She pulled back when he reached his car in the parking garage. When a van screeched between them in the passageway, she lost the opportunity to reveal herself.

Unsettled, Anne walked to a nearby FastBurger. She needed a milkshake and jumbo fries' nasty mix of salt, grease, and ketchup. FastBurger always sliced their fries much too thin to get the desired burst of oil and potato flavor, so Anne took about half a dozen at a time. She quickly drank the frozen strawberry milkshake, drawing out the slurping noise when she vacuumed the bottom with the straw.

Sated with indigestion, Anne ambled back toward her car. On the way, she passed a cathedral where a well-dressed group was flowing out of the massive doorway. They rushed to form a path for the newlyweds' exit. She kept her eye on the bride who emerged from the darkened doorway, her hand entwined with her new husband's. Anne pulled a cigarette from its snug row in the box. The tip glowed, and a thin line of smoke rose in the air. She took in the tobacco with a long, deep draw, then released a plume over her shoulder. She saw herself in the euphoric bride's face and felt the soft lace gown flowing around her. It was Tyler whose gentle hand rested around her waist, his neck red from the uncomfortable tuxedo collar. It was Tyler whose face looked enraptured as he guided her through the pelting rice.

Inside Anne's belly, the fast food grumbled with fury as though it, too, was seething at the couple's joy. She took another smoldering drag of the cigarette and flicked it into the gutter.

Instead of driving home, Anne stopped at Duke's. There were only a few afternoon regulars visible through the haze of the unventilated tavern. The bartender slid her usual glass of vodka rocks toward an available stool. A man she hadn't seen before eyed her from the other side of the bar. She was too busy envisioning the newly married couple's wedding reception to encourage him, as she would have any other day.

"That's enough for tonight," the bartender said hours later. "You're 'bout ready to slip off that stool."

"You know what, Jimmy?" Anne tossed back the last of the vodka, then pushed her tumbler toward him. "That's fine, 'cause I got an appointment tomorrow, and this time I'm showing up."

NINE
Tyler

Tyler shook Suzanne Neuman's clammy hand. His new client seemed uncomfortable in his law office, and certainly not as refined as the firm's typical well-polished clientele. She ran a hand through her hair like she meant to smooth it, but her fingers caught on a tangle. The smoky discoloration underneath her faded brown eyes was visible behind her thick-rimmed eyeglasses, and the creases around her mouth suggested she was older than him by a few years or more.

"Please have a seat." He invited her to take one of the two chairs in front of his desk while he seated himself behind it. Her nervousness and anxiety were palpable. If Tyler were a prosecutor, he'd peg her as a noncredible, easily breakable witness.

"What can I do for you, Ms. Neuman?"

She twisted her fingers until her knuckles cracked, smoothed her dress, and then looked at him with uncertainty.

"I, um, er . . . I have some money from selling property I inherited. I'd like information about creating a will."

"Well, we can get into the specifics a little later." He clasped his hands loosely on his desk and recited the same introduction he gave to all his potential clients. "But there are many components to consider before we create a draft of the will. For instance, any trusts you've already set up, or might need, as well as philanthropic decisions."

Ms. Neuman nodded in all the right places, but Tyler could tell she wasn't absorbing anything he said.

"Would you like me to continue?" he asked. He found himself staring at a patch of little red bumps on her cheek.

"Yes, of course."

"It's important to be aware of how expensive taxes are on an estate and be sure you've considered the aspects and expenses of your care as you age, and the ultimate cost of care later in life. Then we can talk about any descendants you want to provide for and protect."

Ms. Neuman used a tissue to dab at the swelling perspiration below her hairline.

"I know this is a difficult topic," he said. "Do you still want to continue?"

"Yeah." She cleared her throat. "I mean, yes."

Tyler pushed a one-inch-thick packet and a pen toward her. She was blinking rapidly when she leaned closer to the desk, and he could see her eyelids were coated in makeup. She quickly sat back in her chair with her lips pressed together.

"We'll start by having you fill out some basic information. It begins with the simple stuff: your name, address, marital status, and information about children."

Ms. Neuman stood up. Her abrupt movement was so unexpected, Tyler flinched and hit his knee on the underside of his desk. As a reflex, he reached for the sore spot but toppled his coffee mug and stained his suit.

"I have to go," Ms. Neuman said.

What the hell? Tyler wondered. The topic of wills and planning for death was uncomfortable for most people, but no client had reacted quite like that.

His secretary came in with a new batch of documents and mail. "Never seen anyone beeline to the elevators so fast before," Marla said. "She was pretty sketchy, don't you think?" She picked up the forms Ms. Neuman had left on the chair. "Uh-huh, didn't even fill out her address."

"What's this?" Tyler held up a pink envelope from the top of the pile she'd put on his desk. His full name was hand-printed across it.

"No idea. I went to refresh my coffee earlier, and it was lying in my inbox when I came back."

Once Marla left his office, his curiosity piqued. Tyler picked up the engraved silver letter opener he'd received when he made associate and let it glide under the gum of the seal flap. He swiped his fingers inside and then pulled out the one item it contained: a wallet-sized baby photo. The newborn in the picture wore a pink sweater and a flowered hat. Tyler scratched his jaw and flipped it over. The letters "L.B." were written in blue ink on the back.

"Weird," he said aloud.

His calendar reminder dinged for dinner at his friends Moe and Ashley's, so he tossed it and the rest of his mail into a pile by his computer. He couldn't wait to see their son Nicholas, his godson, and give him the miniature-sized Celtics warm-up suit he'd bought. If he hurried, he could stop at home and change out of his stained suit. He hoped Billie's headache was better, and she'd change her mind and come too. Though Billie seemed calm and collected on the outside, in Tyler's opinion, she was ignoring what they'd been through by hyperfocusing on getting pregnant again. They'd been lucky she'd stayed in good health last time, but what if another pregnancy didn't end up as well? He was terrified of a high-risk pregnancy. He couldn't lose her. But he knew it would break her if he shared his fears.

His phone dinged again, this time with a text from an undisclosed number. Tyler assumed the message, Do you love her? was a misdial. *Someone* was having relationship drama. He deleted it, sending mental good luck to the poor jerk it was intended for.

Tyler cursed under his breath when he reached his car in the parking garage. He pulled a paper from under his windshield wiper, but instead of the marketing flier he expected, it was another envelope with his name hand-printed on the front. He felt a cool breeze of unease pass along the back of his neck as he opened it and found a duplicate photo inside. Glancing over his shoulder, he shoved it in his pocket as he quickly got inside the car and locked the doors. Thinking of all the horror movies he'd ever seen, he twisted around to make sure no one was in the back seat. "You're ridiculous," he said out loud with a laugh.

"Again!" Nicholas demanded. He was sitting on Tyler's back, using Tyler's polo shirt collar as his reins.

Tyler whinnied like a horse, crawling and bucking in circles in Nicholas's playroom. "You're knocking me out, kid. Time to dismount."

Nicholas's eyes sparkled when he discovered Tyler's phone on the floor, and he excitedly mashed the buttons. "Hello? Hi, Gan-ma," the boy said in his helium-pitched voice. "I playing horsey with Unca Tyler."

Tyler laughed until the cell beeped. With all the button pushing, it was possible the toddler called or texted someone.

"My turn," he said.

"No." Nicholas pulled away when he tried to take it. Then Tyler tickled the boy until he rolled on the floor and released the phone.

Nicholas hadn't misdialed anything. Tyler had received another text from the unknown number: Didn't you get the photo? A copy of the same photos he'd received earlier appeared below it.

Tyler's mind filled with questions: *How would someone even know about the miscarriages? And who would want to undermine me this way? Could another associate at work be trying to sabotage me?* As much as he wanted to, he knew better than to engage. He'd given the same professional advice to several clients subjected to harassment: "Do not respond." Now that his career was advancing, and with the recent TV coverage, any crank could try to get to him. But, with everything going on at home, a photo of a baby felt very personal.

"Unca Tyler, you mad?"

"No, buddy, I'm okay." He picked up the boy who sensed but didn't have the vocabulary to describe the trepidation Tyler was trying to conceal. "Let's go see if your mommy needs some help cooking."

Tyler turned his house key into the lock, careful to balance the left-over plate of cake Ashley had sent for Billie. He found her curled up in her favorite chair in the family room, watching the latest episode of *The Newsroom.*

"Feeling better?"

"Advil did the trick. How was dinner?"

"Delicious as always." He passed the cake slice to her. "Ashley didn't want you to miss out on her latest masterpiece, lemon sherbet."

"I don't know how she finds the time." Billie sat up. "But I'm glad she does."

"Your fork." Tyler handed her a plastic one wrapped in a napkin.

"She thinks of everything. I could never live up to her, even if I tried." Billie took a bite and rolled her eyes as she savored the fluffy citrus cake he'd tasted earlier. "Hey," she said. "Was that your phone pinging or mine?"

After hours of sporadic sleep, Tyler gave up trying. He couldn't shake the texts he'd received. He was also fighting the urge to examine the photo and figure out its meaning. But Billie's head was on his chest, and he was trying to lie still so he didn't wake her. It was hard to predict his wife's moods sometimes since the tubal, so he'd tried to be careful about the things he said and did around her. He would not risk upsetting her with whatever nonsense this was with the texts.

When his phone vibrated on the nightstand, Tyler grabbed for it. He checked Billie, who rolled over but stayed asleep. He waited to be sure she settled before he dared to read the text: Will I see you soon?

The room got smaller and hotter, the silence deafening. He wanted to throw the phone across the room, but he glanced down at Billie, peaceful by his side. He had to get out of there. He needed to run, more than he'd ever needed to run in his life.

The next morning, Tyler held the fridge door open, letting the escaping air cool him down after a long run. He grabbed a Gatorade and then saw Billie on the backyard deck, sipping from her preferred oversized coffee mug. There were folders and piles of papers strewn across the patio table.

Tyler found her most beautiful as she was now, casual, without makeup, relaxed. His heart swelled looking at her. He loved her more deeply than he ever thought he could. When they'd met at the charity dinner three years earlier, she'd been entirely unaware of how enticing she looked. She'd worn a deep gray cocktail dress and a pair of slinky black high-heeled sandals. When they'd talked at the bar that night, she was open and bold, and Tyler was hooked. She'd bewitched him with her caramel-colored eyes and soft, flowery perfume.

The deck's wood planks were warm under his bare feet as he stepped through the sliding glass doors toward her. He could tell she was too absorbed in her work to be aware of him, so he leaned over her shoulder and kissed her neck. Billie squealed, clasped his forearm, and pulled him closer. He inhaled the fruity fragrance of his wife's hair as she leaned into him. He kissed her cinnamon coffee–flavored lips.

"You're wet and smelly. Off with you, go shower before you drip on my reports." Billie passed a lounge chair towel to him. "Here, take this so you don't leave a trail on my clean floors."

Tyler kissed her several more times while she pretended to be offended. Before he headed upstairs, he stopped in the room they'd converted to his home office. He wanted to review some documents Marla had marked as urgent. He covered the chair with the towel, balanced his briefcase on his knees as he unlatched it, and propped the top open. Instead of taking what he needed, he checked for the little photo he'd found on his windshield. It wasn't there. Tyler played back the events of the previous afternoon, realizing he'd put it in his pants pockets. He'd have to get it out of the laundry hamper where he'd shoved his suit before rushing out to Moe's last night.

Turning on his computer, he moved his mouse around the screen, clicking on various computer files to locate any notes or documents on cases he might have had involving a child. If he could find any hint at all, he'd have a place to start searching for whoever was trying to intimidate him. He opened folder after folder without success. When his mouth felt sticky from not replenishing enough after his long run, he stretched out his stiffened limbs and went to get a drink. On his way to the kitchen, he saw Billie, still on the deck, her head back and face to the sun. He reached into the refrigerator and grabbed another Gatorade, then returned to his desk. This time, he systematically weeded through the profiles and backgrounds of his colleagues at the firm and those he may have fought on behalf of his clients. He jumped when Billie touched his back.

"Where've ya been?" she asked.

The harsh sound of the ringing telephone caught him off guard before he could react. Tyler winced when "Private Caller" came up on the landline screen. "Could be my mom. But let it go to voicemail."

Billie answered anyway. "Hello?" she said. "Hello? Hello? Hello? Who is this? I can hear you breathing. I know you're there. Say something."

He kissed Billie's cheek as he eased the phone from her grip and hung it up. "I'm gonna shower and change."

"While you do that, I'm going to run to the bagel place to get our lunch. I have a few errands over that way. Do you need anything?"

"Nope, all good."

After he'd cleaned up, Tyler opened the hamper to get the photo. The bin was empty. He didn't want to chance Billie finding it before he understood it. He rushed to the top of the steps and clutched the banister as he called down, "Hon, did you take my suit?" He heard the muffled rattle the overhead garage made when it was closing and sprinted to the bedroom window in time to see the back end of her SUV roll out of sight.

"Do you want to eat now or wait?" Billie asked when she came back from her errands.

"Now's good." Tyler sliced and toasted a sesame bagel for her and a marble rye for himself.

"That smells yum." Billie lifted a pitcher of iced tea. She'd already carried some containers of chicken salad and fruit out on the deck.

He kept his face lowered so she wouldn't see his distress. Before they were about to go outside, he took the phone off the hook.

Billie peered at him as she chewed a chunk of pineapple. "You're uptight. What aren't you saying?"

Tyler could feel her leisurely mood dispelling. She'd been through enough recently. There was no way he was going to freak her out by mentioning the disturbing texts or telling her he'd been getting similar calls at work since July. He'd always assumed it was a disgruntled client or someone he'd beaten in court. Until yesterday, there'd been no reason to worry about it. His leg tapped increasingly faster as Billie pushed a melon cube around her plate. The need to take care of her pressed upon him as his concerns heightened. He could handle someone with a grudge against him, but not if they were going to frighten his wife too.

"Nothing at all," he answered. "The sun was way stronger than I expected, and I ran farther than I should have." He felt horrible for lying, but whoever was doing this to them left him no choice. Protecting Billie was all he cared about.

TEN
Billie

Hurling an open box of tampons at the bathroom wall did little to erase Billie's frustration. The lingering hope in the four weeks since her prognosis snuffed itself out. She put the box away with a slam of the cabinet door. Glimpsing her pitiful reflection in the mirror, she wondered what she would say if she were her own client. *Don't give up. It can still happen. There are highly successful fertility treatments to consider. There is always adoption.*

"Don't you do that!" she admonished the mirror. Her nose was turning crimson, and her eyes were glistening. She fanned her face with her hands while inhaling. "Your mother didn't raise a wallower, and today's not the day to start!"

Billie grabbed her makeup to apply her professional face. She brushed, blotted, and dabbed on creams, foundation, and powders to accentuate her high cheeks, which came from her father's side. Her toffee-brown eyes were a maternal family trait. The natural, sophisticated look she created had the authoritative yet understated effect she'd wanted for the morning adoption symposium.

When she finished, she whispered, "Strength, courage, heart." These were the words her mother always spoke before kissing her cheek and sending her out to face a challenging day.

Billie tapped her fingers twice on the hollow of her cheek. Then she went down to the dining room where she'd left her materials. Tyler had his makeshift office, but she liked to spread out across the more spacious tabletop. She confirmed her index card notes were in order for the keynote speech and secured the pile with a rubber band.

As a presenter, being well prepared and organized was fundamental to her, even though she knew, no matter how compulsive and practiced, things might not go the way she expected. She'd learned this from her very first lecture. A small hospital had asked her agency for an adoption specialist to give a speech to the staff. They were hoping to improve the sensitivity and treatment of birth mothers, which had become Billie's forte.

In her usual perfectionist style, which her parents had encouraged, she spent the three weeks prior analyzing data and perfecting her fifteen-minute presentation. "Check your facts. Let's hear it again," her parents used to tell her when she'd had to give an oral report in school. She had lovely memories of them piling books at the head of the kitchen table to be her practice lectern and their encouraging faces as she spoke. Billie still stood at the head of her own dining table when preparing a speech until she deemed her parents would've agreed it was ready.

When she arrived for her first adoption speech five years ago, the hospital's auditorium was empty. The organizer forgot to advertise the lecture. Reassured a group was waiting for her, she went to a staff room where four women sat at a round lunch table, sipping instant coffee from lipstick-stained Styrofoam cups. Before Billie made it through the first paragraph of the intro, the women began thrusting questions at her. They were each experiencing fertility issues and were desperate for insider adoption tips. They'd had no room in their heads for birth mothers. It had been a valuable lesson about speaking to her audience rather than forcing her own platform.

If it hadn't been for that momentary calamity, Billie wouldn't have become the seasoned speaker she was now, or, she believed, a more flexible person. She was, however, having difficulty applying the philosophy to her current nothing-going-right life. Especially today. Her mom had been a social and behavioral science professor at the university hosting the morning symposium. Billie hadn't been there since she'd cleaned out her mother's desk last year. The miscarriage happened a month later. Not being able to talk to her mom about it had ravaged her. Being on her mother's campus was going to be rough, but if she avoided the wing where the office was, she could make her mother proud by portraying confidence and authority, even if she didn't feel it.

"Son of a bitch!" Tyler yelled from the foyer.

"What happened?"

He threw his phone into his briefcase. "Nothing." He glanced everywhere but at her. "I'm going to be late."

"You're leaving without saying goodbye?"

"You know I wouldn't do that." He leaned toward her and, with a softer voice, said, "Good luck with your speech."

"Good luck with your . . . whatever."

He gave her a distracted goodbye kiss.

"Love you," she said.

"Gotta go."

Billie flipped an index card to the used pile on the left side of the lectern. She'd already covered two of the three key topics in her speech. The first was to teach hospital staff to understand a birth mother's psyche and respect her if she can't hold her baby. The second was to enlighten adoptive couples about the different adoption paths and the laws they'd need to navigate.

"So, I've given you a lot of information about the adoption process. I've highlighted the ups, the downs, and the ins and outs of the many types of adoption. It's a lot. It's complicated and overwhelming, but this is why you have adoption agencies and lawyers. Our job is to guide you and support you through it."

When she and Tyler were dating, Billie confided she'd intended to work with pediatric cancer patients. When she'd received her master's in social work, though, hospital jobs were limited. Like her peers, she'd gotten caught in a conundrum: to be hired you needed experience, but you couldn't get experience without being hired. She'd only accepted the adoption position because her rent was due. But after six years in the field, Billie was a sought-out speaker about Massachusetts adoption laws and the arduous process for adoptive parents.

She gave a playful smirk. "By now, I'm guessing you're hoping I'll attend to the questions you secretly came here for, like can I guarantee nurture trumps nature? Or what's the trick to getting bumped to the top of the waiting list? Or, the big one, how can I get a birth mother to pick me? It would be something, wouldn't it, if there was one true answer to any of those? And I will take questions, and give you answers, at least to the ones I have facts for." Billie heard chuckles from the audience. "I think it's important, though, to take a moment to understand a bit more about birth mothers."

As knowledgeable as she was about the legalities of adoption, Billie's passion was educating people about birth mothers, their journey, and the gift of family they give to their babies. She had come into the job with typical preconceived biases that birth mothers were mentally ill, druggies, promiscuous, or simply uncaring, but the majority of women she had worked with weren't so different from those who wanted to adopt. They were students, professional women, and sometimes mothers who found themselves in unfortunately timed situations or financially impossible ones. Through her lectures, Billie made it her mission to undo the stereotypes.

As she initiated the final theme in her speech, that birth mothers matter and adoptions aren't a mere legal transaction, she looked into the audience, expecting to see her mother in the front row. Billie searched the multitude of women's faces in the adjacent seats and the rows behind. It suddenly hit her—she was part of their sisterhood now. She imagined sitting amongst the other infertile women listening to her lecture, likely no more receptive to the birth mother's perspective than they were. Rebounding before the pause in her speech became too obvious, she continued making her points. Then Billie picked up the next card with her closing statement. "In conclusion." She lifted the lined index card, looked at the waiting faces in the crowd, then placed it face down. Taking the mike off the stand, she stepped away from the lectern.

"In conclusion," she tried again, "whether you're seeking to adopt or considering placing your child for adoption, it's because in some way we've lost control of our bodies—we fear each other's judgment, we cloak ourselves in shame or guilt. If you are here because you've tried for at least one year to get pregnant, or you've experienced a long trial of medications and technological procedures, or you're a birth mother or adoptee, take a look around the room. Notice the woman to your left or the couple to your right. They've all been on a roller-coaster ride of hope, grief, fear, and renewed hope. So, if you hit a low phase or feel like you can't talk about what you are going through, remember this crowd and remind yourselves how many others understand. And whatever path led you to this seminar and your interest in adoption, you are not alone."

* *

Waiting in the coffee drive-through line, Billie thought about how well the morning's symposium had gone. When she'd finished, she'd received an appreciative applause and positive feedback from her colleagues who'd been there. But her momentary blip still shook her, and then that she'd gone off-script. *What's happening to me?* The robotic attendant stuck her arm out of the restaurant window, and Billie secured her coffee in the driver's-side cupholder. Checking the time, she decided against stopping at the dry cleaner before heading to work.

With her case strap over her shoulder and coffee in hand, she clicked the key fob twice to make sure the car doors locked. Then she strode to the ninth-floor staircase in the far corner of the cement parking garage. She made it a habit to park there so she could use the steps as the workout she wouldn't have time for later. With clients in less than an hour, she had to hustle. The determined rhythm of her pumps echoed on the descending concrete stairs. Outside, the summer sun warmed her as she speed-walked the few blocks to her office building. A light wind swooped through her hair and sent it swaying in motion with her gait. Her thoughts had already leaped to the information she'd need to assemble for the clients she'd be seeing.

"Afternoon!" she called to Rita, the receptionist, who cheerfully held a pile of pink message slips in the air. There were still some people who preferred direct messages over voicemail. Billie supposed they felt some control, some assurance their message wouldn't go unanswered.

Inside the elevator, she sifted through and prioritized the calls she had to return. The other passengers, home health aides and coordinators, brushed against her as they exited onto the bustling second floor. In contrast, the atmosphere of the third floor waiting area projected quiet stillness. Behind each solid door, social workers provided therapy and support to their clients. The far back corner, reserved for adoption services, was where Billie counseled birth mothers and conducted home studies to determine potential parents' readiness to adopt.

Fresh roses mixed with freesia, a bouquet from Tyler, perfumed her small office. Her husband was a thoughtful man, but the fragrance irritated her. She'd been patient, believing what was bothering him lately had everything to do with her fertility, or lack thereof. She'd hoped he'd open up to her but had gotten nothing except flowers. Billie placed her briefcase under the desk and reached for the phone. She dialed her husband's private line, sat back in the swivel desk chair, and waited for him to answer.

"Hi, sweetie!" he said. "Did you get the flowers?"

"Yes. They're beautiful. You know you don't have to send something every time you get grouchy."

"Well, I shouldn't have been. Besides, it makes you happy."

She smiled at his photo in the silver frame she kept angled toward the window so her clients couldn't view it. His ginger-brown hair was swept neatly to the side, save for a few sexy strands grazing his forehead. The photographer had captured the love in his crystalline blue eyes that day. The breathlessness she'd felt in that moment struck her every time she looked at it. But he was right. He'd been moody since they'd gone to see Dr. Fischman. Instead of watching television with her or cuddling by the fireplace after their evening strolls, he secluded himself in his study. She didn't want to think about his rebuff while they were in bed Sunday morning. Even last night, he'd had a vacant look in his eyes, and throughout dinner he'd only nodded or answered with "uh-huh." She'd tried to give him some space, confident he'd share whatever was gnawing at him when he was ready. Waiting wasn't easy, though, and after dinner she'd pushed open the door to his study. He was sitting in the dark, staring somewhere over his desk.

"Hey!" She'd stood in the doorway, zipping a light jacket. "The sky is filled with stars. Wanna go for a walk?"

Her effort was met with a grumbled "Not tonight," followed by "Would ya close the door?"

She'd gone to sleep without him, unnerved by his broody manner. She knew he had a full caseload and had just completed another intense trial, but he'd never let work take over their personal lives like this before. More than anything, though, she was disappointed that they hadn't had a chance to talk. She'd wanted to tell him her period was overdue. It turned out to be for the best that she hadn't.

"So, how'd the speech go?" he asked.

"It was great."

"And the turnout?"

"Pretty good. The usual fill of people hoping to adopt. I think I got them to relate to the part about birth mothers." Billie glimpsed the flowers and made a mental note to add water to the vase.

"And you were okay being there?" Tyler asked.

"What?" Billie returned her focus to the call.

"Were you okay being there?"

He wasn't referring to the impact of Dr Fischman's news. Billie floundered, trying to sidestep the other reason being at the university this morning had been stressful.

"Mm-hmm."

"Bills . . . level with me." His sincerity was compelling.

"It was weird at first, but I handled it."

"I'm sure it was hard, honey. I would have rearranged my schedule and been there for you if you'd have let me."

"Really?" Billie laughed. "I saw that pyramid of boxes in your office when we went to lunch the other day."

Tyler laughed.

Billie's office intercom bleeped. "I have to go. My afternoon client is here."

"Okay. See you at home, unless you want to go out tonight?"

"In. Hey, Ty?" Her somber tone was unmistakable. "I got my period this morning."

There was a long silence, though Billie thought she could hear the small squeak his chair made when he shifted closer to his desk.

"Listen, there's no sense getting worked up about it until we have the facts. I love you, Bills."

ELEVEN
Anne

Sleep was useless against the wired anticipation. Anne pulled her pillow against her, pretending it was Tyler lying on top of her, their bodies connecting once again. Fits of giggles escaped her at random because she'd set things in motion and Tyler would come to her soon. But he'd already left her hanging for three days, and she couldn't understand why he wasn't there. Her anxiety looming, Anne called her mother.

"Hang on," her mother said. "I'm going to another room. Grant's on the other line with a client."

Grant and her mother had met when Anne was in high school. They'd been living together in Arizona since. It was her fault they'd never married because her mother would've had to divorce her father first. But that would've meant telling him where they were, which was terrifying. Grant was a dependable man who kept his promises and put everything else aside for family. Her mother often said Grant was her one true love. Anne understood because Tyler was hers, but her mother didn't know.

"I don't like the way you sound, honey. You're not sleeping, and I imagine not eating either," her mother said when she switched phones. "Maybe you should take some time off and come out here.

Grant and I would love to have you, and you know you'll relax if you do."

"Yeah, maybe. I might have some vacation days left." Though with all the days she'd been skipping, that was debatable.

"We'll arrange a ticket for you. I'm sure Grant has airline miles we can use. You just get yourself here. You're going to be okay."

But Anne could barely hear her mother as her thoughts argued with themselves. If she did go away, maybe her foolish worry that her father would get her would stop. But she couldn't leave without Tyler.

"I'll call you back." She let the phone slip from her hand without bothering to hang up and moved heavily to the closet to dig her suitcase out of the clutter. Her sluggish body didn't even react to the avalanche of coats, umbrellas, and miscellaneous sharp objects that toppled over her. Her immediate plan was to leave the heap and deal with it when she returned from Arizona, but then she spotted the crushed Buster Brown shoebox. As a little girl, she'd had trouble containing her excitement when she carried the box of shiny "big girl" party shoes from the thrift store. Once she outgrew the shoes, she couldn't bear to throw out the little box. She'd stuffed it with the scraps of her childhood "good times."

Anne sat in the debris, straightened her glasses, and pushed the lid off the shoebox. The photograph on top showed her and her parents making silly faces, sticking their tongues out and crossing their eyes in front of stacked bales of hay. Her father held the giant pumpkin he'd picked at the farm. Afterward, Anne remembered, she and her mother had carved a crooked face into the pumpkin, and then they'd lit a candle in its belly for Halloween. That was the year she wore a shiny blue Cinderella dress and a blonde wig over her dark locks for the kindergarten Halloween parade.

Raking through the assortment, she let her fingers linger on the smooth surface of a miniature silver ice skate that lay in the bottom corner. Her mother had found it outside the local ice rink before Anne's seventh birthday. Her father had insisted they keep it for "his princess." She could still feel his thumb brushing her skin when he'd held her wrist, taken the trinket from her mother, and closed it into her palm.

She shook the box again. A drive-in movie ticket stub, dated 1986, rose to the top. Anne had been eight. The details of that day were still so clear after twenty-five and a half years.

She'd been watching television that morning. Barney Rubble and Fred Flintstone had just lifted their caveman-style car, and their feet were gaining speed when the television screen sucked all the colors into its gut, leaving one tiny bright white dot winking in its center. Anne's eyes had drifted from the blackness to her mother, who stood on the side of the TV set.

"That's enough Sunday cartoons already," her mother said. "You're missing a beautiful day."

She must have forgotten her mother had the day off, because in those days, when her mother was home, Anne usually stayed in her room. It was the only way to avoid the onslaught of "fun mommy" who wanted to spend the day making up for all the activities work made her miss with her daughter. Anne struggled to be with fun mommy. She was both mad because her mother let bad things happen to her and petrified she'd give away her secret and bad things would happen to her mother too. Even as a young girl, Anne understood the safety of isolation.

"Come on, get your sneakers on. Let's go to the playground. The good one on the other side of town." Her mother tugged her arm and tried to lift her off the couch.

"I don't wanna!" Anne twisted free from her mother and scrunched into the corner of the couch.

"My god." Her hopefulness dissolved into a deep frown. "What is with you lately? Huh?"

Anne crossed her arms and waited, but her mother wouldn't back off.

"You used to be such an outgoing kid and were always moving fast this way and that. I could never get you to come inside." She set her hands on her hips and watched something out the big living room window. There were sounds of goofy voices and bicycle bells that meant a bunch of kids were passing their house, probably rounding everyone up to play red rover. Her mother pushed up the sleeves of the baggy sweater she wore in the house, no matter what time of year. Her droopy eyes had dark circles underneath, and her hair, even in a pony, always had flyaway strands. "You don't even play with the neighborhood kids anymore. All you seem to do is mope."

All Anne ever wanted back then was to be left alone. Her mother had made her grilled cheese and tomato soup that day. She'd stayed on the couch, watching her smoosh butter on a pile of Wonder Bread. The slices hissed when she dropped them into the pan. Her mother squeezed the legs of a can opener while turning the thingamajig until the Campbell's lid peeled off. With the soup on the stove, she applied American cheese to the bread and picked up a spatula to flip and flatten the sandwich. Anne had dislodged herself from the couch and shuffled to her chair at the square blue table that had belonged to her grandmother before her mother inherited the house. Her mother said it was a Formica top. That silly word used to make Anne laugh.

Anne still found comfort in a greasy, gooey sandwich dipped in hot tomato soup, but that particular afternoon, while she was eating, the screen door opened and then flapped shut behind her father. He'd been out back mowing the small patch of grass they called a yard. A wet chest and underarm hair escaped from the white sleeveless undershirt her father wore. He'd grabbed one of her mother's dish towels to rub bits of dirt and grass from his forehead and arms. Anne had forgotten to chew, and the last hunk of sandwich clumped on the inside of her cheek. Her eyes fixated on her belly button area when he came around and mussed her hair.

"Hey now, princess! That sandwich looks good!"

"I'll make you some," her mother said. "Give me a minute."

"What are my lovely ladies doing for fun today?"

"Your daughter is being a fuddy-duddy."

"A fuddy-duddy?" he'd said. "We can't have that, can we? How about we splurge tonight and see a movie at the drive-in? All of us can squeeze in the front seat of the car."

Anne hadn't moved. Hadn't chewed. Hadn't looked up. But she'd felt the burn where his stare, with its X-ray vision, saw through her.

He rustled the paper. "Appears to be Elvis month. We can make the first show. It's *Spinout*."

During the car ride, her father sang Elvis songs and imitated his deep velvety voice. He'd even stuck his head out the window and said, "Thank you, thank you very much," when the drive-in ticket booth woman handed him his change. When Anne tried it, she had to press her chin to her throat to make herself sound like a man. After her father hooked the speaker on his door, he'd told Anne to climb over into the front seat. Her mother pulled out a bag of Jiffy Pop popcorn they'd taken turns shaking over the stove and a large bag of Swedish Fish.

Anne didn't understand the movie but remembered feeling that she didn't want their family time to end. But then her father's leg pressed against hers and she'd squashed the half-full bag of candy between her thigh and his, just in case.

* *

Anne swirled her fingers inside the memory box, trying to stir up a later trip, but there weren't any. Elvis had been their last outing before her family began imploding.

Pushing the Buster Brown box back into the closet's expelled mass revealed the old green composition book she'd used to detail her life when she'd been full of secrets she wouldn't share. She leaned into the medley of scarves, dusty boxes, shoes, and cleaning supplies, undecided about destroying the diary and the demons that lay behind its cover. She swept her hand across the front of the book's white-lined space where she'd printed "1991." Anne tossed the book aside and crawled away from the closet, seeking refuge back in bed. Pulling the edge of the blanket, she clutched her old stuffed puppy, rolled herself into a burrito, and then wiggled her head under her pillow.

If she had opened the journal and flipped through, she'd have found the gap where she'd ripped out a page almost as soon as she'd written it. Anne remembered her knuckles had gotten white as she pressed the pen hard into the paper and the things that had begun happening to her when she was seven gushed out. There were little holes where she'd written over droplets of tears. She'd read the page over and over before tearing it to the smallest shreds. But she still knew it. She'd never forget how her breath quickened when she heard the floorboards creaking outside her bedroom. Perspiration beaded on her neck as prickles ran up and down her spine. The door squeaked as it slowly pushed open as he slipped into the darkness of her room. The coarse calluses on his hands chafed her young skin as they ran along her torso. The springs on her mattress whined as he shifted his body until it smothered her. Then he did that horrible thing.

Startled by her own screams, Anne pushed the pillow off her head, peering around her apartment bedroom where the sun seeped through the haze.

“It’s not real, it’s not real,” she chanted. “He can’t get me.”

Next to her bed, the fan’s blades rattled as the worthless oscillator clicked and clicked. Kicking the tight blankets off, Anne tried to shed the panic. Too scared to shut her eyes for even a minute, she remained numb in a tightly curled position. When she finally dared to roll over, she stared at the clock, willing herself to understand what 1:00 p.m. meant, what day it was, and where she was supposed to be. The brightness outside her window indicated it was afternoon, and it was a weekday, she remembered, so she was going to be in trouble for missing work again.

TWELVE
Tyler

"Holy crap, watch it!" Moe said. "You're like a savage."

Tyler and his lifelong friend reveled in their early morning monthly racquetball games. Moe squatted against the blemished, scraped wall after Tyler gained the sixth of the eleven points needed to win their tiebreaker match. They were both drenched in sweat.

"Too aggressive for your wimpy ass?" Tyler responded.

"Wimp? What are you, twelve?" Moe said. They both laughed. "Seriously, though, I've never seen you this pent up. What's up with you?"

"It's work, rough case," he lied.

Tyler took his time getting the ball, which had rolled along the hardwood flooring near the glass wall behind him. The pain and confusion he felt for deceiving Billie eclipsed the refreshing escape he usually found in the court's sallow, fluorescent-hued containment. He'd never kept any secrets from her before. He wasn't even sure why he wasn't telling her everything about the photo and texts; it wasn't like he was doing anything wrong, was he? Besides, Billie seemed fragile these days, and he needed to safeguard her against more stress. Even if he despised himself for it, he knew in his core that keeping his mouth shut was the right thing to do. He positioned himself at the service line and slammed the ball again. He and Moe both ducked after it thwacked the wall and soared back toward them.

"Shit, man," Moe said. "I'm out."

The friends were silent as they headed to the locker room to get changed. Tyler dried off and wrapped the towel around his hips. Lowering himself onto the wooden bench running between the row of lockers, he rubbed his hands against his temples while Moe dressed and repacked his workout bag. A door slammed from the other end of the men's room as Moe approached him and cleared his throat.

"Hey," he said. "I know you and Billie are going through a lot with the pregnancy stuff. If you want to grab a beer and blow off steam without endangering my life, just call."

Tyler almost stopped his friend from leaving but didn't. He trusted Moe, just not with this. First, he needed to figure out what "this" was.

Still draped in his gym towel from the waist down, he sat hunched on the bench in front of his open locker. He realized his friend was right. He needed to talk about what was going on. The distance between him and Billie since the fertility stuff started was only going to get worse if he continued to keep this from her. She was the one he needed to open up to, not Moe. Tyler stood, took his phone from the top shelf in his locker, and messaged Billie.

Hey. Are you up yet?

Up. Not out of bed. You heading home from gym?

Yes. Wanted to say I love you.

Everything okay?

All good. I'll explain later. Dinner date tonight?

He blew out a long breath. *It's the right move*, he thought. The conversation would be hard on Billie, but they would get through it together. He was already feeling better as he got dressed. Tyler lifted his gym bag as the empty locker clicked shut. He cringed when his phone vibrated. Against his sense of logic, he tapped to open the new message from the unknown caller. His heart pounded against his chest when he read the eerie words: I know you've seen her, Tyger.

"Son of a . . ." His sharp yelp reverberated in the abandoned locker room. Tyger was his nickname when he was a teen. The school gym used to rumble as the crowd stamped their feet and chanted, "Tyger, Tyger, Tyger!" whenever he scored a winning three-pointer in his basketball games. Tyler dropped back down onto the bench. The chances the person hounding him was a random client or over-zealous coworker were slim. No, he comprehended now, this person knew him as a child. He pulled a bottle of water from his bag and chugged it down. He could only think of one person from his past who'd want to do this to him.

Tyler thought back to that awful December day in middle school. The sky had hovered between afternoon's light and dusk when he walked out of the gym after practice. He waited out front for his father to pick him up, eventually accepting he'd have to walk home. A gust of wind made him shiver, and he contemplated putting on the team jacket he carried, but it was uncool for guys to wear coats, no matter how cold. He secured his books against his hip, keeping his face angled toward the crunchy ground ahead of him to avoid the biting wind. He was approaching the corner of the brick building when a hand grabbed his throat and slammed his back into the wall.

"Hey! What the . . ." Tyler yelled at a disheveled man with greasy, uncombed hair wearing a navy-blue bomber jacket. Red, raw skin peeked out from behind patches of hair on his unshaven neck. He had a cold, evil look in his eyes, and the smell of stale booze assaulted Tyler.

"Where is she, you little bastard?" The gravelly voice was chilling.

"Get off me." Tyler struggled to pull the man's wrists away.

"I asked you a question." The man's claw gripped tighter around Tyler's throat as he pressed Tyler harder against the brick.

"Where is who?" The words hurt as they escaped his dry, constricted throat.

"Don't bullshit me! Where's my daughter?"

"Don't know," Tyler gasped.

"I'm gonna find her. You understand me?"

"Yes, sir." The rough brick dug into his back as the man loosened his hold and Tyler wriggled to free himself. He was vaguely aware of his own warm urine trickling down his leg.

"You hear from her, you let me know. But you and your friends . . . you stay away from her! Got it?" His hot, vile breath snaked its way up Tyler's nostrils. "If you don't, I'll end you." He squeezed Tyler's throat again and moved so close their noses touched. "You tell anyone about our little chat, and your parents are done for too." His hand released its grasp, and the man strode out of sight. Tyler heard a harsh, creepy voice echoing down the hill, "That's my baby, goddamn it."

Tyler massaged the inflamed skin around his neck before he grabbed his books off the ground and then forced his shaking legs to run home. With each step, he felt a sharp pain in his side, but he kept on running. When he reached the house, he slammed the front door behind him.

"Dinner's ready," his mother sang from the kitchen.

"Not hungry." Tyler bounded up the stairs. He quickly changed the pants and underwear he'd soiled while the life was being squeezed out of him. His nerves were still on hyper speed. He put two fingers on the point beneath his jaw to check his pulse the way the health teacher had taught. It was too fast to count. He took a deep breath, but his throat blazed and hurt when he swallowed. He tried to look at his ribs, but his shirt stuck to his side, and it was painful as hell when he peeled it off. The spot felt wet and gummy, and when he looked at himself in the mirror on the back of his bedroom door, he could see a bloody gash. He flung open the door and flew to the bathroom.

"Aaargh." Gritting his teeth, he tried not to scream while he poured bacitracin over the long, deep wound. He moved quickly as the blood dripped faster than he could blot it. He'd aced first aid in Boy Scouts and knew he needed to put pressure on it to stop the bleeding. Once he managed to get a double layer of gauze taped over it, he placed rolled strips on top of the bandage, wincing as he added a tighter second bandage. Tyler attempted to clean the mess from the floor and counter with a washcloth. He filled a garbage bag with everything he'd used and added the clothes he'd been wearing. He stashed it under his bed, intending to drop it in a random neighborhood garbage can on trash day.

Ignoring the throbbing in his side, he lay on his bed, staring at the ceiling in the darkened room. What the hell? It was not a scary movie. This was his real life, and it happened. To him. Tyler had one hundred percent thought he was going to die, right there with his back against the school building's jagged brick. *Why me? I never did anything to anyone.*

His mother knocked on the door. He hadn't thought to press the lock. If he didn't answer, she'd come in.

"Go away." He didn't want to talk to anyone, especially his parents. His father had high blood pressure, and his mother would make it all into a huge drama and go to the police. Besides, the man said not to. His mother pushed the door open a crack, like she wasn't invading his privacy if it wasn't fully ajar.

"Tyler, what's happened? There are blood drops on the carpet."

"I'm fine."

"You are not . . . You're bleeding! Let me see." She was already at his side, lifting his shirt. "How did you get this slash?"

"It's not a big deal. I tripped and fell on a rock." Tyler looked at the blotch of blood seeping through his shoddy bandage.

"Not a big deal. Right. Okay, tough guy." She placed a hand under his elbow as she supported him off the bed. "Off to the ER we go."

The doctor kept asking, "How'd you really get injured?" as he stitched Tyler up. But he'd stuck to his story about falling on a rock, and in the years that followed, he'd never told anyone the truth about his large scar, not his mother, not Moe, and not Billie.

Fuck me, Tyler thought as he left the locker room, keeping his head down as he sped through the sports facility to his car. With a gazillion scenarios racing around in his head, he thought it was somewhat of a miracle he made it home without skidding off the road.

"Hey, sweetie." He waved at Billie and hurried upstairs to avoid her. She was too perceptive to be fooled for long. "Gonna get cleaned up for work."

Tyler stepped into the shower and turned the hot knob all the way. He stood under the pelleting spray until the water almost seared his skin. He was soaping up his shoulders when cool air enveloped his body and Billie came in. This time he jerked away when she pressed up behind him and kissed the scar on his back ribs.

Her arms stayed suspended, embracing only the sprinkling water. "What just happened?"

He willed himself to answer but couldn't.

"It's fine if you don't want to. Just say so, but you don't need to push me away like that." Her eyes, always full of understanding and patience, darkened. "Have I done something wrong? I'd understand if you're worried about me after losing the baby. I promise my body is okay. But you have to talk to me. Please."

Questions lingered in her expression, but he did nothing to comfort her.

"Wow, okay then," she said, "this is how you want it to be?"

Steam escaped from the shower, skimming across the bathroom mirror as Billie wrapped a bath towel around herself.

Tyler waited to get out of the shower until the bathroom was thoroughly fogged, preventing him from facing his reflection. He was aware of her glances as they dressed wordlessly.

Tyler was neither relieved nor sorry when he pulled into his parking spot in the garage next to his office building. He thought he saw Ms. Neuman nearing the stairwell. Thinking he should make sure he hadn't offended her in any way, he called out to her.

"Sorry, Judge McFarrin," he said when the woman turned. "Thought you were someone else."

"Well, it better be someone fabulous you've mistaken me for," she said, and laughed.

"No one better than you, Judge."

"Flatterer. Maybe you should consider getting yourself some caffeine, Mr. Scott. It'll improve your eyesight. See you soon."

Tyler smacked his forehead and hustled to the elevator in the other direction.

Marla, who always had a positive attitude, was banging her phone against her desktop as he approached. Tyler cleared his throat.

"Unfitting behavior, you don't need to tell me," she said. "The phantom caller has amped up. It's exasperating."

"Continue documenting the calls." He tried to keep his voice flat to disguise the clutching sensation in his chest.

Tyler tossed his briefcase on his office couch and closed the door. He raked his fingers through his hair as he tried to think clearly. The man who'd attacked him was much too dangerous. There was no way he could resolve what was happening alone, and he trusted the firm's investigator. He opened the office door and poked his head out. "Marla, can you get Collin Frost on the phone?"

His intercom buzzed a couple of minutes later. "Line two."

"What need have you today, boss man?" Collin Frost asked when Tyler picked up.

"I'd like you to check on someone for me." Without revealing the reason for his interest, Tyler gave him the man's name, where he used to work, his last known location, and the few other details he had. "Anything you can find, particularly his whereabouts, will be a help."

"I'll see what's what and I'll get back to ya soon."

Tyler prayed soon wasn't too late.

THIRTEEN
Billie

Weary from the long workday, Billie pushed herself up the hot parking garage steps. After hours in the heat, the car door handle scorched her fingers, and a gush of smoldering air escaped from the car. Reaching across the seat, she started the engine, cranked up the air-conditioning, and pressed the buttons to open all the windows. While she waited, Billie thought if she had a daughter, she would teach her better than to stand alone in a shadowy concrete structure filled with odd noises and few vehicles.

The second she walked into the house, she kicked the heels off her sore feet, dropped her briefcase on the floor, and hung the dry cleaning in the coat closet. Tyler had said he'd go to the cleaners for her, but she was in the area and picked it up herself. Billie pulled off a small envelope attached to the plastic covering over her husband's stain-free suit. Once in a while, loose change got past her searches and hid in clothing pockets. The cleaners always returned it in small envelopes clipped to the receipts on the bags. This one was weightless, which meant it was probably a dollar bill. Hastening to the kitchen, she unloaded the food bags digging into her arms and set the oven to reheat the veal piccata dinners she'd brought. She put the food in a glass dish, recycled the containers, and wiped down the counter, leaving it spotless—except for the white envelope from the cleaners. When she swiped her finger under the flap, she found a 2x3 glossy photograph of a baby inside instead of cash. Her first thought was it might be from one of her cases, but it wasn't familiar and wouldn't explain how it'd ended up in Tyler's suit.

She studied the photograph, entranced by the infant clothed in a sweet pink cap with a lilac flower and a pink sweater. The newborn's pureness made Billie's heart contract and burn to spoil her. It was the same yearning pain she felt whenever she saw any baby these days. The photo came from a personal camera, not one of those staged hospital photographer packages her friends sometimes sent with birth announcements. She couldn't make out the faded date stamped on the back, but someone had written "L.B." underneath. After scrutinizing the cherubic face, Billie placed the photo on the counter so she'd remember to ask Tyler about it. Then she went to change out of her suit.

"Hey, something smells good!" Tyler said when he came home.

"Artisimo's piccata with angel hair." Billie tucked herself into her husband's hug. "I was too beat to cook."

While they got the table ready for the takeout feast, she and Tyler chatted about their day in the distant, impersonal way people do when they are avoiding uncomfortable issues.

"I took on a crazy case today," she said.

"All your cases are crazy, but I love hearing about them."

Before she could tell him, she had to create a moniker for the client so she wouldn't divulge identifying information. She thought about Gianna's white-blonde hair. The color, and the tan complexion of her Mediterranean skin, reminded Billie of the palomino horses she'd ridden with her mother along Cape Cod beaches.

"She's fourteen, Ty. She's having a baby and she's fourteen."

"You've had teenagers before, but so young, I don't get it."

Billie dipped her finger in the piccata sauce and touched it to her tongue, letting her senses absorb the lemon butter sauce.

"There was a woman from a California adoption agency at the symposium the other day. She's working with a thirteen-year-old client. Fourteen is bad, but can you imagine going through such a thing at that age? I know it happens. I even refer to the stats in lectures, but in all my years, I haven't had a birth mother as young as that." Billie transferred the food to ceramic dinner plates.

"It's just not right, you know? A baby having a baby," she continued. "Even at fourteen, the Palomino doesn't seem to understand how someone gets pregnant and swears she was never with a boy." When she turned to look at Tyler, he was emerging from the fridge with a bottle of ranch dressing. "She's either in the deepest denial I've ever seen or was roofied and raped at a party. I haven't ruled out the possibility of sexual abuse either." Billie shook her head. "I'm supposed to be objective, but people who take advantage of young girls like that repulse me." The bottle of ranch slipped from Tyler's hand and splattered on the floor. They both grabbed wads of paper towels to clean up the mess.

"Anyway, it's all very troubling," Billie said.

Tyler seemed too focused on his meticulous search for shards of glass on the tiled floor to respond.

"Shouldn't you report the family?" he asked after Billie placed their meals on the table.

"Yes. I hate to do it, though. Once the process starts, it throws a family into turmoil. Sadly, even if it's in the child's best interest, the children you're saving often end up traumatized." *And*, Billie thought, *heaven forbid, I make that call and the determination is no abuse. I'll destroy a family.* Even if Gianna had consensual sex with another minor, it's considered statutory rape by law. Knowing Gianna was going to despise her, Billie had been delaying the inevitable.

She went to the toaster oven to remove the restaurant rolls she'd warmed up. "The reality is, DCF—Department of Children and Families—is way too overloaded and understaffed. Weeks could go by before they assign a caseworker or determine if it's plausible to pursue."

"That's asinine. They're mandated to protect these kids from their abusers. They can't just let grown-ups take advantage of innocent children and walk away. Offenders need to be punished."

"Calm down. It's not news that it's a badly broken system. On the upside, I can continue helping her as much as I can before DCF hauls her away to some foster situation."

It took a moment for Tyler's shoulders to relax, and Billie waited for the heat in his cheeks to fade before she changed the subject.

"Have the partners stopped gloating from last month's big win?"

"A bit. You know how Prachett likes to milk it."

"He does." Billie laughed, both at Prachett's reputation and in relief that Tyler had chilled out. "Do you think you can take a breather now? Maybe we could take a long weekend up in Maine?"

"Not yet. There's another case I'm prepping for. I hope it'll end up settling."

"And here I thought I'd married a man with a cut-and-dried desk career." Billie sighed. "Who's suing who this time?"

"Children of a wealthy philanthropist are suing to expunge the second wife from the terms of the estate."

"Haven't I read about them somewhere?"

Tyler winked as he shoveled a twirl of pasta into his mouth. Billie finished eating and watched him sop up a pool of sauce with a dinner roll.

"I almost forgot!" She scraped her chair backward to retrieve the picture. "The cleaners found this in your pocket. Who is it?" She slid the photo across the table. His chewing slowed as he inspected it.

"Not sure. I thought it was you." Tyler returned to blotting the sauce.

"Well, it's not me. I've never seen this before." She turned the photo over. "And what did you think 'L.B.' meant? Little Billie?"

"Why not?"

"You're not funny."

"Huh." Tyler swallowed the last of the saucy bread.

"I bought some cannoli. Do you want dessert now or later?"

Tyler patted his belly. "Why wait?"

Billie popped a coffee pod into the Keurig and took the box of cannoli and two clean plates to the table. When she brought their coffee mugs, she lifted the photo to make space between her and Tyler.

"Where'd this come from, anyway?" She placed the photo closer to his side.

"In my gym bag. Must've gotten mixed into my stuff when I was helping my parents move some boxes to the attic."

"Why would you think there'd be a childhood photo of me in your parents' attic?"

"You're right, I guess there wouldn't be." When he looked up, Billie was sure he must have seen the questions on her face because his eyebrow twitched.

"How do you think it got in your bag?"

"Am I on trial here, Miss Skeptic?" His laugh sounded forced to her. "Anyway, must be a relative, wouldn't you think?"

"I handled all our wedding invitations and seating arrangements and organized your dad's surprise party with your mother. I know your entire family tree. There isn't a single female I can think of whose initials are L.B."

Tyler swiped his napkin across his jaw. "It's been a long day. Can we just drop it already?" His voice had a slight bite to it, and his eyes were steady and unblinking.

"Aren't you curious who it is? I'm going shopping with your mom after work Thursday. I'll take the photo and ask her about it."

He balled up the napkin and sat back in his chair.

Billie loved a good mystery and would have delved more in-depth, but something about the tension in his body, the fist that squeezed the clumped napkin, silenced her.

"I'm just kidding," Tyler said. "A potential new client gave it to me. I don't know why."

"Didn't you ask?"

"Couldn't. They didn't end up hiring me."

The muffled beeping of her pager called out from inside Billie's briefcase.

"You're on call?"

"Yeah, next two weeks. One of Paige's clients is due this month, and she's finally going on her honeymoon."

As Billie dialed the answering service, she saw Tyler pluck the photo from the table, cup it in his palm, and head toward his study. His need to hide something from her hurt as much as his recent physical rejections.

FOURTEEN
Anne

Forcing herself to get up when her empty stomach protested in the middle of the night, Anne took a carton of milk and a box of Oreos to eat under the covers. On her way back, she stubbed her toe on the composition book she'd cast aside the day before. A heavy weight pressed on her chest as she scooped the notebook under the cookie package, cradling it as she burrowed herself against the bed pillows. A musty smell, reminiscent of the stale odor of the bedroom she'd grown up in, overcame her. It seemed as if she was in her grungy, mold-stained old room, watching herself pull the cute boy inside and push the warped door shut. They threw their book bags on her bed, removed their textbooks, and slid to the floor.

"Won't your parents mind if we're in your room?" he asked.

"Nah." Anne flipped the pages in the book to find the project they had to do. "My mother works night shifts. She takes a pill and sleeps all day. Which is fine 'cause she's bitchy when she's awake. And I haven't seen my father in a couple of months. He took off with a young chick he met at the post office where he works. My mother calls her the 'big-busted bimbo.' He lives with her and her little kids now."

A torrent of mixed emotions surged within her. She worried

about the girlfriend's daughter, who was about to turn seven, the same age Anne was when her father first started his night visits. Guilt consumed her at times for hoping he'd move on to someone else and not knowing how to protect the other girl. With him out of the house, she thought she'd finally be able to sleep, but nightmares kept her awake.

Anne glanced sideways at her classmate. The warm pull to press against him was unfamiliar and not at all like the fear and grime that swallowed her when her father approached. Deep down, she knew the craving was wrong, but she could feel the monster in her—the one forming since her body started maturing and her father's use for her ran dry. And the monster needed feeding. Shoving her notebook off her lap, she pursed her lips and leaned toward him. She let her kiss linger on his sweet, soft mouth before pushing her tongue into his. Moving her body, she sat on his lap and waited until he stiffened; then she guided him up to her bed. She pulled his jeans and briefs down to his ankles, using her feet to push their bags to the floor as she pinned him down.

"I, uh, I never . . . I don't know how . . ." he sputtered between kisses.

"It's okay. I'll show you . . ." Anne lowered her pants. She took his hands, placing one on each breast under her shirt, and began riding him. The bedsprings clacked their grating tune. He sighed, and his arms fell helplessly above his head. His blue eyes were rolling and drowning as his face twisted. She squeezed her eyes shut, confused by and unable to tolerate his pleasure.

"Tell me I'm your princess," she ordered. "Say it now!"

"You're . . . my . . . princess," he obliged.

Anne felt him shudder. She'd done what she'd had to do. She removed herself from her perch, pulled her jeans up, and sank off the bed. She looked back at the boy lying with a surprised yet triumphant grin.

"Well, that was . . . something," he whispered before he turned toward her. "Is it like that every time?"

"Don't be a geek." Anne pretended to search her backpack for a pencil to avoid the emotions she might see in the face of the boy who lay on her blanket.

In truth, it had never been like that before, but she couldn't explain that she'd never felt the peculiar stirring rising within her and then the throbbing. As she thought about it, her crotch felt warm again. Ashamed, she picked up her math book and let it rest on her knees. While her fingers rolled and pulled her ear, she heard clanging in her head. Anne imagined one of those monkey toys with creepy eyes and sinister smirks that rotated back and forth and wouldn't stop banging cymbals until you smashed it with your fist. She bit at a hangnail until it bled. A small part of her felt she should earn some kind of badge for what she'd done to him. But the act that filled his face with that boastful look left her empty. Humiliation slithered across her skin. It grew worse when he sat too close to her on the floor. She could sense his uncertainty in how he kept peering at her like a puppy waiting for a treat. The constant tapping of his pencil against his book made her nuts.

"Can we finish problem seventeen already?" She didn't know why she was short-tempered, but it didn't seem to bother him. "You're on the wrong damn page."

At four o'clock in the morning, Anne rolled out of the blankets and dialed her mother, forgetting Arizona was three hours behind.

"I'm not coming." She snapped the phone base cord out of the socket before her mother could change her mind. She pulled the wine bottle from the counter, hugging the smooth glass between her breasts. It felt as warm against her skin as the air in her apartment. Anne threw her head back, tilted the bottle, and shook the last drop of wine onto her tongue. Without a fresh supply, she had no way to trick herself into sleep.

The aroma of the vendor's hot dogs was less than appealing, but Anne had forgotten breakfast. It perplexed her that Tyler had let eleven days slip by without contacting her, so she'd kept her vigil on the bench. She'd made a point to show up to work for a few days this week to appease Rudy.

"Excuse me," the woman in line behind her said. She was apologizing for bumping her stroller into Anne.

"You have a lot to juggle there." Anne nodded toward the toddler wearing a plaid short set and matching hair bow. The agile baby was attempting to tug her shoes off. "You can go ahead of me."

While the young mother struggled to pay for her hot dogs and drinks without spilling the contents of her diaper bag, Anne surveyed the restless tot's arm for the identifier she could never find.

When she took her meal to her bench, the woman and a spread of mommy accessories were invading her space. The baby was on her mother's lap, gurgling as her greedy little hands grabbed the small pieces of food offered to her. Anne walked past them, crossed the street, leaned on the outside edge of a bus shelter, and ate standing up.

She held the last of the ketchup-stained roll pinched in her fingers when she recognized the woman with the well-groomed presence in front of Tyler's building. Anne already suspected the fashionable woman was his wife. She knew the wife was preventing him from coming to her, and her anger toward the woman sizzled.

Tyler popped out of the revolving door, all smiles and kisses a few minutes later. Instead of going into the parking garage or their favorite café, they walked to the T, the stifling subway system Anne hated. The couple found two empty seats as she hopped in and the Green Line's car doors smacked together. She camouflaged herself behind a wide, scruffy man but kept them in view when they exited on Commonwealth Avenue in Back Bay. They walked a few blocks lined with tight rows of brownstones, which had an old-world quality. Each exterior had its own personality, some rounded, some flat, some red brick, some light sandstone. Some had manicured hedges in front, some iron gates. Anne could imagine herself in a Victorian dress, waiting for a horse and carriage. Caught up in the imagery, she almost didn't see Tyler and the wife enter a brownstone. She waited a sensible amount of time before going up the steps to read the brass plaque outside the door: "Advanced Fertility Clinic of Greater Boston."

The rising clatter of thoughts in Anne's head made her dizzy. *She can't give him a baby.* A low, deep whisper tickled her ear. She twisted around, expecting to see someone standing behind her, but she was alone on the stoop. *You can.* The high-pitched words bounced inside her head. A snake of excitement crawled from her abdomen, wriggled to her stomach, and clutched her lungs. Winded and woozy, she grabbed onto the railing.

"I can." The realization oozed from her vocal cords. A more seductive-sounding thought resounded: *I'm the one for Tyler, not her. Go to him, show him . . . go to him.* The chorus of thoughts continued its chant until Anne backed away from the building and ran.

FIFTEEN
Tyler

While Billie went to the desk to check in, Tyler took a seat in the waiting room. He sorted through the women-oriented magazines on the table next to him, feeling uncomfortable and out of place. Even with the sound off, he felt his phone vibrating when a new text arrived, and he muttered a curse when he opened the screen.

We're looking for the same thing.

Who is this? he typed back.

You know who I am.

Collin Frost had already made it clear the man Tyler feared was neither a threat nor the person harassing him—he'd been dead for years. Only one other person came to mind. It was a far reach, he knew, but since they'd met, he kept thinking he saw her in random places. It seemed unethical to reveal a client's name, but she hadn't actually hired him, so he wasn't breaking any rules.

Ms. Neuman? Tyler typed, deleted, retyped, and sent. He flicked the screen off when Billie sat in the chair next to him.

"They say we shouldn't have to wait too long."

"Okay." He held his cell up. "Work stuff." It was a safe gamble she wouldn't question him. Billie was the most understanding woman he'd ever met. He couldn't remember a single time she got annoyed or resentful when he had put his career over their personal life. Just another reason why he couldn't break her heart and admit he was reluctant about being a father. He'd only agreed to this appointment to give a semen sample for analysis because he owed it to his wife.

Not Neuman.

Tell me who you are.

He knew he shouldn't keep engaging. His pulse raced when the door from the waiting area to the examination rooms opened. He wasn't sure if he was getting overheated because of the texts or the task he was there to complete. The person who walked out wasn't medical staff. They weren't looking for him or Billie.

The texts seemed to have stopped, and Tyler hoped he'd called the person's bluff and they'd quit. He thought he should be better company to Billie and wondered if his wife felt as composed as she looked. She had her legs crossed, and her arms fell loosely on her lap. The pose was much like how she sat waiting for the previews in a movie theater. There was no hint of anticipation or apprehension. Maybe, after all the years of routine gyno appointments and recent miscarriages and testing, she'd grown immune to strangers touching and invading her body. It was something he'd never get used to. It was emasculating and left him feeling powerless and angry. Those feelings heightened as he imagined being alone in a cubicle with a cup, porn magazines, and nurses, patients, and office personnel within two feet of the closed door. Did employees make bets on how long it took each schmuck to reappear?

You already know, the mystery person texted in response to his question asking who it was.

But Tyler didn't know what or whom he supposedly knew.

"Do you have any mints?" he asked Billie.

He waited while she pulled a tin of Altoids from her bag and held it open for him. He took three and shot them all in his mouth, quickly forgetting that a person should never bite an Altoid. It felt like there was a fire shooting cool-mint flames when he breathed in. His eyes watered as the peppermint sailed through his sinuses. Billie was shaking her head, watching him with obvious amusement.

"Don't you dare say I told you so."

"Oh, but I have." She giggled.

Tyler looked back at his cell, wondering how he could get the upper hand. He was fed up with the mystery texter, and it was past time to put an end to it.

What do you want?

I gave you the answers.

I don't know what you're talking about.

Tyler waited to see the three little dots indicating someone was typing, but they didn't come. He kept rereading the chain of texts going back to the beginning, trying to piece it all together. It had all started last week, with one person, one appointment, and one object: Ms. Neuman, in the office, with a hand-delivered envelope. He felt like he was playing a scary version of the board game Clue, except someone had rigged the deck.

Tyler texted Suzanne Neuman's name and description to Frost and asked him to look into her. He slipped his hand inside his jacket pocket and touched the corner of the snapshot he'd kept with him since he took it back from Billie. He visualized the unidentified baby, still perplexed by its significance.

The photo? he asked.

A minute or two went by.

When are you coming to me? I've been waiting.

What game is this? he demanded, though he wasn't sure that translated in a text.

Don't be mean, Tyler.

He had gotten nowhere, no identity or motive, or even how they had his cell number. If it was a friend messing with his head, it wasn't funny. But it didn't feel like a prank. This person had an agenda, and if he or she intended to unnerve him, they'd won. None of it made any sense to him.

Tyler was still holding his phone when it shook with an incoming call. He waited until it passed, and the missed call notification appeared. Then came the voicemail alert, which added to his increasing sense of dread. He clicked to view his voicemails, knowing he was looking for trouble.

The message was from Marla to let him know Prachett was concerned if he would make it back in time for the four-thirty meeting. And she alerted him that Huck's secretary was nosing around, asking indirect questions about why Tyler took most of the day off. He knew Huck had sent his secretary to snoop. The senior partner had been scrutinizing everything his mentee had done since his warning at the Fourth of July party six weeks ago. There was no doubt Huck was adding this as a black mark to the growing list of why he wasn't getting the partnership. *This day can't get worse.* Tyler brushed his hair off his forehead. His mood lightened for a moment as he mentally played out a scene where he stood in front of Huck and described every detail of what the partner's prized, well-educated, brilliant lawyer with the most potential was about to do with a plastic cup.

Tyler powered off his phone. It didn't seem like a good idea to continue getting stressed before his impending performance for an ample sperm contribution he didn't want to give. He needed to clear his mind. He wanted to walk away, but he had no choice but to stay and go along with the analysis.

SIXTEEN
Billie

When they came to the fertility clinic the first time, Billie hadn't realized how barren the waiting area was. Brown vinyl cushions were in tight rows against taupe walls. There was little staff activity behind the glassed-in cubicles where patients signed their names on the check-in form. On the TV across from where she and Tyler sat, an effervescent Rachel Ray was demonstrating something simple one could make at home, and Billie just wanted her to be quiet.

Tyler was scrolling through his phone. Moe had probably sent the latest batch of Nicholas's second birthday portraits. Tyler was ecstatic when Moe and Ashley named him as the godfather of their baby son. He took his role seriously, and it was impossible to stop him from spoiling the boy. Billie had encouraged the indulgences, which delighted her too. They'd brought an infant Celtics outfit, including green booties, to the hospital when Nicholas was born. And then Tyler had insisted on buying both a toddler-sized basketball and an official one for the boy's first birthday. At the time, it amused Billie to watch her husband roll on the floor with the baby and incite crawling races before Nicholas was walking.

In the past few months, as they'd waited for the methotrexate to flush out of her system, Billie kept making more and more excuses to avoid Moe and his family. It was wrenching to watch Tyler fawn over Nicholas when she knew he ached for his own. As much as she loved them all, every time she saw or heard Tyler's stories about Moe's family, her insides burned. But now, as he scrolled through his phone while waiting for the doctor, she couldn't interpret what he was feeling. His expression looked . . . hopeful or wishful. Or what was she seeing?

"Billie?" Neila, the nurse practitioner, called out.

Billie rushed to follow, almost forgetting Tyler was with her. Dr. Fischman had told her to come on the second day of full menstrual flow to have a follicle-stimulating hormone (FSH) and estradiol blood test. The results would show her ovarian ability to produce eggs and their quality. Tyler would be down the hall depositing his specimen sample, and she couldn't help but feel a sharp stab of guilt. She'd offered to go in with him to make it fun, but he'd gruffly declined.

After she'd dressed, Billie headed to the doctor's office where she'd been told to wait. She eyed the woman coming toward her with one hand cupping her rounded belly from underneath while the other hand caressed the mound in gentle circles. Billie bitterly forced a smile as she pressed herself against the wall to let the other woman pass. *Just once*, she thought, *I'd like to know that feeling.* To come out of an ob-gyn or fertility specialist's door with something to look forward to. Twice, she had experienced only a glimpse of that eager anticipation.

Tyler came into Dr. Fischman's office and took the only other vacant chair. He seemed weary, and she worried what he'd just been through had bruised his self-esteem.

"I'm sorry you had to do that," she said without looking at him. "Was it awful?" She turned her ring around her finger while she waited for his reply.

"It's over now, Bills."

"Well, they shouldn't have made you do that when they already know it's me who's the problem." Billie meant to be empathic, to take the blame, and to make him feel better. They sat silently for a minute, side by side in the doctor's office, holding hands between their chairs.

Tyler opened his mouth to say something, hesitated, and cleared his throat with a muted cough. "Maybe we shouldn't have stopped the birth control when we did."

"That's ridiculous. It's what we both wanted."

On the last night of their honeymoon two years ago, she'd been standing at the bathroom sink, about to press a tiny birth control tablet from a new pill pack, when Tyler curled his muscled body around her. Her head fit perfectly between his shoulder and neck, just at the spot where she could nuzzle his jawline. He'd had a strange look in his eye that night, seductive with a slice of mischief as he carried her to bed and the pills dropped to the floor. Had they actually agreed to leave it all up to chance?

"If we hadn't stopped on the honeymoon, we'd be sitting here two years from now. I'd be thirty-four, and the chances of conceiving would be worse."

"Why do you think the doctor wants to see us?" Tyler asked after a while.

"I'm not sure I want to know. I don't think I can bear more bad news." Billie eyed the slatted shade covering the window and considered cleaning the dust off it. "What if we got up and left before he gets here? We could get the car and drive up to Vermont or even Canada and get away from everything." She was about to add, "I miss having fun together," but Dr. Fischman came in and leaned on the front edge of his desk, his arms folded across his chest.

"So, I wanted to touch base," the doctor said. The warmth he attempted to exude with his relaxed posture conflicted with his stern expression. "And review the next steps with you. You should continue tracking your menstruation so we get a handle on your typical cycle and continue the basal temperature charting for now. One of the next tests we'll run is a post-coital. You'll need to come in several hours after intercourse to retrieve the cervical mucus."

"How romantic," Billie mumbled.

"What does that kind of exam tell you?" Tyler asked.

"Well, the simple version is it gives us an idea whether the sperm and mucus are compatible to allow passage to the uterus."

"And if they're not?"

"It's just one piece of the puzzle. There are many variables we have to evaluate to determine the best plan of action. But let me be clear, I'm not going to cut corners and go from zero to ninety. Depending on the ovulation graphs and kits, I'd prefer to start with the least invasive approaches, like the synthetic meds, and see what kind of response we get. I'll be in touch. Good to see you folks," he said, which made Billie feel like they'd overstayed their welcome. As they left the office, she could feel Tyler's hand shaking almost as hard as her own.

Tyler and Billie walked back to the T together, yet apart, each lost in their private thoughts as they absorbed their discussion with Dr. Fischman. The summer heat had found its way into every crevice of the underground platform. Two college-age kids a few feet away intently tapped their phones, never communicating with the other. *Perhaps*, Billie thought, *they can't face what needs to be said to one another either.* While he stayed behind the caution line, Tyler kept bending forward as if looking for the train could speed up its arrival. She turned away from the tracks to listen to a guitarist who leaned against the subway wall. His straight white teeth caught her attention as the words from Jim Croce's "Time in a Bottle" flowed from his earthy voice. She wondered what his story was as the platform vibrated beneath her feet.

Billie and Tyler sat side by side, their bodies leaning into the other as the T wove through the tunnels heading downtown. Tyler placed his hand on her arm when the train stopped at the Government Center station.

"Let's stay on one more stop."

Unsure what he was thinking but willing to go along, she sat back against the plastic seat.

"This way," Tyler said, taking her hand as they emerged from underneath the city. They followed along Hanover Street into the North End, passing Italian restaurants with European-style facades beneath brick apartment buildings. There were corner Italian groceries with large glass storefronts displaying salamis, cheese, and olive oils. Tyler turned onto Parmenter Street, and then, after two more turns, they ended up on a cobblestone alley. At its end stood a small villa-like building that had outlived the development surrounding it.

"Vanni's." Tyler said the name as though he'd found a lost family member. "I can't believe I haven't brought you here before."

"Hey, I know this place," Billie said as they took a booth in the back corner. After their walk in the sun, she appreciated the cold vinyl seat. "Sometimes when I was little, I'd spend the night with my grandparents in the South End. One day I'll show you the building if it's still there. They lived in a row house. It was decaying on the outside, but the inside was beautiful with fine lace curtains and an old wood hutch displaying a tarnished silver tea set and tiny frames of my ancestors. Grandma kept the small home almost too tidy and organized."

"So, it's hereditary," Tyler said. "I always wondered why you alphabetized the spices."

"You're hilarious. Anyway, I've told you sometimes my grandparents took me to the Duck Pond at the Commons. But once in a while, I'd have a special day, just me and Grandpa. We'd take the T and come here for a slice."

Both grandparents died before Billie was ten. She hadn't been back since, but until college, every year on Grandpa's birthday she insisted her parents get pizza. She never said it out loud, but she'd always imagined carrying on the Duck Pond–pizza day with her own children.

"Should we get Vanni's famous barbecue-chicken pizza, or do you want Sicilian today?" Tyler asked.

"You might as well get the barbecue. I don't have much of an appetite."

While their pie was baking, Billie fidgeted with the shakers of Parmesan and crushed red pepper flakes. Tyler reached across the table and pulled her hand into his own. She sensed he was looking at her, waiting for her to lift her eyes and see him. He continued stroking the back of her hand until she did.

"What Fischman said . . . I know it's not the news we were hoping for. But we're in this together, Bills. We'll deal with it. Whatever comes, we have each other."

She reached her other hand out to caress the hands that held her own. It was a strain to smile at her husband. Then she released him, grabbed a wad of napkins from the dispenser, and dabbed her tear-soaked cheeks.

The waiter placed salads and fresh garlic knots before them. When he returned with the pie, Billie's mouth moistened at the fresh-baked bread, cheese, garlic, and tomato combination. Without thinking, she dove into the fat slices.

"What's that look? Are you doubting me?"

"I don't know what you're talking about," Billie said through a gob of pizza. But after he kept looking at her with his chin down and eyebrow raised, she had to give up.

"Ugh, you know me too well."

"This is going to be a tough ride. You know that better than anyone, but you have to have faith in us." With a pointed look, he added, "In me."

"I do, of course, I do. I always have. Maybe not as much as you did the night we met." Billie brightened as she teased him.

"Well, I was right, wasn't I? I told Prachett I'd just met my wife." The laugh lines around Tyler's eyes deepened.

"God, I still have no idea why you weren't scared off. You and all your gorgeousness made me so nervous. I think I told you my entire life story over one glass of wine."

"I learned a lot in one cocktail hour," he chuckled.

"Did you now?"

"Absolutely. You told me you liked comedy, horses, and basketball."

"Is that why you took me to a Celtics game on our first date?"

"It was a brilliant move." Tyler looked pleased with himself.

"While you're enjoying your ego trip, you have a glob of cheese right here." Billie touched the side of her mouth to show him.

After he pulled the small paper napkin across his mouth, his expression filled with sincerity. "The only thing I needed to know about you, which was and still is obvious to everyone, is what an incredible woman you are."

"Me? How about the guy who's given countless hours making young kidney patients feel special?"

Standing with him at the bar the night they'd met, she'd stopped blabbering long enough to ask what brought him to the event and discovered his heroics.

"My cousin had lupus and needed a transplant," he'd said. His expression softened when he added, "Dr. Pearse handled the surgery."

Billie remembered telling Tyler how she'd loved interning for Dr. Pearse and his pediatric kidney patients in grad school. And even though the adoption job wasn't what she planned, the Burkhead Family Service Agency's work helping couples find babies they were desperate for intoxicated her. In the beginning, it made her sad that there were people who couldn't experience the joy her mother described when, after years of dwindling hope, her baby finally arrived. But Billie couldn't resist the chance to make that happen for other people.

"If memory serves," Tyler said, "you also told me about your best friend in elementary school who was adopted and how you adored her family so much you pretended they adopted you too."

"I still can't believe you didn't run."

"There might've also been a sordid story about your college roommate."

"I remember what I said. She was the first person I knew who had an abortion. Maybe part of why my job seemed appealing was the impact she had on me when she made that decision. I didn't believe in abortion so much back then, but I respected my friends' choices for themselves. I can't say if I would've placed a baby for adoption, I only knew I'd want to be able to choose if it were me."

Tyler stared above her head in a way that made her uncomfortable.

"You know," he said, "we've never really talked about that. Did you ever get in a, er, situation?"

Billie bit into the soft pizza crust she'd intended not to eat. She took her time before swallowing the bread while contemplating her answer.

"There were times, maybe once or twice, where I was afraid. But no, I was never pregnant. I guess now we know why." She tore at the rest of the crust, refusing to succumb to the self-pity. "What would you have chosen?"

"I don't know." He lifted his hands and made a quick half shrug. "I've never had to think about it."

She looked at him and felt a wave of tenderness.

"What?" he asked.

"I was thinking about how I knew from our first little chat that I would have no choice but to love you."

"It was the scar that did it for you. Admit it."

Billie looked across the narrow pizzeria table at the husband she loved so deeply and fiddled with her wedding ring.

"How could I not marry the kind of man who cared so much for others? But yes, I do love that scar."

"I could show it to you now." He emphasized his suggestive tone with a wink, but she didn't respond in the all-in, let's-hurry-home way she always did. She could feel herself dimming and saw Tyler stop thumbing through his wallet to pay the bill.

"Why would you want to?" Billie heard her voice shake. "You haven't seemed too interested since the tubal."

"God, no. Please don't think that."

"I feel like you deserve someone who can give you a family."

"Never ever say that. Never. I love you, and I want you, and you are all I'll ever need."

SEVENTEEN
Anne

The clerk at the liquor store pissed her off. He was too young to be asking for proof of ID. Anne complied, though—anything to get herself the wine she needed after fleeing the fertility clinic steps. Most kids had no clue what details to check on a license, and this guy was no different. He made a show of looking at it, handed it back, and reached for the wine she'd placed next to the register. His arm moved each bottle along the conveyer belt the way a sloth might. No, a sloth would be faster. Her head was aching, and her skin grew hot and flushed. The urge to scream crawled up her throat.

She knew better than to draw attention to herself in case he refused to give her the booze. The store was small and run-down, which was what she liked about it. The bigger place she used to go questioned the frequency of her visits and the volume of her purchases. That was why she only bought four bottles this time. A case, as often as she came in, might be too conspicuous. Jimmy, the bartender, had once explained how, by law, bars, restaurants, and liquor stores couldn't sell alcohol to an intoxicated person. The old guy who owned this place and usually worked the register was too tired to care to whom he was selling. But an eager-to-please young kid went by the books. While she hadn't had a drink yet today, if she gave the clerk any reason to suspect, he could deny her. It was best to appear bored.

Anne considered upping her game to Scotch since the wine failed to take the edge off anymore. Scotch would be more pleasing, but its price wasn't. Maybe she could convince Stanley to prescribe something stronger to paralyze her pain and let her rest. She crouched against the rough stucco wall outside the store exit, keeping the shopping bag balanced on her knees, and pressed her phone to her ear. She hadn't expected him to answer her call.

"You've missed appointments, Anne." His patronizing voice always sounded like he was talking through a mouthful of marshmallows.

"It was a mistake." She tried to make herself sound regretful and childlike. Heat radiating from the concrete sidewalk clung to her legs as though they were poultry in a broaster. "There's been a lot of pressure." She had to come up with something he'd believe. "At work, I mean, there's been layoffs, and . . ." She slowed herself down. Too much information made for a bad lie. "Well, I'm feeling like, I don't know, it's stressful, and I can't sleep."

"You're going through a lot. We should discuss it at your next appointment."

"I'll be there at my regular time next week, for sure." Her skin was burning, but the bottles would drop if she scratched at it. "But the thing is, um, my refills have expired. Can you call in the Prozac and maybe the Xanax too?"

Stanley insisted on seeing her in person before prescribing anything. She was furious but had to keep herself together. People walking into the liquor store were sneering at her.

Anne slid into her car and placed the clinking brown bag on the passenger-side floor. As she righted herself, her hand grazed the composition book that lay on the unoccupied seat. She had no recollection of taking it out of her house or putting it in her car. Its presence seemed to dare her to open it. Trying to resist, she grasped the neck of a wine bottle. The cap released a satisfying *pfft* as she unscrewed it. After several gulps of the bitter, cheap fluid, she gave in to the book's lure.

The creamy yellow of the neglected pages was uninviting, but Anne recognized her youth's precise handwriting. Each student in eighth-grade English class received a fresh composition book.

"And this is for journaling," the teacher had said. "As part of your writing assignments, you will make at least one entry each week. It can be about anything you want, and the books will be confidential between you and me only."

Anne hadn't wanted to share anything but knew her father got pissed whenever she had bad grades. As she turned the first handful of pages now, she admired how her young wit had handled it. Each week noted in the journal repeated: "Dear Book. That's all. Anne." Once or twice, she'd written, "Hello, Book. Goodbye, Book." She'd drawn little happy-faced stars in the corners of the November sheets, the month of Tyler's birthday.

Flipping more pages of the makeshift diary, she found her first true entry, which she never got to hand in. December 7, 1991. The memory was as vivid as when she lay on the couch in John DeAngelo's basement, Tyler sitting on the floor leaning against the cushion right by her. The shaded floor lamps gave the room a hazy orange glow. A couple of guys were playing pool. They all sang along to the popular Rod Stewart disc crooning from the CD player, except for Moe and CeCe, who were making out on a bean-bag chair in the corner.

"Holy shit!" Tyler cried. He pulled his legs up as she suddenly puked on his blue Converse sneakers. Strands of her hair stuck to her cheek, and the back of her throat burned. Anne pressed her wrist to her mouth, hoping to hold back the rest.

Tyler grabbed her heaving shoulders, pushed her into the bathroom, and closed the door to avoid the grossness. She heard him gagging as she lifted the toilet lid and knelt beside it.

“Shut up!” he yelled at Moe and CeCe, who belly-laughed at his plight. She figured he was trying to get his Converse off without touching her vomit.

Every few minutes, he came to the bathroom door to ask if she was okay. Her moaned responses seemed to satisfy him each time. She lay on the bathroom floor, her cheeks resting on the cool porcelain of John DeAngelo’s toilet. When the next wave of nausea swelled, she breathed in, hoping it would recede quickly.

“Hey, you all right in there?” Tyler knocked three times on the door. Anne hoisted herself up, turned on the faucet, and rinsed her mouth before she emerged. The kids looked skeeved out by her, all except Tyler, who stood pleasantly by the door. His gentleness was new and strange to her.

“I’ll walk you home,” he said.

“Feel better,” CeCe called. She elbowed Moe, who was staring at the freaky white skin and tangled hair Anne had seen in the mirror.

“Yeah, see ya!” Moe said.

Tyler clutched the rolled top of a brown grocery bag John had dug up to carry the soiled sneakers. His thick Nike socks padded his feet against the rough sidewalk.

The fresh air helped perk her up by the end of the first block.

“I guess that’s the last time I’ll steal Mr. DeAngelo’s beer,” she joked.

“I told you and Moe not to do it,” Tyler said with more concern than consternation.

"Did you see the look on John's face when he saw me puke?"

"He's gonna have to clean it up, or his parents will know you guys got into their alcohol!" The duo's laughter echoed off the houses in the sleepy neighborhood.

"I always thought you and John were related. You guys could be twins."

"Everyone thinks so. I'll bet if another blue-eyed redhead moves into town, they'll say we're triplets or something."

"I'm so dumb. I shouldn't have mentioned it."

"Hey, don't put yourself down," Tyler said. "I think you're really smart."

"Why are you being nice to me?"

"Why wouldn't I be?"

They followed the cracked slate paver walkway leading from the street to her house.

"Thanks for including me with your friends," Anne said when they got to her door. "Even if I . . . you know."

"Sure, no worries."

"Anyway, thanks for taking care of me."

"See you tomorrow," he said.

The house was quiet when she lay down in her room. She rubbed where her stomach still hurt but had a warm feeling knowing Tyler cared about her. Maybe he even loved her? She toyed with the notion of being Mrs. Tyler Scott. The words were like magic when she whispered them aloud. Anne had always scorned the girls in her class who scripted their future names on their notebooks, like "Mrs. Luke Perry," punctuating the curlicues with hearts. But now she imagined how pretty her name would look with "Scott" at the end. The pleasant comfort of her thoughts was enough to soothe her to sleep.

Anne felt queasy again the next day and stayed in bed. The

feeling harassed her all day, and by the time her mother woke late that afternoon, she was pasty and her stomach felt weird.

"You're probably getting the flu," her mother said. "I bet you'll have a fever by tomorrow. Damn it, I can't afford for you to be sick right now."

Anne didn't go to school the next day or the next. There was no fever, but she looked pale and the nausea continued. She felt weak and light-headed when she sat up, so she stayed in bed. Her mother kept plying her with soup and ginger tea and made sure there were plenty of premium crackers nearby. Sometimes, in between laundry and dishes and errands, her mother just sat with her, rubbing her back in smooth circles.

At some point in the hours that are neither day nor night, when the world outside her apartment was mute, Anne rolled off her couch. Her mouth felt parched and rough, her breath putrid. She had vague, blurred visions of leaving the liquor store, of peeling off her street clothes as she zigzagged into the room. She examined her body, patting her skin, skimming her belly rolls, finding she wore only her bra and panties. There was no point in standing, so she crawled toward the sink. Her knee hit a cluster of empty bottles as she heard them roll and scatter.

"Jesus friggin' Christ," she griped.

The countertop seemed too high for the effort of pulling herself up, except for the urgency of her thirst. When she turned on the faucet, the neglected old pipes creaked in protest, like they sympathized with Anne's distress.

She flopped back on the couch and pulled the throw blanket around her, which sent the diary sliding to the floor. She brought it up to her lap, opened the cover, and turned the pages to where she'd left off. Unable to bear the misery of the memory she knew was waiting for her, Anne closed the diary again. Her lungs tightened as though clamped inside one of those vises they used in woodshop class. Frantic for something to numb her brain, she plowed through the cabinets in the kitchen and then under her bathroom sink, where she found a sticky bottle of nighttime cold medicine.

"Well, this will do!" she said aloud.

She contemplated the half-empty bottle for a millisecond, wondering when she'd been sick and purchased it, or if a previous tenant left it there years ago.

"Whatever." She shrugged, then sucked down the sickly sweet liquid.

It didn't take long for her head to feel thick and her limbs to be nearly immobile, not unlike the way her body was that December. Anne opened the diary to the page describing the coma-like sleep she'd been in when her mother shook her awake with a hand so cold her skin stung. She'd tried opening her eyes in response, but the morning light hurt, and they rebelled.

"Go away, Ma. I wanna sleep." The ratty blanket she'd pulled over her head muffled her words. "Go to bed and leave me alone."

"I'm taking you to the doctor," her mother said. "This has gone on long enough. You're nauseous all the time, barely eating, your head hurts, and you can't stay awake. I'm worried. One of the girls switched shifts with me. I'll sleep when we get back. Let's go."

Her mother tugged and pulled until Anne dislodged from the covers. She got a clean T-shirt and jeans on her, then all but dragged her to the car.

The car sputtered and protested but got them to the pediatrician's office. The doctor, a white-haired man with large, dry hands, pushed on her abdomen, gently squeezed the glands under her jawline, and pulled on her bottom eyelids.

"Say ahh," he said.

He gagged her with a wooden stick on the back of her tongue, then looked in her ears and nose with a funny-looking, tubular-handled gadget with a long beak. It reminded her of the grey heron from a school lesson on birds. He washed his hands in the sink and used crinkling paper towels to dry them.

"Get dressed, and I'll come back to talk with you both." He nodded at her mother and closed the door behind him. Anne had put her clothes back on and was lying on the cushioned exam table when he returned. Her mother was sitting on a wooden chair on the other side of the room, pulling on her hooped earrings.

"The nurse is going to come in and draw some blood." He spoke to her mother. "I suspect she's severely anemic, and since her belly is tender, I think she should see Dr. Polk for an ultrasound to rule out any cysts." His voice had a practiced blend of authority and empathy. "I've called his office, and he can squeeze you in this afternoon if you go straight from here."

Dr. Polk was a tall, skinny man who smelled like soap. He examined Anne and touched her in places she didn't want him to, but she was afraid to say so. She stayed calm by fixating on his lab coat and the black letters printed after his name, *OB/GYN*. To distract herself she came up with words that the letters could stand for: *Obnoxious Bastard Gets You Noodles? Old Boy Gives You Nerditis?* He finished the nasty stuff quickly. Then he did an ultrasound, which made an eerie whoosh and reminded her of the sound of a submarine descending into the deep, dark water.

Later, Dr. Polk met with her and her mother. He sat dead still with his hands clasped on the desk in front of him. His eyes latched onto her with such intensity, he didn't blink once.

"The exam and tests I ran confirm that you're about seven, maybe eight weeks pregnant."

Her mother's mouth fell open. She looked at Anne with wild eyes that turned red and watery. Dr. Polk and her mother talked rapidly, seeming to forget she was there. Words like "baby," "options," "cost," "clinic," floated around the room beyond her grasp.

After they left, Anne, drained and wanting to avoid the world, fell asleep with her head against the icy car window. They were both too worn out to talk once they were home. Her mother heated some canned tomato soup and placed their bowls and spoons on the Formica table. The refrigerator stopped humming when she opened it to fill the plastic cups she'd earned with FastBurger purchases. When she sat across from Anne, a stream of air released from the plastic cushion on her chair. Her mother looked ragged and had dark, puffy circles under her eyes. She kept wiping her palms on her dress.

"How did . . ." Her mother stuttered, shook her head, and blew on a spoonful of hot soup. "Who was . . . Never mind." She stirred her spoon in her bowl again. "God. I don't even know what to say. This is way too hard to understand."

Trying to ignore the sniffles between her mother's words, Anne concentrated on the evenly timed plinks of water dripping from the faucet into the soaking pot.

"I'm shocked. It never dawned on me. We never talked about this stuff."

Anne slurped a spoonful of the creamy red liquid into her mouth. She was listening but didn't want to see her mother's sad face.

"This is just disappointing," her mother continued. "If I'd been home, I could have taken care of you, taught you better."

If you'd been home. Anne sagged back in her seat. *Daddy wouldn't have done what he did, and maybe then I wouldn't have had sex with that boy.* But she hadn't been there, and her father had always warned her she'd better not tell her mother.

"This is our special secret, okay?" He'd say it the same way he might wish someone a happy birthday. But then his voice always deepened, and he'd add, "Because something bad will happen to Mommy if anyone finds out. You know that, right?"

Her mother dropped her spoon into the bowl, sending splotches of red around the table. A few sobs escaped her throat. "Your childhood is gone. I'm just heartbroken."

"I'm sorry." Anne cried too. "I didn't mean to."

She loved her mother and always tried to behave so nothing would happen to her. No matter how many times she'd wanted to tell her mother, wanted her mother to save her, or wanted her mother to figure it out, she had kept the secret. And it didn't matter—she had gone and been the one to hurt her mother anyway. Anne wiped her nose on her sleeve.

"I'm sorry I'm so bad. You can hate me now. I do."

The dim kitchen lighting, created by a long-ago blown bulb, seemed to soften the stress lines in her mother's face. Their water cups shook when her mother pushed away from the table. She came around to the seat next to Anne, scraping the chair's legs against the gold vinyl flooring as she drew it closer.

Her mother patted her arm and stroked her hair. "There now. That's all just me thinking out loud when I shouldn't have, and I've gone and made things worse. I'm more confused than I've ever been, and scared, and I realize you probably are too. Look, this is where we are. It doesn't matter how we got here. Right?"

Anne's shoulders twitched in a semi-shrug of agreement.

"So, let's make a pinky swear. Look at me, honey."

Anne's eyelids were heavy, but she managed to lift them.

"We agree, here and now, we're in this together. Okay? That means good or bad, we talk, share, and handle whatever we have to, 'cause we have each other." She stuck out her pinky.

"I wasn't sure I wanted to make a pact with her," Anne had written in the diary. "I already had a pact with Daddy, and that one sucked." At the time, though, she'd realized that no matter how often she'd been angry because her mother wasn't around when she needed her, her mother had never hurt her on purpose. She'd thought maybe her mother would finally pay attention to her and take care of her.

She had eyed her mother's hand with caution. Even if her mother let her down, she'd had no choice but to accept her offer of comfort; there was no one else. Anne lifted her pinky the way she had that day when she'd hooked it to her mother's waiting finger. Something had happened after that, before she'd finished her soup, but she'd blocked out whatever it was. She continued reading the rest of the journal passage: "Mom made a phone call. She stretched the cord around the hall corner to get out of earshot, but I heard it anyway . . ."

Anne remembered the rest. "She's covered by my stupid drunk of a husband's insurance," her mother said. "That asshole won't even pay for a divorce. He'll blame me for this, and God knows what he'll do to her. Is there any way you can get me extra shifts? I have to find the money. He can't know."

"I'm going into work tonight," she said when she returned the phone to its cradle. "I need to talk to my boss to figure out how I can get more hours to help pay for all this." Her mother quivered and patted Anne's hand, which lay limp next to her soup bowl. "Don't you worry, honey. We'll talk about it tomorrow when I know what he says. We'll figure this out, okay?"

Anne nodded and went down the short hallway, past her mother's bedroom to her own. She lay on her bed, listening to the sounds of dishes being washed and then her mother's closet opening and shutting as she changed for work. With the lights off, Anne's room was turning a dusky shade of gray. She was taking comfort in its dullness when her mother rapped gently on her door.

"I'm leaving now. I'll wake you when I get home."

Anne pulled the blanket to her chin and rolled toward the wall, waiting for the tinkling sound of her mother grabbing her keys. She heard a sickening thud, and icicles pricked her skin before her brain registered her father's raspy voice.

"Where's my princess?" He shouted with a rage she had never known. She wormed off the bed, crawled into her closet, and piled her clothes on top of her.

"What the hell are you doing here?" Her mother's voice seemed shaken and angry.

"Put down the phone!" he roared.

"I'm calling the police!" she yelled. "You have no right to barge in here."

Anne heard the clash of metal and plastic as he ripped the phone off the wall and smashed it on the floor. The bone-chilling sound of her father stomping toward her room was unmistakable. She tried to hold her breath to stop the tremors that had taken over her body. He pushed the door open so hard the floor beneath her quaked.

"I know she's here!" he howled.

"What do you want from us?" Her mother's voice was rising to a screech.

"The fucking pharmacy called my number instead of yours. They said my daughter's prenatal vitamin prescription was ready. I was sure they screwed up until I went down there and saw it for myself." Anne heard something rattle and then a thunk as if, she guessed, he'd thrown the bottle. "*Pregnant!* How could you let this happen to my princess?"

There were noises Anne couldn't make sense of. Slapping. Gasping. Her father's laugh. Her mother yelping. Heavy footsteps. Things slammed.

"Put down the knife, you bitch!"

Anne's fetal position drew so tight her knees dented her forehead.

"Get out! Get out of my house!" her mom shrieked.

"I'm going to find her, and then I'm going to crush your useless life out of you!" he hollered. There was a long pause before the front door boomed shut.

The closet door groaned when her mother opened it.

"He's gone," she said.

Anne peeked out of the clothes mound, thankful her mother guessed she was in her winning childhood hide-and-go-seek spot. Her mother moved away from the closet, then paced the few feet between the walls.

"I don't know what to do. Think, think." She banged her fist against her forehead.

Anne stayed on the closet floor, listening as her mother talked to herself. She sat on the edge of Anne's bed, rocking back and forth until she put her head in her hands.

"I have to go to work. I can't lose my job. My paycheck is the only thing keeping us afloat since the dirtbag moved out."

Is she having a complete breakdown right in front of me? When her mother stood and picked up the pacing, this time in small circles, Anne shifted closer to the back of the closet.

"I have to figure something out. I'll have a clearer head at work. Okay, I'm going. Oh, no." She stopped mid-step and looked into the closet. "If I go to work, what will I do about you?"

Before she could come up with an idea, her mother knelt next to her. "Come with me and sleep in the nurses' lounge."

Immobile and unwilling to leave her fort, Anne could barely shake her head. "Let me stay in the closet, Mom," she said. "Please?"

Her mother pinched her forehead. She covered her eyes with her palm. Her chest rose and fell like ocean waves coming ashore.

"Okay, yes, hide in there."

Her mother walked off toward the hall and then came back and looked down at Anne for a moment. "Promise me you won't come out until I get home."

"I won't."

Her mother seemed uncomfortable with the deal but closed the closet door. Through the thin walls, Anne heard her mother continue speaking out loud as she rushed around the house, and from the sound of it, she was crying.

"What the hell is happening?" her mother asked herself. "I have to figure out what to do. I have to. I will, but how?"

Her voice faded away, and then Anne heard the front door locks fasten into place. The only sound within the house was the constant refrigerator hum. She was once again alone when she heard scratching outside her window like someone was trying to get in.

Anne remembered many blustery nights in her childhood when she'd laid in her bed, fascinated by this tapping and high-pitch scraping of the tree branches against her window. She'd found the random creaks soothing. But that night, in the closet's lonely confines and thick pile of clothes, she felt each screech. At one point, she thought she heard the front door open but told herself it was another burst of wind. She burrowed herself further under the clothes after another long ear-piercing scrape against the window.

"It's just the tree. It's just the tree," her lips soundlessly repeated. Yet in Anne's imagination, the noise came from the long, scraggly fingers of a witch running her nails against the closet door, or worse, her father, once again slipping into her room.

Something hard on the bottom of the pile pressed into her back. She felt around and pulled it up through the jeans, shirts, sweaters, and shoes. Following the shape of the thin metal with her fingers, she knew it was a wire hanger. Visualizing it in the darkness, she twisted the head off and clutched it, so it projected out of her fingers Captain Hook style. It helped to imagine how shocked her father would be if he opened the door and she tore at his face, or even better, his eyes. It would give her time to get past him and run outside. She listened to the walls moan as minutes passed, willing herself not to scream when the closet door flew open.

"Are you all right?" her mother asked. "I must have been out of my mind to leave you in there, or alone in this house. I was almost at the hospital and turned around." She reached out a hand and helped Anne to her feet.

Anne was stiff and had to hop from foot to foot until she could bear the pins and needles in her legs. "I'm fine." She wrenched out of her mother's hold.

Her mother's cool, smooth hand touched her chin.

"Look at me, sweetheart."

When she did, Anne thought her mother seemed more together, but her bloodshot eyes still looked scared.

"I will never leave you alone ever again." She let go of Anne's face.

Just before dawn, Anne and her mother left the nurses' lounge and went back to the house. "Now, I need you to listen to me," her mother said as they stepped inside. "Everything's going to be okay. I have a plan, but you have to do as I say. There's no time for questions." She thrust a duffel bag toward her. "Fill this fast! Your clothes, underwear, whatever you can fit." Her mother spun around, eyeing Anne's meager belongings. "Take only what you must, nothing else. Hurry."

This wasn't the first time her mother had threatened to leave. It was the way her parents had always ended their fights. Until her father actually did. She never once thought her mother was courageous enough to do it, not even after her father's rampage about her pregnancy hours before. But her mother held a passport and both of their birth certificates, and by the look in her eye, this time was different. Anne did as she was told, adding only some books and a stuffed puppy Tyler had won when she went with him and his friends to the school's fall festival. She walked into her mother's room, feeling lopsided from the bag's weight slung over her shoulder. Her mother was breathless as she threw her clothes and toiletries into a green-and-tan suitcase.

"Go, go." Her mother hoisted her bulging bag off her bed.

As Anne neared the front door, she saw her mother grab a can of Maxwell House coffee from the closet that doubled as their pantry. It took a few tries for her shaky hands to remove the plastic lid and withdraw a wad of cash hidden inside. Once she secured it in her pocketbook, her stern expression made Anne feel panicky.

"Get in the car." Her mother's directive was urgent. "Let's get the hell out of here."

The engine turned over before she even had the door closed. Her mother peeled out of the driveway, and the last memory Anne had of the place where she'd grown up was the smell of burning rubber.

EIGHTEEN
Tyler

After Vanni's, Tyler hustled back to his office to prep for the four-thirty conference call with Prachett and a potential new client. If he could just focus, the account would be exclusively his. When he caught himself adding the wrong files for the meeting, he released a barrage of curses and punched the wall. He leaned on the edge of his desk, rubbing his knuckles, which were sure to bruise. It had been a long day filled with humiliation, the mysterious texts, and the truths he needed to share with his wife, particularly the memory that still terrified him.

"Prachett's waiting."

He hadn't noticed Marla come into his office. He slipped the little photo he'd been staring at between the documents on his desk.

"I don't know what's up with you," she said, "but get your head in the game, pronto."

"Yeah, got it." He went to the men's room to splash some water on his face, but he couldn't put away his past.

He remembered being summoned to the coach's office, a small box at the back of the boys' locker room. An array of dust-coated trophies sat on a flimsy shelf and a window ledge. Tyler had shifted his feet in the cramped space, waiting for the coach to explain why he was there.

"Fairmont game's coming up. Last one before Christmas break."

"Yes, sir."

"Crowd gets bigger every year, what with the rivalry and all."

"We'll whip 'em, Coach. You know we will."

The coach scooched his chair as close to the desk as his beer belly allowed. Tyler squirmed, wanting to avoid the man's scrutiny.

"Where's your head been, kid?"

"What d'ya mean? I'm focused on the game and playing great."

"Your moves are pretty solid, and your teamwork is always the best. But c'mon, buddy, I've coached you since Pee Wee basketball. I know you, and your head is somewhere else." The bulk of the coach's weight leaned into the chair, and he clasped his hands behind his neck.

"I'm good, Coach. I swear." Tyler wished the room had more air. He'd thought he'd played it cool, thought he'd gotten past the spasms when players edged behind him. Even if his three-pointers weren't sinking like they should and his assists had slowed, the team's average was still solid. But the coach had seen through it all and was calling bullshit. If he didn't find a way to stop the coach from grilling him, this was going to get back to his parents. Then it would all blow up, and the man might come after him again.

"If something's going on, you know my door is always open," the coach said.

"There's nothing. I'll pick up the slack. I promise. You can count on me."

Tyler made it to Prachett's office as the partner, already seated at his round meeting table, greeted the client on speakerphone. He laid his notepad on the table, readying himself for business, but his mind went back to a night a few weeks after that Christmas break when he and his friends Moe and CeCe went to Garby's Diner after a game.

"Have you heard anything new about that girl Laura?" CeCe had asked. She sucked a thick vanilla milkshake through a red-and-blue-striped straw.

"No." Tyler set his cheeseburger onto his plate and pushed it toward the middle of the table. As far back as first or second grade, Laura had been the gloomy, quiet kid whose existence was part of the whole but unacknowledged. Though no one had paid much attention to her for years, his classmates couldn't stop gossiping in the ten days since she and her mother dropped out of sight. Laura had been his math lab partner that year. He'd tried to be nice to her and included her a couple of times when his friends hung out. He had stared at his reflection in the frosted diner window and saw the wild look on the face of the man whose voice and smell still spooked him. Was it Laura's name he'd shouted when he sprinted down the hill?

"My mother says Laura and her mom are probably hiding 'cause her dad's a total turd," Moe said. "She thinks maybe they went to one of those women's shelters."

"I think that's the saddest thing I ever heard," CeCe had said.

Prachett threw a crumpled paper ball, which hit Tyler's nose and made him blink.

"Mr. Scott, you want to respond to that?"

They'd been discussing their proposed strategy with the client when Tyler had spaced out again.

"Yes, I agree," Tyler said. "I can take it on. I won't let you down, Coach." He avoided Prachett's confused expression and hoped his boss would think the comment was a joke. *How could you be so stupid?*

As soon as the meeting, which he'd inadequately faked his way through, ended, Tyler left the office building and walked around the park across the street. His breath quickened and his throat throbbed as he remembered when, just before his freshman year at BU, his small town was abuzz with news of a local man's arrest. He was stunned when his mother showed him an article and the man in the grainy black-and-white photo was his attacker. They had him arrested on charges unrelated to Tyler, but he had a name: Curtis Bennett.

"Oh, shit." Tyler reversed direction and bolted back to his office.

"Mommy, that man said a bad word," a little boy on the park path behind him said.

Marla followed him into his office. "Did something happen? Can I help?"

"Get out!" he shouted.

"Okay. Okay." She lifted her hands to surrender. "No offense, but you look like a madman. Don't let them"—she jabbed her thumb above her shoulder toward the outer office—"see you unhinged." She quietly closed the door on her way out.

Ignoring her warning, Tyler frantically searched his desk, making a mess of his files and scattering them onto the carpet. "It has to be here," he mumbled. He checked his briefcase a second time and felt inside the small pocket meant for business cards where he usually kept it. Nothing. Searching through the papers again, he shook the fastened documents until the baby photo fell out. He lifted it off the floor, turned it over, and read the initials on the back out loud: "L.B." Tyler slid his back down the side of the desk until he was sitting. "Laura Bennett." He rapped his fist against his forehead. "Shit. Shit. Shit."

Billie didn't speak to him during dinner that night, and her questioning glances were full of misery. He wasn't trying to hurt her any more than he already had, but he wouldn't let himself explain why he wasn't sitting still or why he couldn't look directly at her. He almost wished she'd be angry and yell at him the way he deserved.

Tyler didn't even help her clear the table before he closed himself into his study. He sat at his desk and rotated his chair toward the shelves lined with books and photo albums behind him to avoid the ominous sensation coursing through him. He pulled on the slim brown spine of his junior high yearbook. Faces and memories passed by as he leafed through the pages. He stopped on the eighth-grade class photos taken in the first few weeks of the school year and found Moe's bloated-cheek mugshot. They'd conspired to spit a mouthful of Yoo-hoo when the camera clicked, but Moe missed his cue and the chocolate drink had dribbled down his chin. Tyler, whose cheeks burned as he tried to hold in the liquid, ended up spitting it onto the girl in line in front of him. His only time in the principal's office had been so worth it.

Turning back a few pages to the beginning of the alphabetized names, he landed on a freckled face with mysterious brown eyes and a puzzling half smile. The face was no more or less stunning than the other girls their age; rather, it occurred to him, Laura had an endearing stray cat quality. Tyler's brows squeezed toward his nose as he wondered about her and the photo. The old questions their hometown had obsessed over swarmed in his head. *Where had she gone? Were the rumors true?* His muscles tensed. He and his friends had accepted the theory that Laura and her mother had escaped the despicable Mr. Bennett and were safe somewhere. But Tyler knew better than anyone what Laura's father was capable of.

Returning the yearbook to the neat row on the shelf, he reached for his bar mitzvah album. He opened it to a full-page shot of him standing on the temple's pulpit, his hands resting on either side of the oak podium where the rabbi usually stood. It was three weeks shy of his thirteenth birthday because the religious ritual was scheduled based on the Hebrew calendar. He'd felt so grown-up, yet in retrospect, he looked so childlike. His crisp suit and starched shirt collar were stiff and itchy as he read the bar mitzvah passages he'd practiced. His friends all sat in a pack in front of him, including Laura, whom his mother made him invite. He didn't really remember what she looked like that day, though he would never forget when he'd stumbled over his speech, stuttering and repeating words because she'd flashed the same sultry pout she'd given him when they'd hooked up a few weeks before.

After the ceremony, Moe approached him and mussed his hair. "Smooth move," he said.

Tyler's ears burned, but he chuckled anyway.

John DeAngelo said, "N-n-n-nice job!"

Then the rest of Tyler's closest friends surrounded him and imitated his errors too. He'd withstood their ribbing, knowing it would never stop if they saw him cringing. He was almost relieved when his mother called him to the dreaded receiving line. But Tyler was polite as he greeted his parents' guests making their way to the cocktail reception that followed the service. A little while later, his father pulled him, Moe, and John into a corner.

"By your mother's Jewish law, you're a man now," he said. "But you're only half Jewish. Isn't that right, my boy?" He tapped Tyler's shoulder with an open hand. "You want your Scottish side to be a man too, don't cha?" He gave a jolly laugh.

Tyler and his buddies kept looking at each other. He knew from their wide eyes and swallowed smirks that, like him, they were unsure what secret club they were about to join but sensed it was going to be a good one.

Tyler's dad was the cool one who all his friends gravitated toward and confided in when they couldn't talk to their fathers. With his mother's endless offering of food and his father's jokes and stories, his house was where his friends gathered. His dad was so much fun it became ordinary for him to hang with them in the basement, playing pool or watching sports. Somehow his father skillfully straddled the line between being one of the guys and a respected adult. With a conspiratorial wink, his father pulled an engraved stainless-steel flask from his pocket.

His father's unruly eyebrows, which had always given him a sleepy look, lifted and the creases in his forehead became more pronounced. The pink tinge in his round cheeks seemed to deepen as he came even closer to Tyler, Moe, and John.

"This is how my father introduced me to manhood, and his father before him."

His dad liked to kick back a drink here and there, but he'd never approved of Tyler touching the stuff before. In the past, he'd come home from family bar mitzvahs gloating about how he and their relatives had given the honoree and his friends a round of shots. Once Tyler was mature enough to understand, it horrified him that his father was corrupting the kids. "It's all in good fun, Serious Sam," his father had said. Because his mother had been giggling, he'd calmed down and gotten used to his father's antics. Douglas Scott's shenanigans were part of why he was invited to every party.

"Here ya go, boys." He passed the flask of Drambuie to Tyler, who took too big a sip.

"Easy there, slugger," his father guffawed. "We don't want your mothers all coming after us now, do we? Just a taste." He took it from Tyler and handed it on to Moe and then John.

As the liquid's singe mellowed in the back of Tyler's throat, he and a bunch of boys snuck outside to smoke the cigars they'd swiped from their fathers' stashes. Their anticipation canceled out the below-average November temperature. His cousin Charlie had just passed the lighter to him when someone tugged at his elbow. It was Laura, who was peeking out of the door.

"Come on," she whispered.

Tyler followed her inside to the janitor's closet. She kissed him, a long, slow French kiss. Then she pulled his pants down and gave him the best bar mitzvah gift an eighth-grade boy could wish for. He was aware of the absurd grin on his face as he paraded around the party for the rest of the afternoon.

A few weeks after his thirteenth birthday, the streets were full of slush and neighborhoods lit up with colorful Christmas lights. Except for Laura's house. Tyler's mother had sent him over with some of his family's old decorations to brighten the holiday for her. They never locked their door, so he'd grown comfortable walking in without knocking when he went over to study. Often he'd arrive to find Gene Kelly singing in the rain on the dusty living room television that seemed to be stuck on The Movie Channel and Laura lying on the ugly diamond-patterned love seat in front. Her parents hadn't changed the previous owner's furniture. It looked like the set of *The Brady Bunch* reruns he'd seen on late-night TV. He remembered how eager he was to string the twinkle lights and bring Christmas spirit to the home. But the worn front door at Laura's house was locked when he arrived. No one answered his insistent knocks. He stood on the curb, looking at the dark, still structure before he gave up. Several days in a row, no one answered his calls. Even though they'd had sex once, twice if you counted his bar mitzvah, they were pretty much only lab partners, not friends. But she didn't have any real friends, and Tyler wanted to help. He wanted to know if she was okay.

His mother would have had a meltdown if she'd discovered he'd snuck out his bedroom window and jumped off the low end of the garage roof. He'd risked it to talk to Laura's mother. He knew his way, even in the dark. Most everyone in their small town worked at the hospital at one time or another. Moe's dad was a cardiologist there. Tyler had often slept at the Culligans' house when Moe's dad covered nights. Moe's mother bellyached every time while scrambling eggs and baking Pillsbury cinnamon rolls for his dad's 6:00 a.m. arrival. Tyler checked his watch. If he ran the two and a half miles, he'd arrive minutes before Mrs. Bennett's shift ended.

Tyler's fists bulged in his team jacket pockets while he leaned on the wall outside the hospital entrance. His fingertips were numb from frigid gusts of predawn winds. Each time the mechanical doors whirred, they coughed out people bundled in scarves and coats. He could tell the hospital staff by their medical pants and soft shoes. The housekeeping crew wore dark gray.

"What are you doing here at this hour?" a woman asked.

Fixated on the door, Tyler hadn't noticed his friend Angie Finelli's mother stop next to him.

"I'm waiting for Mrs. Bennett."

"Kathleen's taking time off." Mrs. Finelli's mouth puckered like she'd sucked a lemon.

"When will she be back?"

"The boss told us she's taken a leave of absence." Her stern look resembled the one his Latin teacher got before she sent kids to the principal. "That means she'll be gone a long time." Mrs. Finelli seemed sad. "Could be she's never coming back."

His fist tightened, and he kicked the toe of his sneaker against the concrete. The hand Mrs. Finelli placed on his shoulder felt like a gym weight.

"Tyler," she said, "go home."

* *

Now Tyler closed the heavy album and swiveled his chair back toward his computer. He typed Laura's name into the search but left his fingers hovering over the enter button. Then he pressed the delete button, as if wiping out memories were as easy as that.

NINETEEN
Billie

Billie got under the covers and nestled on Tyler's warm chest. With an unlit new moon, an opaque shade of onyx filled the bedroom.

"You know the stuff Fischman told us yesterday about the slow road ahead?" Tyler asked.

"Hmm."

"I guess I'm having a hard time understanding the risks your mother took, and now there are more serious ones you'd have to go through."

"My mother couldn't have known how a choice she made when she was so young would impact our lives decades later. She made a decision that would ensure a healthy pregnancy." Billie paused. "The uncanny thing is, while it gave me life, it took hers."

She altered her position under the sheets to face him. A light stubble gloved the soft face she had kissed a million times in their few years together. Though she could only see his form from the bedside clock's green glow, she felt his eyes absorbing her vulnerability. She tuned out the concept of her misshapen uterus and felt beautiful and safe again. His solid, reassuring arms surrounded her with security until the steady rise and fall of his chest lulled her toward sleep.

* *

Tyler's words about a mother's decisions affecting future generations were still on her mind the next day when her client Gianna flopped into her office armchair. Billie sat in a matching chair next to the young girl whose large build was exaggerated by the pregnancy. Gianna removed the hood of her Mickey Mouse sweatshirt, revealing her long, matted palomino-colored hair.

A local hospital had referred the fourteen-year-old to the adoption agency after her parents brought her into the ER with severe stomach pains. No one was prepared for the discovery that this adolescent was almost eight months pregnant. When he'd made the referral in early August, the resident had reported a hostile scene. He said the mother had spit at her daughter, hissed, "You're filth," then scowled from the farthest corner of the ER cubicle. The father had wailed, "How could you? If Nonna were alive, she'd kill herself from the shame you've brought to our family."

It was clear no one was sympathetic to the scared young teen who didn't comprehend what was happening. No one had asked if she was okay. Billie had resisted the yearning to take Gianna home and nurture her the way the girl deserved. She'd always maintained the professional distance needed to remain objective for her clients. But in the five weeks Gianna had been coming twice a week to see her, the pull to protect her had only gotten stronger.

In their first session, Gianna had told Billie that while her parents were "freaking out," she lay on the ER stretcher, in a paper hospital gown, quietly gouging her wrist into a bolt on the side of the metal frame.

"I couldn't feel anything," she explained. "I thought I'd feel that."

Gianna had pushed up her sweatshirt sleeve to reveal a host of scars all along the underside of her arm. Billie noted the marks. Most were near the bend in her arm. The one by her wrist was raw, but the others were white, meaning they weren't recent. They weren't deep and ran horizontally. Vertical cuts along an artery would have been a suicidal flag. What Gianna had done to herself was a cry for help.

"I never feel it. I keep trying, but nothing works. What's wrong with me?"

Billie could feel the tragic emptiness emanating from her imploring green eyes. If she wrapped her arms around her, the way she badly wanted to, the girl would surely run. She forced her hands to remain in her lap, aghast at her desire to behave inappropriately with a client.

Much of Billie's role was to prepare and inform her clients. Her therapeutic social work skills were essential, particularly for birth mothers who faced intense loss and grief with their choices. But she worried that her training wasn't rigorous enough to break through Gianna's profound traumas. This case required a consult with their staff psychologist. If the timing to refer Gianna for more intensive therapy wasn't precise, she or her parents might bail out of services. It was also Billie's professional intuition that the girl, who barely opened up, even to her, would not soon develop a rapport with someone else.

Billie glanced at Gianna's belly. She was carrying a little small for someone due so soon, but she'd had good medical care since she selected the adoptive parents.

"Did you see the obstetrician this week?"

"Yeah." A frightened child's look replaced the toughness she exuded. "He said I'm one centimeter."

"Do you remember what that is, and what will happen next?"

Gianna shrugged in her typical vague way. The almost imperceptible raising of her eyebrows and increased blinking were the only hint that she might want to know. She'd demonstrated a shocking lack of knowledge about puberty and her body. With the help of the book *Our Bodies, Ourselves,* Billie had educated her about reproduction and birth. The day she explained ovulation, Gianna had leaned close to her and attentively looked at the pages. The moment had given Billie a strange insight into the kind of mother she would be herself one day.

Being only one centimeter dilated could mean the birth was weeks away, or it could be imminent. Before the session ended, Billie reviewed what would happen when labor began. She reassured Gianna that she was available by phone, but no matter how many times the girl asked, she wouldn't be at the hospital. Billie struggled with her desire to be at Gianna's side, to hold her hand through the birth, to comfort her, but she couldn't. Other adoption agencies believed their presence offered support to the birth mothers who too often didn't have anyone with them, or lent a shoulder to the family, if there were any. They argued their physical presence ensured that the adoption procedures continued seamlessly and that hospital staff didn't impose their oppositional personal beliefs on the birth mother. The legal department at Burkhead, however, believed such practices left the agency vulnerable and prohibited any such engagement, lest someone claim the adoption worker's presence influenced the birth mother's decision. Billie had always been careful to follow the rules. Being at the hospital would infringe on Gianna's time with the baby—if she desired it—and the time needed to make sure adoption was the right choice.

"If you proceed with the adoption, I'll see you here when you're well enough to leave the hospital, and we'll sign the papers that I've reviewed with you."

"But you're the one taking the baby to the family?" Gianna asked, a trace of anxiety in her voice.

"Yes, since you've elected not to meet the adoptive parents, the baby will be released to me at discharge."

Gianna chewed on her bottom lip and scratched at her knee. Her emotions were as anemic as her pallor. "Good." She flipped her hood back over her head and left the office.

Billie made some notes in the case file and squeezed it into the cabinet drawer. With minutes before her next appointment, a new couple coming for the first phase of the home study assessment, she grabbed a scratch pad to start a grocery list. She scribbled down rice, sesame seeds, and orange juice before the intercom rang.

Tyler set the table while Billie stirred a pot of wild rice and kept an eye on the teriyaki salmon baking in the oven. Even though she'd made the dish dozens of times, she still checked the recipe card, which she propped near the stove and the lined-up ingredients. Tyler leaned against the kitchen counter, deftly staying out of her way as she danced between the appliances. Over dinner, he shared tidbits about his day. Billie had hoped for some deep dirt or drama to explain the growing . . . what was the right word to define his recent weirdness with her? Detachment? Apathy? Coolness? Whatever it was, he seemed easygoing, more himself tonight. His willingness to go for an after-dinner walk delighted her.

They strolled down their street, each enjoying the serenity of the fall breeze. Oncoming storm clouds had swallowed the moon, leaving porch lights and streetlamps to create a dimly lit path through the darkened neighborhood.

They walked past the last ranch-style house left in the area. In the daylight, it seemed dwarfed next to the modern traditional houses that surrounded it. Old Mr. Farrow, a renowned penny-pincher, refused to modernize even the HVAC, so the windows were open into the height of winter. Tonight they could hear Mrs. Farrow playing a show tune on their woefully out-of-tune piano.

"How was the home study you started today?" Tyler asked.

"The Toughnuts?" Billie usually used kinder aliases, like "the Palomino" for Gianna, but tonight she'd blurted out the nickname. Tyler laughed.

"That's pretty harsh," he said, though still amused. "Was it that bad?"

"Yes. No. It was challenging."

"Well, now I need details." He slipped his hand around her waist.

The closeness made her feel like the world was righting itself again. Whatever he was going through about their infertility, maybe he was coming back to her. She pressed against his side, savoring the familiar intimacy in case his mood flipped again.

"So, at first Mr. and Mrs. Toughnuts seemed sociable and warm."

Like most first-time couples, they'd sat in Billie's office chairs feigning casual comfort. But fluttering eyes, hands sweeping away unseen wrinkles, and uncertain smiles betrayed their composure.

"They were smart and both asked educated questions about adoption guidelines and what to expect from the home study. When they answered the initial basic questions I asked, they even had a sense of humor."

"They sound fine." Tyler fanned his hand to ward off a hungry mosquito.

"I thought so too until I asked the wife to tell me about her upbringing and relationship with her parents."

"What did they do?"

"The wife's mouth sort of scrunched together." Billie imitated the gesture, though she wasn't sure Tyler could appreciate it in the near darkness. "She said, 'This is getting quite personal. My parents have nothing to do with this.'" Billie had glanced to be sure the tissue box on the side table had ample supply. It was foreseeable that one or both of them would react. This process was an intrusive reminder of how their bodies had failed them. Of the bereavement they constantly felt for their planned future. It was understandable that the questions she asked would elicit some emotion. Usually, it was tears.

"I mean, you know I have to ask those kinds of questions to get a sense of how they were raised and how that might or might not impact the kind of parents they hope to be. I described why we like to get a picture of the composition of the extended family and the type of interactions the child will grow up in." The husband, an assistant district attorney, had sat forward in the chair, his elbows on his knees and his hands clasped. It had made Billie wonder if he sat like that in court, preparing to pounce on a witness. "Mr. T. grew red in the face, and his breathing became huffy when I dove deeper and asked what they thought were their strengths and weaknesses as parents. And then, with angry accusation, he asked, 'Are *you* a mother?'" His legal instincts had aimed and stung Billie's weakness.

"That's unacceptable. He had no right to say that." Tyler stopped walking, and under the ray of a lamppost, she saw his jawline tighten. His protective instincts were on alert. "Why isn't it enough that you have a master's in social work and a background in child development?"

"I also pointed out I have many years of experience working with couples, birth mothers, and babies. But that incensed him more." Billie closed her eyes and took a deep breath. "He practically spit when he said, 'A degree doesn't qualify you to judge us. If you had a child, you would never ask these questions. You have no idea what it's like to sit here, having your life dissected because you can't be parents.'" She felt Tyler's hand wrap around hers. His shoe scuffed on the pavement, sending a pebble ricocheting along the road before them.

"Oh, Ty, it hurt so much. All I could think of was how much I wish I could have said, 'Yes, I am a mother.'"

"One day soon. It will happen."

Billie felt her lips pull into an I-want-to-believe-you smile. She stuffed her fists in the front pockets of her jeans as the wind picked up. The unseasonably warm first weeks of September were shifting into fall.

"Smells like rain," Tyler said. "Short route?"

She had hoped to walk around the pond a few streets over, but they agreed it wasn't worth the gamble and looped back toward their house. They were less than a block away when they heard the first rumble of thunder.

"Did you see that?" Billie asked.

"See what?"

"That shadow, like something was moving across our yard."

"It's probably just a bear."

"When have you ever seen or heard of a bear in or near this town?"

"Could happen. What about the one in Brookline back in June? Ha! Lawyer shoots and scores!"

The absurdity of Tyler's reaction erased her flare of concern.

A barrage of brisk rain followed a brilliant flash of lightning. They dashed inside their house, laughing as they removed their wet shoes.

"I'm going to take a hot shower," Billie said.

"I'll come with you."

Afterward, sated and cozy in her crescent moon flannel pajamas and fuzzy socks, Billie went to the kitchen to microwave popcorn. In the family room, Tyler chose one of his favorite movies, *Back to the Future*, and popped it into the DVR.

"Admit it," she teased, "you're madly in love with the DeLorean."

"Now, don't be jealous." He leaned toward her and nibbled her neck.

Billie purred. As the opening credits rolled, she snuggled closer to her husband.

Tyler had already left for the city when she woke the next morning. She dressed in her favorite camel-colored pantsuit, then went down to the kitchen to start the Keurig. The sky was overcast and the air damp when she went out to get the paper. The tips of her Ugg boots darkened as she walked across the dew-covered lawn and pulled the lever to open the mailbox. As she turned to go back, Billie saw a smattering of cigarette butts in the grass below. Recalling the dark form outside their home the night before, she hurried back inside and ran around, closing all the curtains in the house. Startled by the ringing of the phone, her pulse sped up. She grabbed what she needed and headed to work, double-locking the door behind her.

TWENTY
Anne

As her mother sped away from their home, Anne had tried to watch the sunrise but surrendered to her fatigue. About an hour later, she woke to find they were in the driveway of a charming white cottage with black shutters surrounded by low shrubs and wildflowers. A full-cheeked woman, older than her mother, ushered them inside. The warm house smelled of fresh-cooked bacon and something equally mouthwatering but sweeter.

"I've made some eggs and blueberry muffins for you," the woman said. "Come, sit down. I'm sure you must be hungry."

The woman, who insisted they call her Mama Sue, was the sister of Anne's mother's boss. He knew she'd take them in and protect them.

"Under the circumstances, we gotta think of your safety," Mama Sue said, "and keep my busybody neighbors from poking in our puddin'. It'll be best if we say you're family, and you should use my name."

Unsure of what was going on, Anne watched her mother. "You would do that for us?" her mother asked. Her forehead creased like she was confused too, and her voice seemed frail.

"Can you do that, child?" Mama Sue fixed an encouraging look on her. "Call yourself Suzanne Neuman?"

"How about just Anne, hmm?" her mother asked.

The idea of being anyone but herself and belonging to someone else's family was like an early Christmas gift. Anne earnestly nodded, trying to keep the muffin she'd bitten from slipping through her mile-wide grin.

She had never slept as comfortably as she had that first night in the crisp, clean sheets on the cushy mattress in her private new bedroom. It seemed surreal to wake up in the bright room with pink peony wallpaper. She stretched and yawned as she sank her toes into the plush carpet and then stumbled down the stairs in her pajamas, following the mysterious aroma coming from the kitchen. Anne's stomach growled when she saw the picnic-style table, loaded with pancakes, syrup, bacon, eggs, and orange juice. She readied herself for a wave of nausea, but the morning sickness didn't come.

"Well, good morning, there! That's a fine case of bedhead you're sporting!" Mama Sue said.

Anne groaned and rubbed her eyes. It was way too early to be good-natured.

"Your mom's already been up and headed out to meet my friend, who found her a housekeeping job. She and I chatted this morning and think it's best for you to stay here for the duration of the pregnancy. We've agreed she'll contribute part of her earnings to the household, and you'll chip in by doing chores. Well, whatcha standing there for? Take a seat and eat up. We've got a big day ahead, and you're gonna need the fuel."

Anne slid onto the bench and devoured the delicious meal. Then she observed the woman who'd sweet-talked her into a food overdose. Mama Sue looked like a cartoon grandmother she'd seen on TV. Her thick, short hair reminded Anne of women in magazines who'd just pulled out the curlers they slept with. She flitted around the kitchen, clearing plates and pans, stopping now and then to wipe her hands on her country apron. Her flabby underarms vibrated with each movement.

"Where ya going, hon?" Mama Sue called as Anne headed toward the family room. "We clean up after ourselves here."

With an exasperated huff/eye roll combination, she lifted her dish and utensils and laid them on the sink counter. Mama Sue nodded toward the table, still littered with serving plates and a jug of syrup. After placing those next to the other pile, Anne tried to escape again.

"Not so fast." Mama Sue pulled open a drawer under the countertop. "This is where you'll find the tinfoil and plastic wrap for leftovers. Tupperware containers are in this cabinet down here."

"There's so much. It will take all day."

"We help each other. Teamwork. That's the way we do things in this house," Mama Sue said. "You can put the fruit salad in a large Tupperware and tinfoil the leftover bacon. All of that and the orange juice go in the fridge."

Anne followed instructions until there was nothing left to salvage. "Can I go now?"

"What's your rush? You haven't washed your dishes."

"I've only ever left dishes in the sink." She thought back to the teetering piles of food-stained dishes, bowls, and cups her mother had always sudsed up and rinsed clean without complaint.

"Tsk, don't worry, you'll learn. The sponge is in the caddy here." Mama Sue pointed to a holder hanging near the faucet. "Now squirt a tad of dish soap on it."

She liked Mama Sue's gentle nature. The way she dropped hints to teach the proper way to do things made the chore less annoying. And it was nice when she handed the wet dishes to Mama Sue to dry with her rooster-decorated dish towels. By the time Mama Sue showed her where everything belonged so they could put them away, Anne was almost having fun.

"Follow me. There's an extra pair of boots for you by the door." With a quick push on the storm door handle, Mama Sue was outside, and Anne hastened to catch up.

The backyard was larger than any of the ones in Anne's neighborhood. One side was a vast garden where Mama Sue grew vegetables. There was wire fencing around a small shed on the other side. When they walked into the penned area, two chickens scampered away.

"That's Henny, and that's Penny. Keep 'em happy, and they'll keep giving us breakfast eggs."

Something warm and fuzzy brushed Anne's leg. "What is that?" she gasped. The creature was white with black dalmatian-like splatters.

"Meet Gary the Goat. She's in charge of our milk. Go on, you can pet her."

"Gary's a girl?" Anne hesitated and then tapped Gary's back.

"One of my previous foster kids named her." Mama Sue chuckled. "You and Gary are going to get along swell. It's going to be your job to milk her every morning."

"Uh, no . . . what?"

"Here, watch."

Mama Sue pulled a round cake pan from the shed and placed it under Gary. Then she clasped one of Gary's dangling boobs. Watery white liquid splashed into the pan.

"Now you try."

They switched places.

"Take Gary's teat from the very top."

"I'm not touching Gary's tits!"

"Teats, not tits," Mama Sue laughed.

The goat's tiny hairs prickled when Anne encircled her fingers around the cool skin. Then she imitated the motions Mama Sue showed her, over and over, until her hands became useless clumps of uncoordinated rubber. She was sweaty and infuriated by Mama Sue's unflappable patience.

"I can't do this!" she whined.

"Try again."

Anne's thumb and forefinger squeezed Gary's teat from the top. Her other fingers pumped into her palm. There was a squirt and a splash as Gary rewarded her with a teaspoon of milk.

"I did it! I did it!" Her jubilation at the splotch of goat milk sent her into spasms of laughter.

"Taste it." Mama Sue's eyes twinkled.

It was hard to tell if Mama Sue was pranking her, but so far she had no reason not to trust the woman. Anne dipped her finger in the pan and brought a small dab to her mouth. It was creamy, sweet, and warm. The odd new flavor stayed with her for a second before she remembered it had come from inside a goat.

"Gross!"

The lovely sound of Mama Sue's laughter was the best thing Anne had ever heard, yet she couldn't enjoy it. She'd never allowed any adult to trick her into getting close, not a teacher or a doctor or someone else's parent. She wasn't sure what this lady was after, but she'd learned long ago there was always something, and Anne wasn't giving it.

When they returned to the kitchen, Mama Sue made Anne wash her hands, then told her to sit at the table. She left the room for a minute and returned with a stack of books. A copy of *Little Women* was on top.

"These are for your studies." The pile thumped on the table. "I'll be homeschooling you while you're here." Mama Sue pulled out a prearranged schedule that included math, history, science, grammar, and literature.

"Why does it say piano? I don't play." But Tyler played. At least, she thought he did. She'd seen a dark, shiny piano and matching bench in the big living room in his house, although she'd never heard anyone play it. Mama Sue's old upright piano, with scuffs and scars from the unnamed kids who'd lived there before, was squeezed into the corner of her front room.

"I'm going to teach you."

Anne had struggled between the urge to laugh and the urge to toss something at the woman. Behind oval wire-framed glasses, Mama Sue's malted milk ball eyes were inviting rather than intimidating. Yet the rigid line of her mouth set beneath her sagging cheeks implied she was no-nonsense.

Anne began drawing *X*'s on her refrigerator calendar, which still displayed August 2012. She flipped the page to September, its banner filled with autumn-colored leaves, and kept marking until she finished on September 10. *Yesterday was a month since I met with Tyler.* Her anxiety, coupled with her intensifying preoccupation with him, had caused her to lose track of the days. She'd forgotten a meeting with her boss and two appointments with her psychiatrist. In her opinion, there wasn't much sense in going to see Stanley anyway, since he didn't do much for her. *Oh, but the pills*, she thought. She craved them. But he'd used this stall tactic before: insist she come in before giving her a scrip, then make her suffer through a few sessions while he assessed her state of mind and sent her for blood tests before determining the right pills or dosage. No, Anne decided, it wasn't worth it.

As was her morning habit in the past two months, she turned on the television. She knew now that shooting her father had only been a nightmare, but she was waiting and wanting, with her entire being, for confirmation his death was real.

"Can't you just this once answer my prayers?"

Anne merged onto Route 128, intending to show up for work, but passed the exit that led to Rudy's Plumbing. With the last of rush hour traffic to contend with, it had taken over an hour to get downtown. Her timing couldn't have been better. She was about two blocks away from his office when she saw Tyler and his wife walking in her direction. She hurried to the nearby newsstand and picked up a magazine from the top pile to hide her face.

"Hey, you going to pay for that or what?" The vendor reached his hand out for payment.

She tossed the magazine back on the stack, furious he'd drawn attention to her. "Like I'd want a copy of *Teen Vogue*?"

With a slight turn of her head, she checked to see if Tyler had noticed, but he was at the corner hugging his wife. Watching their embrace filled her with revulsion. It was usually lunchtime when she saw them together, not this time of morning. They must have had another doctor's appointment. Dried leaves that had accumulated by the edge of the sidewalk crackled as they swirled in a draft behind the newsstand where she took cover. As the woman walked away, Anne could sense her happiness. The woman carried a briefcase and went in the opposite direction from the parking garage. Then she passed an entrance to the T. Anne walked along a parallel path across the street.

The whoosh of cars passing, bus hydraulics expelling, and people's chatter came between her and the bouncy-stepped woman who walked like she never questioned who she was or where she belonged. Unlike Anne's ill-fitting jacket, the woman's unfastened beige coat accentuated her confident posture and stylishly flapped as her arms swung gently with her stride. *She's probably never slouched a day in her life.* The brisk fall day with its pale sky seemed to invigorate rather than rattle her the way it did Anne. Winded, she leaned against a metal stop sign until the woman turned a corner, and Anne had to trot after her. She caught up as the woman's beautiful brown hair and designer suit disappeared into an old stone building. The structure looked ancient amidst the modern-day high-rises flanking it. Anne choked when she saw "BURKHEAD" carved in enormous capital letters above the door. She ran faster than she ever had in her life, racing to get away from the name she'd thought she'd buried decades ago. Burkhead. The place the woman who took her baby had worked.

Drifting through the city in a daze, Anne had a vague perception of bumping into outraged people as she tried to find her way back to Tyler's building. She assumed she'd driven herself home. How else would she have landed in a heap on her kitchen floor? Sucking air through her teeth, she rubbed the tender goose egg on the crown of her throbbing head.

Nightmares corroded her sleep with distorted visions of her father climbing on top of her small body, his scratchy chest hairs pressing against her, and the sour smell lingering in her room when he left. Anne woke, bawling for Mama Sue. She kicked her legs to push the sweat-soaked sheets to the end of the bed and turned on the lamp. The light illuminated the diary now lying on the night table, and she knew that was where she'd find Mama.

As her night sweats slowly subsided, her body shivered. She pulled the damp bedding back over her and rested the composition book on the blanket.

12/20/91: "Dear Book, Mama Sue's house is big and clean. My room smells like lavender. I ate a ton of her food today, and I didn't throw it up! But I'm so tired. I want to sleep all the time, but I guess since she's letting us stay here, and got my mom a job, I'll try to do what she wants."

1/14/92: "Dear Book, my mom doesn't seem so afraid my father will find us anymore. She likes her job and works during the day now, so we can hang out at night. It's nice being with her and sharing my books like *Little Women*. We both love Jo. Gary the Goat and I are getting along. She's kinda cute. Mama Sue's a good teacher and says I'm a fast learner. We've been spending time in her garden. We built a little shelter so the onions and squash will grow. Mama lets me cook with her, but I have to stop eating everything. I'm getting fat and farting all the time."

Mama Sue would've giggled at that. Anne hugged herself, wishing till it hurt they could talk again, and she could hear one of Mama's silly phrases that held some life lesson when you untangled it. She would tell Mama all about how seeing Tyler made her nervous and how mad she was that his wife was stopping him from being with her. Maybe seeing Burkhead was a sign from Mama that the woman knew where her baby was. Anne rolled the top of her ear between her fingers until she knew what Mama Sue would want her to do.

TWENTY-ONE
Tyler

The morning had been filled with people's congratulatory remarks. All of it came from the office next to Tyler, and the accolades were for the associate who'd scored the firm's newest big account. Everyone had been sure Tyler was the top pick. It was the second client assignment he'd lost since the botched conference call with Prachett in August. He'd believed he had been doing a solid job in the last three and a half weeks and proved his worth to the partners, but their message was clear: he wasn't doing enough.

By midday, Tyler, in desperate need of air, walked to Faneuil Hall. He left the bulging container of Chinese food he'd bought for lunch untouched, much to the delight of the two bees circling above it. As he watched them, he overheard the family at the table next to him discussing their tour of Tufts's campus. He empathized with their kid; it had been a lot of pressure when he'd gone through it his senior year. In particular, he'd struggled to formulate his college application essay.

He remembered a day he'd spread college pamphlets and wads of crushed paper across the kitchen table. His father was hovering behind him, pretending to drink a mug of coffee, when his mother came home from her Saturday errands in a tizzy.

"Roberta!" his father said. "What's wrong?"

"Your eyes are gonna pop out, Mom," Tyler said.

"Is everything all right? You look funny," his father added.

"I was at the nail salon," she stammered. She looked back and forth between her husband and son, then collected herself. "I don't know if I should bring this up. No, Tyler doesn't need to hear this. It's just gossip. Never mind."

"What?" he and his father shouted in unison.

"Alice, my manicurist, well, she said, 'Say, wasn't your boy the same age as that Laura Bennett?' Remember her, Tyler? She had such a crush on you."

In the more than three and a half years since Laura vanished, the concerns and gossip had lessened, and Tyler rarely wondered about her anymore.

"Anyway, then Alice went on, in a voice as quiet as a parrot trying to whisper, and told me Kitty, that's the father's girlfriend, was in the salon yesterday for acrylics. Alice said Kitty was a mess, with mascara-smeared red eyes, and ranting like a wild child, and Alice could barely work on her. And the manicurist at the next table started snickering . . ."

"Roberta," Tyler's father said with a headshake. "Stick to the topic."

"Alice said Kitty was freaking out." She stopped talking, trying to catch her breath. "Apparently, Curtis Bennett is being investigated for sexually assaulting a kid in the neighborhood!"

Pinpricks infested Tyler's body as soon as she said the man's name.

"Mrs. Hartman," his mother continued, "was at the drying table, blathering, 'I always said there was something wrong with that one. The way he looked at ya.' She said it gave her the creeps! And then Mrs. Feingold took her hands out of the pink sudsy liquid and slapped the table . . ."

"Roberta!" his father yelled.

"Well, Mrs. Feingold said, 'He's a drunk, he practically lives at Herman's Bar.'" She mimicked Mrs. Feingold's nasal voice. "Then Alice said she told Kitty to get her own kid to a therapist right away, 'cause who knows what he could've done to her. But Kitty wasn't having it. But I think Alice is right. She said, 'If he messed up the neighbor, you can bet she wasn't the only one.'"

His mother was silent for a moment, her eyes flickering from her husband to Tyler. "Then Mrs. Feingold said something that really made me think. She said maybe that's why Laura and her mom ran away all those years ago."

"Tyler, buddy, you okay there?" His father's voice sounded far away.

"That's not possible. Is it?" he asked. *Would her own father do that to her?* Laura had taken the lead the one time they'd had sex. He'd never stopped to think about how she'd learned to do that. His stomach churned as he compared what he'd done with Laura to her father's disgusting behavior and vowed never to tell anyone about it. Tyler looked ruefully at his dad. "I didn't help."

His father placed a hand on Tyler's shoulder. "You were thirteen, son. Even if anyone had known, there wasn't anything you could've done. She had a good friend in you, and I'm sure she was grateful for that. We should all give thanks she escaped. It's in the past, and that's where it should stay."

TWENTY-TWO
Billie

Billie's agency had a good working relationship with Central Hospital, where Gianna delivered her baby. Central always let the babies stay the four-day grace period before the birth mothers could sign the adoption documents. She'd kept in close communication with the hospital social worker, who told her Gianna had been quiet and emotionless but had followed the nurse's instructions during labor, and the delivery had gone smoothly. Billie almost wept, picturing the young teen lying on the bed, staring at the ceiling, barely experiencing or, more likely, expertly blocking the pain she'd long ago stopped feeling. The nurses said Gianna held the baby girl briefly after the birth but asked not to see her again. Neither of her parents had gone into the delivery room.

Gianna was at the agency now, a mere ninety-six hours after giving birth. She looked drained, paler than usual, and her sweats were limp and saggy on her barely post-baby body. Her parents, Emilio and Karla, accompanied her to the conference room. Her mother, a small, curvy woman with a bleached blonde bun, reeked of tobacco and scarcely spoke to Billie or her family. She took a chair at the far end of the long table, reciting a prayer, first in Italian and then in English. Karla's voice diminished with each repetition until she all but disappeared before the meeting was underway. Emilio, on the other hand, was tall, portly, and imposing. Messy dark curls lumbered atop his head, and bushy eyebrows punctuated his mean brown-black eyes. He'd gripped Billie's hand in an aggressive handshake before he took a seat.

Gianna sat in the corner chair next to the head of the table, where Billie had preset a stack of papers. At the bottom was a manila envelope with a string wound around its button. It contained a completed request to terminate the birth father's rights, which she would submit with the legal papers sent to family court. The court required proof that the agency had made a reasonable attempt to contact the father. It was a simple process. "Reasonable" meant a tiny fine-print classified ad in a local newspaper, with a few brief sentences that began, "To the father of baby girl born 9/13/12." It stated that the Burkhead Family Service Agency was seeking to petition the court to terminate his rights. It would list a date by which he would need to make contact if he contested the petition. Billie was unaware of anyone who knew to look in the classifieds for such a notice. Thus, she'd never experienced an objection.

Billie pulled the pile of folders closer to her, still baffled that Gianna hadn't opened up about who the birth father was or even admitted to having sex. The disconcerting feeling she got whenever she'd done something mortifying swelled as she thought back to a session when she'd tried to reach Gianna with a story about a "client." "Her stepbrother often touched her body in private places and told her it was a secret game. He made her believe something bad would happen if she told anyone," Billie had said. Gianna didn't take the bait, so she tried again.

"Has anyone ever asked you to keep secrets or done anything to you that makes you feel afraid?"

She thought for sure Gianna was going to tell her story, but there was no sign of nervousness or hesitation when she said no. If her experience hadn't told her otherwise, Billie would have believed it. But Gianna's unwillingness to talk, or her significant denial, was a common way a child protected herself, and a huge red flag that pointed to sexual abuse by someone close.

"What about your father? Was he the one who got you pregnant?"

"How can you say that about him?" Her lips scrunched like a spiteful dog about to bare her teeth. It was the first time Gianna had shown anger.

"I shouldn't have said that." A wave of shame washed over her. "It was wrong of me."

Billie had crossed an uncrossable line. If Gianna's father had, in fact, abused her, and the case went to court, they would say she'd coerced Gianna with the suggestion. The state could never charge her father. Worse though, in Billie's opinion, she'd likely breached the trust developed between her and Gianna. *What is happening to me?* She craned her neck to loosen the growing tightness in her shoulders. How could her feelings for a client, the desire to care for her, get so mixed up? Her behavior had been irresponsible.

Now, at the document signing, Billie narrowed her eyes to observe Emilio, who'd shifted his chair as near to Gianna as he could. His broad shoulders hunched forward as he trained his eyes on the table before him. His leather skin puckered. A grating, tic-like clearing of his throat penetrated the silence of the room.

"How are you feeling?" Billie asked. Gianna just gave a slight lift of her shoulders.

Billie sensed the negative energy lingering in the space between Gianna and her father's arm. Her client had shut down, much like the child who'd first arrived in her office.

"So, these papers are the ones we reviewed already together. I'm going to go through them again, so everyone is clear on what they say."

Billie saw Gianna pull her sweatshirt sleeves tighter into her clenched hands.

"I know this is hard. And I imagine you're exhausted after the past few days. Are you sure you want to go on?"

"She's doing this." Emilio's deep voice struck out like the smack of a wooden gavel. He softened before adding, "There's nowhere else for the baby to go."

"Gianna." Slowly, the girl lifted her head, allowing her vacant eyes to meet Billie's. "This has to be what you want. Once you sign the papers, there is no changing your mind." Her tongue felt dry and rough when she swallowed. "Are you certain?"

Gianna whispered, "I'm sure."

Billie buzzed their secretary to notarize the documents as they were signed.

Gianna put down her pen after the last signature. "You're bringing her to the family, right?" Her head was so bent it seemed like she was talking to her lap. She appeared way younger than her fourteen years.

"Yes. Then I'll be monitoring her and the family for the next six months," Billie assured her.

When Gianna and her mother exited toward the elevators, Emilio lingered. Billie's spine stiffened when he clutched her arm.

"I can tell she trusts you." His eyes glistened with emotion. He pulled a wrinkled cotton handkerchief from his pants pocket, keeping it crumpled in his fist. "Thank you."

Emilio turned away, pressed the cloth to his eyes, then joined his family, leaving Billie confounded. He wasn't an ideal parent, but the concern and vulnerability he showed for his daughter had put a chink in her theory that he'd abused Gianna or fathered her child. Could she even trust her instincts anymore?

Three hours later, Billie carried the agency's infant car seat into Central Hospital for the baby's discharge. When she entered the nursery, she instantly knew the infant with the tiny nose, alert gray eyes, and pure blonde fuzz on her head; she was going to look very much like Gianna.

Billie carefully snapped the car seat into its base in her back seat, trying not to disturb the infant, and pulled the belt strap tight to secure it. Then she clipped a yellow "Baby on Board" caution sign to her rear window. The desire for that little placard to be a permanent fixture in her life caused her to hesitate for a moment. When the baby cooed from beneath the car seat straps, she stroked the newborn's downy cheeks and kissed her soft head. She let her lips linger, longer than she should have, and inhaled the baby's fresh, powdery pureness. Billie triple-checked she had all the extra little bottles of formula the nurses had supplied and the plastic sealed orange-pink nipples that screwed onto them. Then she tucked a soft blanket with pale pink, yellow, and blue hippos around the infant sleeping in her car. Billie beamed at the innocent baby, feeling overwhelming pleasure in being her caretaker, at least for a short while.

At the parking lot exit, she resisted the impulse to flick her directional to the left, toward her home. She fantasized about their arrival, how Tyler would come out of the house to greet them and help carry the supplies. They would radiate with exhausted glee as they bustled around, fulfilling the baby's needs. A horn blasted from the car behind Billie, jolting her from the imagined homecoming.

* *

Billie shivered at the blast of cold that skidded down her neck as she left the agency. She pulled her scarf tighter to thwart the unusual October chill and increased her pace toward the parking garage. With her head down, she only caught a glimpse of a shadow. She wasn't sure what about it made her do a double take. There was nothing there except the corner of the building and some shrubs. Still, she thought of the stubbed cigarettes she kept finding by their mailbox and the constant hang-ups.

The phone calls that started in August, around the time she and Tyler noticed the silhouetted figure outside their home, had escalated in the past three weeks. Early morning and late at night. The caller always hung up. It was all so creepy that now she imagined things in other places. She knew she was overreacting, yet every noise or echo made her stop and check behind her as she climbed to the garage's top level. The idea of parking on the ground floor was becoming more desirable. Billie's heels wobbled as she walked faster. She was heading to a client appointment she knew would be pleasant and kept her focus on that, feeling more settled by the time she drove under the lifted parking garage gate.

She was in a good mood when she arrived in Meade, a sleepy southern suburb. It had been two weeks since she'd brought Gianna's baby, now known as Isabella, to the Renati family. One of the cherished benefits of her job was the mandatory follow-up visits after a baby was placed. She got to watch and document the baby's development and bonding for six months. If all went well, then the agency could petition the court to finalize the adoption.

Donalee and Gabriel welcomed Billie with enthusiastic hugs. Now, situated on the couch in their cape-style home, she watched Donalee extract Isabella from an infant rocker. She cradled the baby to her, looked up at Billie with joy, and then exploded with tears.

"Don't mind me," she laughed, "I'm such a mush."

Gabriel slipped his arm around his wife and stroked Isabella's head.

"We'd almost given up. And then you guys called." Gabriel fought back his emotions. "Isabella has won our hearts. She's a part of us." He kissed Donalee's cheek, which unleashed more tears from both of them. "She's not quite three weeks old, but our love for her is deeper than we ever imagined. Everything has changed, in the best way possible."

The moment was as rewarding as an adoption specialist could hope for, yet there was a soft tug on Billie's heart. If she could have seen it, Gianna would have been pleased.

Billie had explained the different types of adoption options to Gianna when they'd met last summer. In general, a closed adoption meant the child would be placed with the next person on the waiting list. Often the couple were unaware until after the child was born and the birth parents had signed the documents, thus relinquishing their parental rights. In more popular open adoption situations, the birth parents and adoptive parents found each other through a lawyer or other legitimate network, and, in many cases, met and continued contact. A semi-closed adoption, the route Gianna had taken, allowed the birth parents to select from the adoptive parents on the waiting list in advance.

So the Renatis, as the prospective parents, had been alerted to the upcoming birth. It was obvious from the abundance of baby supplies and infant toys that they'd taken advantage of the extra prep time. The semi-closed scenario had also allowed them to pay the birth mother's medical expenses, and they could be on a first-name basis if they chose, but Gianna opted out. In an uncanny moment of foresight, she'd worried how she'd react if she heard their names in passing. Later, Donalee and Gabriel would send updates and photos of Isabella to the agency, which would be held for Gianna if she wanted. Billie thought about her as she watched the Renatis' unrestrained adoration for the baby. Gianna had selected ideal parents for her child, the kind the young birth mother had probably wished for herself.

TWENTY-THREE
Anne

Ignoring the nor'easter warning, Anne turned off the car radio. The rain beat on the windshield, no longer in large, loud drops but in fire-hose force. The wiper's back-and-forth creaks were useless against the mid-October storm.

Their shades were still open, but Tyler and his wife became blurred dots inside their warm, dry living room. It was almost seven, which meant they'd move to the kitchen in the back of the house to prepare their dinner. Cuddling in front of a movie would replace their eight-thirty walk. Anne's body heat fogged up the windows, and the defroster was on the fritz. If she opened the window, she'd get drenched. But she couldn't leave.

Anne peeled the lid off the tepid hot chocolate she'd gotten at a little bakery off Route 9. She'd eaten the fresh-baked doughnut she'd bought with it in three bites. But the hot chocolate tasted nasty, as any store-bought would, compared to the special kind Mama Sue used to make for her. Hers had maple syrup and a sprinkle of nutmeg. One time, Mama served it to her after an OB appointment. They'd been sitting across from each other in the kitchen.

Anne remembered saying, "The doctor said the butterfly feeling in my belly is the baby flutter-kicking. That's weird."

"It is." Mama Sue laughed. "At twenty weeks, it's normal, though." She moved to the chair next to Anne. "Do you want to talk about it?"

"Huh?"

"About the baby?"

"What's to talk about?" Anne got jittery. Her mother never asked questions or talked about it, which was just fine. She was used to keeping things private.

"Well, do you understand how you got pregnant?"

"Tsk," Anne chortled, "duh."

When Mama Sue didn't look away, Anne tapped her spoon on the whipped cream topping her mug. "Not really." Mama Sue's soft voice tugged at her, but all she did was shrug.

"Was the boy someone special?"

Anne's eyes welled. That was happening a lot lately. For no reason, even at sappy commercials. She used a shred of a paper napkin to dab her lids.

"Can you tell me about him, hon? Without telling me his name?"

She couldn't figure out why Mama asked it that way.

"No," she said.

"Well, how 'bout this? Can you tell me if there was a special boy in your life?"

"There was a boy I had fun hanging with. He's a cool kid. Smart. And he was nice to me."

"Could this be from him?"

"God, we're only in eighth grade."

Although Mama Sue's unruffled manner compelled her to open up, Anne didn't want to tell her Tyler was her boyfriend. That he thought she was pretty and made her feel like nothing bad would ever happen to her. She didn't want anyone to know she missed him so much it hurt when she thought about him, which was always. There were too many times she'd passed by the telephone and almost called him to apologize for not saying goodbye. She'd written him dozens of letters but always tore them up. Anne had forbidden herself from contacting him because she was sure if Tyler knew where she was, her devil-father would get it out of him. But she also didn't want to tell Mama Sue the truth so she could keep Tyler close to her.

"Did you understand what was happening when you had sex?"

"Yeah, sorta. I know more than my friends." She laughed a little but stopped when Mama's eyes narrowed.

"Do you think he should know you're pregnant?"

"*No!*" The ferocity of her own voice startled her, and her armor went up. But Mama wasn't angry.

"It's okay," she said. "Tell me why you're so against it."

"Because." Anne's lashes were wet and heavy when she blinked, her voice a faint whisper. "He'd be in trouble. My father is dangerous."

Mama Sue stared at her. Not in a shocked kind of way, more like she was infiltrating her thoughts.

"Did your father ever hurt you?"

Anne nodded.

"How did he hurt you?"

Anne looked away.

"Did he ever hit you?"

This time, Anne shook her head.

"Did he ever touch you, in, um, places he shouldn't?"

Anne held her breath but locked eyes with Mama as the room rotated around her.

"Honey, did your father make you have sex with him?"

Anne's breath sped up so fast she couldn't exhale. She searched those cocoa-brown eyes, wondering if they would be disgusted by her.

"You can't tell anyone . . ." When her voice faded, Mama came to her side of the table and hugged her. Anne's long sobs and anguish released into the soft folds of Mama Sue's arms.

"You're safe here. You're okay," Mama cooed. "I love you, Anne, like you were my own daughter. Thank you for telling me. Thank you."

The storm had intensified to the point where Anne could no longer see Tyler's house, and it became futile to try. She drove home, her clothes saturated with rainwater from the five seconds it took to get from her car inside her apartment. Her wet clothes dropped on the bathroom floor as she clumsily pulled on an old pair of polyester pajama bottoms and a sweatshirt. She left her hair dripping down her back, wiped her glasses with a dishrag, and grabbed a bag of Cheetos before settling on the floor. She leaned against her love seat and read the next passage in her diary.

4/23/92: "Dear Book, my boobs are gigantic! They hurt, though. Sometimes I get these funny little wallops from the alien inside my stomach. The doctor said it's normal to feel kicking at twenty-eight weeks. We all decided it's safer if I don't keep the baby. We met with a social worker about it. I pretended I didn't know whose baby it is, so he won't be on the birth certificate. He can't ever know. I bet Mom thinks her daughter is a slut, or a kid at a party did something to me. P.S. I'm scared she'll catch on about the stuff with my father. Like, she wants to know the truth but can't bring herself to ask. I'm pretty sure Mama has kept my secret so far, though."

6/20/92: "Dear Book, it's hard to remember not living here and not being part of Mama Sue's family. She's been a grandmother, aunt, and mom rolled up into one. Sometimes even my mother seems like her child. We've both learned to cook and sew from her. We've shared the literature books, and the three of us discuss them afterward. This week we're reading *Rebecca of Sunnybrook Farm*. So good! I made a delicious cheesecake for Mama Sue's birthday. I have my very own garden patch now, but it's pretty hard to bend over this belly to tend to it. And Gary loves to dart around, hoping I'll chase her, but then nuzzles me when I can't. I think she understands I'm not moving too fast anymore."

Not wanting to go on to the next part, Anne launched the diary toward the wall. It was too hellish to feel it again, but she'd gone too far. She remembered climbing the steps to her room, collapsing at the unexpected pull in her abdomen, and crying out at the spurts of water that puddled out of her. Mama Sue appeared in a flash and scooped her arms around her.

"It's going to be all right," her calm, soft voice whispered in Anne's ear. "Squeeze my hand and let's walk to the car."

Her mother met them in the hospital's birthing room, and the women stood on either side of her, holding her hands as she writhed through the contractions. A tall man with a stork-designed medical cap stood at her feet.

"I'm Doctor Calder," he said. He spread Anne's legs and checked her. With one gloved hand below, his left hand massaged her abdomen. Staff hustled around him as he spoke to them and spread the goo she knew was for an ultrasound.

"Two milligrams propofol." The man's mouth moved like a puppet from behind his mask. The nurse rummaged through a cabinet.

Her mother was watching them with a keen eye. "What's wrong?"

"The baby's breech; I'm going to try to manipulate the head into proper position. We're giving her something to diminish the pain."

"If it doesn't work?"

"If we can't, we'll have to do a cesarean."

The wild look in her mother's eyes added to the pain, which rose again. Anne groaned, and Mama Sue wiped a cool cloth on her forehead.

An unsympathetic-looking nurse holding a syringe pushed her mother to the side.

"Childbirth isn't meant for girls your age. It's too hard. I'm going to give you something to calm you down," she said.

The onset of another crippling cramp erased Anne's fear of the mean nurse. She could feel the bones of Mama Sue's fingers compressing as she clutched them.

"It's called twilight sleep." Mama's voice was soothing. "You'll be awake, but you won't remember the pain."

"We don't call it that anymore." The nurse moved away, and her mother returned to her side. Then Anne felt like she'd just woken up but hadn't realized she'd been asleep. She was still in the hospital room and heard a vague sound of a baby wailing.

"It's a girl!" one nurse cheered. Moments later, they placed a squishy baby in Anne's arms.

"I don't want to touch it," she cried. "Take it away."

"Look, Mama," her mother said in an excited whisper as she changed the baby's diaper the next day. Anne feigned disinterest but glanced over and saw her mother pointing to a blot on the baby's lower arm that looked like a heart.

"That's a beautiful birthmark," Mama Sue said. "It means she'll always have a loving heart."

Her mother carefully dressed the cooing infant in a pink hat and a matching sweater that Mama Sue had taught her to crochet. Mama Sue had added the lilac flower that adorned it. Then her mother coddled the baby while Mama took photographs. Tears escaped both women's eyes as they walked into the hall, forgetting to shut the door. Anne had a clear view as they handed the bundle to a sour-faced lady in an itchy-looking gray suit jacket and skirt, with sensibly heeled shoes.

Two days after the baby had been extracted from her body and sent to her new life, Anne returned to Mama Sue's. Her boobs felt like watermelons, and her abdomen pinched and ached. She was sore and bleeding where the baby came out. She couldn't sit right from it all. Over the next few weeks, she regained her strength and felt more like herself. Her sad self. It was strange and awful to think about the nameless baby, so she didn't. There was no mention of her in the house. As time passed, Anne reconciled it as a miserable illness.

Soon after "the illness," her mother met Grant, a pharmaceutical representative from Arizona. Anne caught her mother grinning for no reason, a lot, and humming too. She'd even worn makeup and dressed nicer. And when she was with him, her mother laughed, a rare, pure sound of pleasure. When Grant asked her mother to move to Phoenix with him, Mama Sue insisted Anne stay with her until she completed high school.

"She's been through enough changes, don't you think?" she had said in her kindly way.

"I don't want to be away from you," her mother had said, "but I have to do what's best for you. You've thrived since we've been here, and it's made me see I never watched over you or taught you about life the way you needed. I don't want you to lose that. You need to complete your schooling, and," she blinked away tears, "Mama Sue can take care of you better than I can right now."

"I get it," Anne replied. "It's better for you too."

While she'd helped her mother pack, she found the baby photos Mama Sue had taken. There were at least a dozen, printed in an array of frameable sizes and a sheet of wallets. Anne had been about to tear them up, but her mother placed a gentle hand on her arm.

"One day," her mother said, "you'll be glad you have them."

She and her mother had spoken on the phone all the time. Anne could tell her mom was happy, and Grant treated her well. He and her mother visited a couple of times a year when he had business nearby. They'd invited her for Thanksgiving and Christmas holidays, but she was never willing to leave Mama Sue, even though Mama had her brother and his family for company.

Life went on like that right up until the day during Anne's senior year when Mama Sue called her down to the living room.

A breeze wafted through the open windows, and she could smell the dry maple leaves that had spent the day falling. She scrunched into the lumpy couch and gasped as her mother walked in from the kitchen.

"What are you doing here?" Anne ran to her mother, who embraced her in a warm, secure hug. "Where's Grant?"

"He went to see a client. He thought we should have some privacy." They sat together on the couch, and she took Anne's hands in her own. Mama Sue made herself comfortable on her other side.

"What's going on?"

"I wanted to be here to tell you myself." She fussed with her hair, then retook Anne's hands. "There's no easy way to say this. Your father's been arrested."

"He . . . what?"

Anne hadn't thought about her father much in the years she'd lived at Mama Sue's. The nightmares had all but stopped except for a couple of times when she was in town, caught a whiskey scent, or heard a gruff voice. Then she'd get unsettled for a day or two, afraid of meaningless shadows and sounds that her all-consuming anxiety magnified. Mostly, though, she'd felt secure in her home here. So much so that often when she slept, calmer, comforting scenes replaced the torment. In them were grown-up versions of her and Tyler in their cute house with the grassy yard, which he mowed each week. They would take their toddler daughter, a miniature version of her, and younger son, a replica of him, to the nearby playground. Tyler would snuggle her as they admired and waved to their squealing, carefree children.

"I came because I didn't want you to hear it from someone else," her mother continued.

"Who would have told me?" Anne hadn't spoken to Tyler or any of his friends. None of them knew where she was. And the kids in the local high school didn't have a clue about her old life.

Though they lived more than an hour west, her old school's basketball team was a big deal in the region, and Tyler was its star. It wasn't hard to find news of him in the sports section of the paper she read for current events in history class. Once, Anne had gone to a regional tournament to watch him play, although she'd stayed obscured in the top bleachers. Afterward, she waited outside the gym for a closer glimpse of him but left when she spotted Moe and CeCe in the crowd. Then she'd seen his school's homecoming photo in the paper. He looked handsome in a suit and tie, and he had his arms around a pretty girl who leaned into him. The small print said she was Angie Finelli. Even though she understood four years had passed, the betrayal still overwhelmed her.

"It seems a neighbor is accusing your father of sexually molesting their daughter. I'm sure they're lying. I can't figure out why."

Anne's gut contracted like a giant fist was squeezing it. Everything was spinning around her. Mama Sue's firm hand on her shoulder kept her grounded.

"It's time, Anne," Mama Sue whispered.

Anne could feel her eyes widening as she looked at Mama. Her head dropped so low her words went into her chest. "It's not a lie," she muttered.

"What are you saying?" Her mother's hand flew to her mouth. "Did you see something?"

Anne remained motionless.

"That *bastard*!" The veins in her mother's forehead bulged as anger revealed itself. Then the dial changed, and sadness overcame her.

"Oh, my baby, I'm so sorry. It's my fault. I should have been there for you. Should have seen it. You must have been so frightened and alone." She pulled Anne into her chest and fastened her arms around her daughter.

Anne stiffened in her mother's hug. It felt like multiple bolts of lightning were striking her.

"Oh my God!" With a gasp, her mother pushed her back, holding her at arm's length. "He didn't? Is he, is the baby . . . his?"

"She isn't." Mama Sue shook her head.

Anne felt a rush of cold pour from her brain to her toes. It froze her face and tongue. She shut down and remained like that, not speaking to anyone until Mama Sue encouraged her mother and Grant to return to Arizona a few days later. "Give her some space. I'll watch over her."

Anne was sitting on the steps, peeking down through the handrail slats while they talked. Her mother was clutching her own shoulders and weeping. The cyclone of emotions swirling inside Anne held her body immobile. A part of her wanted to comfort her mother and reassure her that Mama was right—she should leave. At the same time, she wanted to drum her fists into her mother's chest, scream out and blame her for not knowing. *I hate myself so much.* Mama Sue had often explained her father was sick, and none of it was her fault. But even at seventeen, she didn't always believe it, so the knowledge was of no comfort.

That night, Anne woke, hollering into the blackness of the pre-dawn hour. As she had every time since the nightmares returned, Mama Sue, covered in the sedating smell of her bedtime peppermint muscle cream, came to sit by her side.

"It was so real," Anne said. "I could feel his breath, smell his foulness."

"He can't hurt you anymore."

Her routine returned to normal for a while after her father's arrest. Anne did her early morning chores, milked Gary, who'd become her best friend, went to school, and did her homework. When she finished, she'd spend time outside with Gary. She was a silly goat, jumping in the air and nudging against Anne's legs to propel her around. Gary always seemed to sense her mood if she was feeling down. The fuzzy goat stood next to her, nuzzling her nose against her or nipping on her sleeve when Anne sat on the tree stumps she'd placed in the penned area for Gary to climb. In the evenings, she and Mama Sue played the piano together or discussed books assigned for English class.

One afternoon, while she was studying, she overheard Mama on the phone with her mother.

"I agree. She sounds better. Looks better too. Not so glum, and her appetite's back."

But Anne had known she wasn't right. She felt unsettled all the time, gutted with the sense that something terrible was about to happen. Looking over her shoulder had become as familiar as the anxiety that taunted her. She'd felt the same way when Mama Sue made her go to the public high school, which had a small population of tight-knit students she never fit in with. But in her junior year, Anne and a round-robin of hormonal boys who wouldn't admit to knowing her found the physical satisfaction they needed in the back of the secondhand Mustang her mother and Grant had given her when she got her license.

This arrangement suited her until her classmates became obsessed with their SAT results. While they orchestrated their futures, Anne's past was creeping back, and the careful web of armor she'd woven was unraveling. Since the news of her father's arrest, the nightmares bled into daytime. She was dizzy from lack of sleep. Sweat dripped from her forehead without warning. Teachers marked her homework incomplete, and her grades slipped. They'd become frustrated with her spacing out in class, and she snapped at them when they tried to get her attention. She'd landed in after-school detention a bunch of times. Her renewed fear that her secrets about her father and her baby would get out was impossible to contain.

After her father's October arrest, news outlets kept the story relevant until a spring trial date was declared. Then they went ballistic with constant articles detailing what had happened with the neighbor's seven-year-old kid. There was information on everything but her name—she was too young—but it was all there: how her father lured her to his house when his family was out (he'd promised her an ice cream sundae), how he'd sat her on his lap (to read her a story), how he'd kissed her cheek and then carried her to his bed and held her down. The report indicated the little girl had learned about "special secrets" at school, so she'd confessed everything to her mother as soon as he let her go.

Presumably, it was her family's attorney that was leaking the information. There were a handful of mentions about Anne, with speculation about where she and her mother were and why they disappeared. One article in the *Gazette* went so far as to suggest her father had murdered his first family and disposed of them in mail carrier bags.

For months Anne was terrified some reporter would come close to unearthing the truth, and the police or lawyers might find her and drag her into her father's sins, or worse, force her to publicize her story. But Mama Sue's ESP to change her name years before had spared her and her mother.

The trial began in March. With it came an outraged community crying for the lynching of the man who, it turned out, raped not only his neighbor's kid but also his fiancée's daughter. The almost stepdaughter was brave and testified. News reports were full of the atrocious scandal, and newspaper articles detailed all the highlights.

Anne followed the events from a safe distance. Except for the last day—sentencing. It was a few weeks before her eighteenth birthday, but the only thing on her mind that August morning was the longing to see her father in pain. Before she left, she opened the liquor cabinet in the small hutch next to Mama Sue's piano and removed the gin. She unscrewed the cap and took a swig, the way she'd been doing since day one of the trial.

Wearing a blonde wig and a pair of large sunglasses, Anne drove back to the town she'd thought she was done with. She passed her old school and the streets where she and Tyler had walked. She sped through a stop sign in front of the movie theater where their elbows had touched on the armrest. Garby's Diner, renamed, according to a modern neon sign, Cooper's, where they'd shared fries and milkshakes. Anne passed it all without flinching.

Inside the courthouse, she slipped into the last row of seats. Her eyes fixed on the back of one head: his. After four years, there was less hair, but it was still a recognizable mess. The suit jacket on his wilted shoulders was stained and worn. But it was him. The lurching in her stomach confirmed it. When she'd imagined being in the same room with him again, she'd worried she'd lose control, and the bailiff would drag her off for attacking her father. It turned out she was anything but a maniac. She felt nothing except a deadened resolve. Anne waited for him to stand, for the judge to sentence him to twenty-five years, and then she left as inconspicuously as when she'd arrived.

On her way out of town, Anne eased up on the gas and slowly rolled in front of a familiar mint vinyl house. There were no cars in the driveway and, after watching for a length, no movement inside. She pulled the metal mailbox tab. She fondled the long envelope with Tyler's name written in her best script. Then she slipped it in the mailbox and pushed the little door until it tapped closed. A slight August breeze caressed her bare arms as she drove away from her childhood memories.

TWENTY-FOUR
Tyler

On the first Saturday in October, Tyler went to his parents' house to help his dad organize what Goodwill would pick up and what would go with the junk hauler after they'd downsized to a two-bedroom town house in a fifty-five-plus community. His trendy parents now had a koi pond in their backyard and access to golf, tennis, swimming, restaurants, and a grocery.

They'd only moved a few days ago, yet the air inside the house was musty and still. It was a far cry from the old days when he'd walked in and smelled fresh-baked desserts. He remembered coming through the garage door after a full week of freshman orientation and collegiate-level parties. Being home and in the air-conditioning had been an immediate relief.

"Leave your laundry by the machine," his mother had said.

She'd been moving around the kitchen, collecting bowls and utensils she'd used creating that day's goodies. Whatever she was baking was full of cinnamon and butter. Tyler's best guess was snickerdoodles.

"You're a mess," he said.

"Never you mind. You won't be making fun of me when the

cookies are ready. They're almost done. And not to worry, I made extra for you."

"You're the best. Hey, don't hug me. You'll get that schmutz all over me."

"Oh, poor college boy." His mother reached up and smudged his face with cookie dough.

Now Tyler opened the sliding glass door to make sure there'd been no damage to the backyard after the recent storm. He'd already helped store their lawn furniture in the haul-away pile in the garage weeks before, so those were safe. The cover on the BBQ was intact, and the old oak tree limbs still hung on. A thin layer of pine needles and small sticks topped the grassy area where his dad used to pitch balls to him. From his vantage point in the kitchen, the boundary fence seemed to have withstood the weather too. Tyler looked toward the far corner he, Moe, and John had hurdled to sneak cigarettes. With a nostalgic smile, he remembered the rebellion lasting through the one pack Moe swiped from his sister before the boys admitted they hated it.

Tyler checked to be sure the dining room was empty, then moved into the foyer. Dust swirled when he plopped his parents' unforwarded mail and newspapers on the table across from the front door. There'd been an antique mirror hanging above, which he'd always thought was absurd because you couldn't see your face. His parents had removed the items on the tabletop and kept the heirloom vintage rosewood box from some great- or great-great-grandmother that used to lie between a lamp and a plastic fern. His mother always left mail and reminder notes for him in that box.

He pulled a frame hook from the drywall, thinking again about the day he'd come home from college orientation. The alluring, sugary aroma of baking cookies filled the air when he'd walked through the foyer carrying his overnight bag to his room.

"There's some things in the box for you," his mother had called after him.

When he'd removed the lid, he found an alumni announcement from high school, a notice about voting registration, and something addressed to him in marker.

"Did you see the mail?" His mother was still washing dishes, and she'd raised her voice over the running faucet. "Dad didn't think you'd want me to open any of it."

"Hey, Mom?" An unpleasant odor caught his attention. He'd tossed the mail on the table as he rushed to the kitchen. "Is something burning?"

"Damn it!" Her irritation was evident. "The parchment paper I used to line the cookie sheet caught fire."

Smiling at the memory, Tyler checked the upstairs bedrooms. Before heading back down, he saw the tiny bleached spots on the carpet between his room and the bathroom where he'd left the trail of blood. He and his mother were probably the only ones who ever noticed it. He leaned on the banister and could almost smell the offensive bleach fumes again. The aftershock of that day, the lies he had told, and the edginess crept back to the surface.

At the bottom of the stairs, he turned into the family room. There were indentations in the carpet where the piano had been. His cousin, Charlie's sister, had called dibs on it as soon as she found out he and Billie weren't taking it. Tyler pulled a quarter from his pocket to rub the marks out.

"Might as well leave it," a familiar voice said.

Tyler whipped around. His father was sitting in his favorite high-back chair in the corner by the windows. "I didn't know you were here."

"Your mother dropped me off." His father patted the chair's leather arms. "Just giving her one last spin. Would have taken her if we had room."

"Hard to say goodbye to this place." Tyler pulled the matching ottoman from under his father's feet and sat with him.

"Memories are memories. They're with you wherever you go."

If only it weren't true, Tyler thought. He ran his hand through his hair. "You're very philosophical today."

"Perhaps." His dad shrugged his shoulders. "Or maybe that's what relaxing and having fun does to a man. You should try it. Speaking of relaxing, what's going on at work?"

"I don't know. It's not looking good. I'm not sure the partners are going to support me."

"Why not?"

"All the time off for fertility stuff hasn't been helpful. And maybe I've been distracted."

"Anyone would be, I suppose. Dealing with infertility must be tough."

"It's not that, exactly," Tyler said.

"What about, then?"

"It's nothing."

"It's something if it's interfering with your career. Let's hear it."

His dad had always listened to people's issues with patience. He was nonjudgmental and usually reserved before reacting. Tyler wasn't sure he knew how to voice his fears.

His father's thick brows furrowed, amplifying the deep age lines on his face. He leaned over the arm of his chair and popped the lid off a small cooler on the floor. The ice shifted as he pulled out two beer cans. "I was saving these for later, but now's as good as any."

"Not for me. It's barely past breakfast."

"You sure? Looks like you can use it."

"I'm just exhausted, that's all." Tyler buried his face in his hands. He'd been holding himself together with false bravado, phony smiles, pretending to be successful, not wanting to let down his wife, his parents, his bosses. The pressure building inside him was on the verge of shattering him like a pane of glass.

"Let's hear it then." His father sat forward in his chair and gently touched Tyler's knee. "What's really going on?"

Tyler looked at his father for a long while, taking in the softness of his face and the hint of his sandalwood aftershave. When he was a kid and something was bothering him, he'd crawl onto his father's lap. His father would hold him and say, "You can tell me anything, son," and he'd always make it better.

"If Billie doesn't get pregnant, she's going to want to adopt." Tyler swiped the bangs off his forehead and took a deep breath before continuing. "What worries me is anything could happen to my child. If Billie and I have a baby, it could inherit some disease from me." He gulped back memories of Charlie's last days. "But if we adopt, the medical history could be limited." He rubbed his hand over his face when he felt his eyebrow twitch. His father would recognize Tyler was skirting the issue if he noticed.

"Are you saying you don't want a child unless it's biologically yours?"

"No, Dad. I think I'm saying I don't want kids at all."

"I see."

Tyler watched his father's expression for signs of anger or disappointment.

"Help me understand a little better. Because you can't control their DNA, you've decided you won't have children?"

"Okay, I hear how stupid that sounds. It's more than that." The *tap-tap-tap* his foot was making as his leg bounced grew louder. "I'm terrified something could happen to my child, and I wouldn't know how to do anything. And I don't think I'm cut out for that. I don't think I could live with not being able to keep my child safe."

"Are you sure you aren't just scared, Ty? Anything bad can happen to anyone at any time."

"I know, better than you think. But dads are supposed to make sure they don't." Tears pooled in his eyes. "And you didn't."

"Me? What?"

"Back in middle school." Tyler felt helpless as everything he'd bottled up for years spilled out. "Remember when I got hurt and went to the ER?"

"Came back with a ton of stitches, as I recall."

"You were late to pick me up that day." Tyler's fingers curled into his palm. "So I blamed you."

His father winced as his head jerked to the side. "For falling on a rock? How was that my fault?"

"That's not what happened. I was too scared to tell you and Mom the truth." He looked up at his father. "Do you remember the Bennetts?"

"Who doesn't? That man was a sick piece of work. Their daughter was in your class, wasn't she? What do they have to do with why you were angry at me?"

"Everything and nothing."

His father listened patiently as he retold the story about Mr. Bennett ambushing him.

"You've been living with this all these years? That's horrible." He squeezed his hands together so tightly his knuckles turned white. "I'd known something was going on with you but imagined nothing as awful as this. You'd shut down, and I didn't know how to pull you back. I thought it was a teenage mood thing."

"Yeah, well, back then it all got mixed up in my head." Tyler sniffled. "I thought if you'd been there, then he'd never have gotten to me." He wiped the tears cascading down his cheek with the back of his hand. "You were supposed to save me from harm. But you weren't there."

"If I could have shielded you from every scraped knee, every heartache or pain in your life, I would have done everything in my power to do it. And Lord knows what I would have done to that son of a bitch if you'd told me."

"I know you would have. Though at thirteen, I didn't understand." Tyler glanced out the window. Everything that had happened with that man and his daughter had deeply affected his feelings about himself and becoming a father. He felt like a coward now for not disclosing why Bennett targeted him, but he needed to be careful in how he explained himself. His own connection to Laura back then wasn't something he'd ever want anyone to know.

"It all really messed with me," he explained. "I decided the only way to be a good father, to never fail at providing the safety a child deserves, is never to have kids." Tyler turned away from the window and looked back at his father, who was still listening attentively in his well-loved leather chair.

"Even with the best of intentions, we screw up," his father said. "Sometimes kids get hurt by our mistakes or ignorance. But we pick up, hope we've learned something, and give it our newest best shot. Parenting isn't easy, not always fun, but I wouldn't trade being your father for anything."

"Thanks," Tyler said. "I appreciate what you're saying. Now get your fifty-five-and-over butt off that chair and help me lift it."

"Yes, sir!" His father laughed. "But Tyler?"

"Yeah, Dad?"

"You need to talk to your wife."

TWENTY-FIVE
Billie

Using a pink highlighter, Billie underscored the results of her first daily urine ovulation predictor test in her appointment book. After five days of fertility pills, she'd had to wait four more to start charting. Once the tests showed a positive rise in her luteinizing hormone, then, that day, she and Tyler would have to have sex. With the first entry completed, she worried the medicine and her body would fail, and the levels would stay flat.

After she'd put the kit away, Billie brushed her hair and went downstairs. She checked the locks on all the windows and doors and made sure the shades were down before leaving for work. It had become a habit since the evening she and Tyler noticed muddy footprints in their backyard.

Billie had hoped Tyler would've returned from his run before she left because she wasn't sure if he'd taken the key. It was risky to leave the patio door unlatched for him. Should she chance locking him out? She went into Tyler's study to look in the leather catchall tray he used when he emptied his pockets. His oversized Audi fob lay next to his wallet and some loose change, but, to her relief, his house key was not there. As she stepped away, she saw something on the carpet, and when she lifted it, she recognized the baby photo she'd asked him about last summer.

"What are you doing in here?" Tyler asked.

"You scared me to death, Ty."

He took the photo from her. She wasn't sure which of them was thrown more off guard.

"Well, I don't need you messing up my things."

"Since when can't I be in here?"

"I didn't mean it." He swept his hair off his forehead. "It's just . . . I don't know. I guess I didn't expect to see you."

"I wish I knew what was going on with you. I've been more patient than you deserve at this point." She pointed to the desk drawer where he'd just slipped the wallet-size photo. "And what's the deal with that?"

"Nothing. You're making drama where there isn't any."

Billie wanted to avoid a fight before she ovulated, but Tyler's eyebrow twitched, confirming he was full of it. Did he really think so little of her he thought he could get away with his recent actions and lame excuses?

"I don't know what you're up to, but quit insulting my intelligence."

Billie waited, but Tyler didn't come after her when she stormed off to the garage. She opened his car door and felt around in the side pocket, the console, under the seats, and then looked in the trunk. Her search for something to nullify her sense of paranoia, or anything to help keep her faith in him, was fruitless. What else was her husband lying about?

"Madison?" Billie reached her hand out to the young woman when the elevator arrived. "I'm Belinda Campbell."

Madison clung to the strap of a cornflower-blue crossbody shoulder bag that covered her midsection. Her left hand intertwined with the fingers of the young man standing next to her. Uncertain, the two twentysomethings stood for several seconds as the elevator doors thunked closed behind them.

"This is Steve," Madison said in a small voice. "Steve Quinn." She looped her hand under his arm. "I hope it's okay he came with me. He wants to be a part of everything."

Billie did a quick scan. Steve had a well-kept, preppy look with a fair-skinned, boyish face. He barely looked up from the floor, but when he did, she sensed kindness.

"Glad to meet you, Steve." It was unusual and intriguing for a birth father to be involved. Based on her experience, his presence meant he was invested in Madison and their baby, and they might not follow through with an adoption. She led them to her office, which greeted them with a potpourri of freesia from the new rose arrangement and the cinnamon she'd added to a recent refill of coffee. She gestured for the couple to sit in the two armchairs.

Billie pivoted her desk chair to face them. The bangs of Madison's shoulder-length black cherry–colored hair fell just above her blue eyes. Her creamy skin and freckles enhanced her wholesome look. Steve seemed fused with the armchair, as though willing himself to fade away. The office was quiet except for the sound of voices in the hall and a distant phone ringing. Madison pushed some hair off her face and then quickly pinched her outer ear.

"Tell me how you came to our agency today." She spoke softly and glanced at Madison's stomach. Her blue-flowered cotton dress revealed a bulge, which Billie judged to be the beginning of the third trimester.

"Back in August, there were these fliers in the Woodson student union. We're students there. The fliers were about an adoption thing at the university nearby. I'd realized I was pregnant by then, five months, but hadn't told anyone yet because we weren't sure what we were going to do. Steve came with me to your speech so we both could understand what adoption meant and what we'd all go through." Madison peeked at Steve with an adoring look.

"The way you explained things, I don't know . . ." Madison trailed off, but after a few blinks, she rallied. "There were a lot of facts, but you made it less murky. And I felt like you were talking to me, like you cared about who we are. I think I was afraid it would only be about people greedy for babies, and I wouldn't matter. You get that there are people and feelings involved. And you made me see we were going to need our family's support too."

"We spent many sleepless nights discussing it after that," Steve said. "And took our time thinking it through and making sure it was the right thing for us. And then we talked to our parents. That wasn't, still isn't, so easy."

Billie nodded. "Do your families support your decision for adoption?"

"My parents were sad but understanding," Madison said. "Of course, they'd rather we focus on being kids, not raising one, but said they'd be here for us, whatever we choose."

"Mine were less accepting," Steve said.

"Your mom's coming around a bit, though, don't you think?" Madison asked. "After both our families talked together, his father told us in private he thinks adoption is the best choice, but he won't say it in front of his wife."

"He's learned not to contradict her." Steve chuckled. "My mother and father were raised by strict Irish Catholics. My mother believes it's the parents' duty to raise their children, no matter the circumstances, unless it's not in the child's best interest. But in our case, she seems adamant that our reasons are selfish, and therefore it's not okay in her book."

"And what are your reasons?" Billie asked.

"Steve and I met our freshman year. We're sophomores now. He's an engineering student, and I'm in the nursing program. Our plan was to get married and have a family after we graduate. And then this happened." Madison stroked her belly before tugging her ear again. Steve rested his hand on her back, his touch seeming to encourage her.

"At first we talked about keeping it," he said. "Making this decision is the hardest thing either of us has ever had to do. But we agree it's the right choice."

"Can you tell me more about why that is?" Billie asked.

"My parents are older," Madison said, "so I don't feel right asking them to help raise a baby now, and Steve's family lives too far for us to rely on them."

"We don't have much money to live on," Steve explained, "and both our families used their savings to pay for us to go to college. This child deserves a nice home and financial support."

"We want the baby, we really do," Madison said. "It breaks our hearts to do this, but a baby can't live in a dorm room, you know?"

Steve shifted closer to Madison and laced his fingers through hers. "We will get married and be good parents one day," he said. "We want what's best for our baby, but we can't give that to him or her right now."

Madison reached for a tissue from the box Billie kept on the end table and dabbed her eyes. "You can help us find the right home for our baby, can't you?"

"I have the perfect home for your baby, with me and Tyler!" Billie's throat clamped. She wasn't sure whether she'd actually spoken her thoughts out loud. Her eyes darted between Madison and Steve, but her clients were calm, waiting for her response. She gripped the side of the chair, mentally steadying herself.

"I'll do everything I can to explain the process and make sure you make the best, most informed decisions you can." Billie leaned forward in her chair, closer to her new clients. "I'll be honest with you, though. If you go this route, it won't be easy. It's vital that you're satisfied with the choice you make."

Madison curled the tip of her ear between her fingers and looked at Billie. "I understand how hard it will be." She swallowed. "I'm adopted, so I know this will affect the baby its entire life." She swatted her bangs, which fell back on her forehead. "At first, I thought there was no way I was going to do to my baby what my birth mother did to me. I mean, I love my parents, they're great, but I grew up thinking someone didn't want me. Now I understand she couldn't raise me. Mothers take care of their babies, and that's what she did." Steve rubbed her arm before she continued. "She gave me parents. She gave me a good life. That's what Steve and I want for our baby too."

After her session with Madison and Steve, Billie entered some notes in the case file.

"Earth to Billie." Paige stood in the doorway. "What are you spacing out about?"

"Oh my God." Billie laughed. "How long were you standing there?"

"Long enough to see you're in a fog."

Paige positioned herself in a client chair. "Nice apology flowers. What'd Tyler do this time, cough?"

"We had a little fight this morning. But it's beyond absurd. Every time he expresses any normal, negative, human emotion lately, he sends them to make up for it. It's not like I'm going to love him less or disappear because he's in a bad mood." *Unless the bouquets are meant to assuage his guilt for loving me less.*

"Too many flowers should be every wife's curse," Paige said. "Tyler's a great guy, and he's devoted to you. He gives the rest of the husbands a very high bar to achieve."

"What if he isn't? Devoted, I mean. I don't know how to explain it. He isn't just moody. It's hard to pinpoint, but he's been weird, almost indifferent."

"Aw, Billie, I'm sorry. I'm sure he's just negotiating the fertility process. You know husbands and wives don't come to terms with it in the same way or pace. Not everyone has the advantage of knowing what to expect the way you do. Give him some time. He'll come around when he's ready."

"I wish he'd just talk about it instead."

"I get it."

Billie and Paige indulged in a comfortable silence for a few seconds.

"So, is that what was absorbing you when I came in?" Paige asked.

Billie couldn't divulge that terrible moment with her clients, or make Paige comprehend the unethical craving rising inside her and threatening to boil over. How could she tell her coworker she was considering taking a sabbatical before she did something worse?

"I saw a new birth mother and her boyfriend today."

"Really? We haven't had one of those in a while. The last birth couple didn't go through with it, right?"

"Exactly. These two seem to be a strong couple and are handling the situation with unexpected maturity." Billie lifted her shoulders in a quick shrug. "I don't know if they'll go through with adoption, but if they do, I'm not sure their relationship will survive the stress, pain, and loss they'll face. But"—she wrinkled her nose—"here's the kicker, she was adopted herself."

"Fascinating." Paige nodded. "From here?"

"Yes. What's unusual is she's very levelheaded about it. Wouldn't you say most adoptees we've seen won't place their babies because they don't want their child to feel abandoned the way they did?"

"Definitely."

"Well, this one is completely understanding. It's so healthy I'm sincerely questioning it." Billie shook her head and laughed.

"I'd have to agree," Paige said. "In the case studies I've read and from the adoptee support groups I've attended, what an adoptee goes through is very complex. Lots of older adoptees talk about a deep-seated feeling of not being wanted or not belonging. And then imagine knowing your parents have chosen you. Christ, what pressure that has to be on a child. I'm generalizing, of course, not all adoptees will have these feelings, but mature or not, this client has some issues to unpack. I'm glad you caught this one, not me. I prefer uncomplicated cases."

Tyler was already home when Billie got there. He'd picked up Chinese food, and they worked in tandem to spread the containers, serving spoons, and paper plates on the table.

"I made sure they didn't forget these this time." He handed her a set of chopsticks and kept one for himself. She appreciated her husband's understanding of her love for the precision and control of the wooden utensils.

Billie opened the small waxy bag with a pair of fried egg rolls, still hot to the touch. She placed one on each plate along with an individual container of duck sauce.

Moving together like they'd choreographed a dance, they passed and scooped the containers of Kung Pao chicken, sweet and sour pork, and lo mein onto their dinner plates.

"Neila from Dr. Fischman's office called earlier to see how I was reacting to the meds. He won't need to up the dose if I ovulate. Do you think we should make an appointment to discuss other options?"

"We're only in the early part of this phase. Isn't it too soon to consider anything else?"

"Maybe. I don't know," Billie said. "The other avenues are all extremely long roads. Maybe we have to be prepared so we don't waste precious time."

"What options would we consider?"

"I guess IVF. You'd have to give me shots."

"That could be interesting." Tyler reached for the lo mein.

"Shut up." Billie playfully slapped his wrist.

"Let's be realistic, though. It's terribly expensive, and the results aren't guaranteed."

"But we have insurance. Isn't there enough in our savings to cover the co-pay?"

"Actually, I've been doing a little research," Tyler said. "We have some coverage that might only allow one round."

"We'll have more money when you make partner, so we can at least try, can't we?"

"First of all, *if* I make partner."

"Of course you will. Why wouldn't you?" Billie had never heard him doubt his career path before.

"And second, you know as well as I do, Bills, Fischman isn't sure IVF is the right way to go since the problem isn't only getting pregnant, it's staying pregnant. He said chances are high we'd have to do several cycles or more."

"But there's a chance. How can we not try? I don't think I could live with the what-if, if we didn't."

Billie twisted her napkin until it ripped in two and continued fidgeting with the pieces as Tyler's words sank in. What he'd said was not news to her. She just wasn't willing to accept it. She was going to have a baby, no matter what the cost.

"I can ovulate and produce viable eggs," she said. "So, if the issue is carrying, then we can hire a surrogate, can't we?"

The surrogacy option meant letting go of everything she'd imagined the physicality of pregnancy and her initiation to motherhood would be. The hardest part was accepting the idea of sharing her pregnancy journey with a partner—a stranger. But her desire to be a mother was intense enough to forfeit those ideas and dreams. She considered the sacrifices surrogates make so women like her can have a family. The selflessness a surrogate would have to have to stand in for another woman was someone Billie could embrace.

"I know what surrogacy is, but what would it mean for us?" Tyler asked.

"We'd be candidates for gestational surrogacy. I'd take some meds to develop my eggs, which would be retrieved and fertilized with your sperm. So biologically, the baby would a hundred percent be ours. Then they transfer one embryo to our surrogate."

"Meaning, we'd have to choose which embryo is the lucky one to have a future? And what if that chance fails? Or we run out? And think of the costs, Billie. I understand enough now to know what you're not saying: it will require IVF, plus fees to a surrogate and an agency, legal fees, medical fees for us, plus one. And still there are no guarantees that something won't go wrong."

"What if it goes right, Ty? Think of the positives."

"We're a family, Billie. I'm happy the way we are. Why can't it just be the two of us?"

"Are you saying you don't want kids now?"

"What I'm trying to say is the risks of you getting pregnant again—I don't want to lose you—"

"We can adopt," she interrupted. "We'll love our baby no matter what route it takes to come to us. And we'll be the best parents we can be."

Tyler grimaced as he checked a text, then flipped the phone so its face was toward the table. He squeezed her shoulder and kissed the top of her head before going to the freezer to fix them each a bowl of mint chip ice cream. After he sat back down, he ate spoonful after spoonful while Billie watched hers slowly turn to mush.

"We could do a designated adoption," she said. "There wouldn't be an endless waiting list. We could find a match on our own, pick the birth parents ourselves, meet them if we wanted. Then we'd know everything about them and their background, including their medical records."

"What's the likelihood we'd even find someone?"

"What if I already know them?"

"Go on," he said.

"The birth couple I'm working with would be a good fit. They're physically healthy, intelligent, and stable. And they've been smart about prenatal medical care. It's possible the fertility meds are screwing with me, 'cause I almost asked them to let us have their baby."

"You did not!"

"No. I wanted to, though. But wouldn't that be something, Ty? If they agreed to let us adopt their baby? I know enough reputable adoption attorneys who handle designated adoptions, where the birth parents and adoptive couples select each other. But we'd still need an agency to do a home study, or the state won't approve it. It could be tricky, but we'd make it work."

"Couldn't you get fired?"

"Maybe. But I can take a leave of absence. I'm willing to quit working to be a full-time mom."

"We can't afford any of this on one income, Billie. What you're talking about isn't possible."

Billie looked away from him. "I know," she muttered. "But it's nicer to imagine than our current reality, isn't it?"

TWENTY-SIX
Anne

Anne shook off the recurring shock wave that rose whenever she thought about coming so near to the Burkhead building. Even the thought of seeing Tyler had been too much for her. She'd kept herself in a drunken coma for over a week after.

Most days in the three weeks since she'd eased up on the drinking, she maintained her covert lookout of the office building until Tyler came for his lunch. Though she was growing increasingly peeved at him for ignoring her, she didn't want him to see her anger. It wasn't his fault, anyway; it was his awful wife. Anne had seen the woman with him once each week. She hadn't seen them go to the doctor together since she'd followed his wife to Burkhead last month. They either stayed inside his office building or ate at their café, as they had just done.

Keeping a decent distance behind, Anne followed Tyler's wife for the fourth time. The wife had an enviable, confident presence with her high-end coat and leather shoes. Even her hair shone as it caught in the wind. Anne thought they might be close in age but knew she didn't look it. Her lifetime of wounds, pills, cigarettes, and booze had added years to her blotched, bloated face. Sometimes she saw an old woman in Duke's window before realizing she'd seen herself in the glass. She pinched her hips. At least with all the fresh air and keeping in step with Tyler's wife, her waistline was melting.

People, men in particular, passed by the wife, looking at her with appreciative glances that never found their way to Anne. Being invisible was familiar and comfortable.

Unable to withstand the urge, she got close enough to catch a whiff of the wife's gardenia perfume. The scent was reminiscent of Mama Sue's backyard. The woman turned onto a street leading away from Burkhead, and then another. Anne matched her strides past building after building and when she shifted direction instead of waiting at red lights. Were they even going anywhere? Wherever they were, street noises had given way to the sound of children's voices. The wife slowed as a schoolyard came into view and leaned on the surrounding fence to watch the students jump off the geodome and drop from the monkey bars, all running toward the teachers whose whistles urged them to line up. She opened the gate to the abandoned yard and walked around the equipment on the rubber surface. She held onto the swing set pole for a minute or two before sitting on one of the soft plastic swings.

Before she walked in, Anne twisted her hair into a topknot and hid it under a sun hat someone had left on the fence. She knew it was too gutsy, but seeing Tyler's wife alone in an empty playground was as tantalizing as a fresh bottle of Scotch.

A few minutes went by before the woman noticed her.

"I'm sorry. Is it against the rules for me to be here?" she asked.

Anne enjoyed being mistaken for a school employee. "I won't tell anyone, but you seem sad." She took an adjacent swing. "Is there a problem with your child? Maybe I can help. What grade is he or she in?"

"Oh," the wife said, wincing. "I'm not a parent here." Her voice became near soundless when she added, "I'm not anyone's parent."

“Well,” Anne replied, “not everyone should be a mom.” The painful look on the wife’s face pleased her.

After the wife left the playground, Anne waited on the swing until the right time to follow her, this time on a direct route to work. About half a block before the building, someone waved at the wife and called her name. It sounded like they said Lilly, although a bus had honked at the same time, so she wasn’t certain. To confirm it, she tried to leave a pretend message with the agency’s lunchtime answering service, but they’d never heard of a Lilly Scott. Her recourse was to go to Tyler’s house. Going through his mail was far easier than getting his cell phone number back in August the day she’d posed as Suzanne Neuman. While she’d waited for Tyler, his secretary walked away from her desk, and when Anne added the envelope to the inbox, she saw the secretary’s cell. She’d pressed the home button, clicked on contacts, and found his private number.

Tyler’s name was on the few bills she pulled out of the mailbox. She grazed her fingers over the one nonbusinesslike envelope addressed to Mr. and Mrs. Tyler Scott before opening it. The crisp paper with a Pearse Children’s Foundation logo and a handwritten note began: “Dear Billie and Tyler.”

Anne made one of her rare appearances at work late that afternoon. She wanted to make the call from behind her desk. Maybe it would help her stay in control. Rudy seemed startled to see her when he walked past her. Had he fired her? With squinted eyes, she checked her desktop. Her few personal items—her mug, her goat-shaped pencil cup, and her cat mouse pad—were all there. Rudy did not comment as he moved into his office. As soon as he closed himself in, she dialed Burkhead.

“A friend suggested I contact your agency and ask for someone named Billie.” She punctuated the sentence like it was a question.

"Yes," the receptionist said, "she works in the adoption unit."

Anne couldn't feel anything from the neck down as she recalled the old image of her swaddled newborn in the Burkhead woman's arms.

"She's not in the office right now, though. I'd be happy to take a message."

"That's okay. I'll call back." Even to Anne, her voice seemed reduced to a squeak.

After work, Anne passed a Marshalls on the way to Duke's. She doubled back to the bargain department store, where she sniffed samples of perfume until she recognized the sweet floral aroma that emanated from Tyler's wife. Next, she went to the women's clothing section, where she found a blouse and slacks similar to the ones Billie wore.

"Billie." Forming the word felt salty and bitter.

Anne took the items into the dressing area and closed the heavy curtain around her. She pushed the box of perfume to the bottom of her pocketbook, concealing it under some crumbled tissues and her scarf. She tried on the blouse, tore off the tags, and then put her own sweater over it.

"I'll take this." She placed the slacks on the counter and handed the cashier the one credit card she had left that wasn't yet frozen from debt.

Instead of going to the bar after her shopping spree, Anne went to CVS. She hustled past the rejected costumes and scant bags of trick-or-treat candy still on the shelves two weeks before Halloween. Then she swiped a box of L'Oréal chestnut-brown hair dye.

That night, Anne became overwhelmed by a craving to see Tyler's wife at work. She needed to touch his wife's things, to understand how the bitch had conned him into marrying her. If she could get inside the building, she could snoop around and find his wife. The powerful desire was overriding all other thoughts.

Battling insomnia, Anne watched a movie on the Hallmark Channel about an unhappy teenage girl who goes up to the attic for a smoke after a fight with her mother. While there, she rummages through some old cartons and pulls out a silver shirt box held together with a wide ribbon. Riveted, Anne leaned forward. She could tell from the change in background music that whatever was inside was a game changer.

The girl slowly pulls out of the box her baby clothes, blankets, and stuffed animals. Underneath are legal documents the girl doesn't understand at first before piecing together that she was adopted and her parents never intended to tell her. Furious, she empties the box and finds a first birthday card. The camera zooms in on the handwriting inside: "To my darling baby," and then a name and address. Anne could feel the excitement growing within her as the movie spawned a luscious yet perilous idea.

TWENTY-SEVEN
Tyler

Collin Frost stretched himself out in such a way the hard conference room chair looked as comfortable as a La-Z-Boy recliner. He repeatedly removed a hand from the zippered side pocket of his motorcycle jacket to comb his fingers through his mop of hair. Collin's lackadaisical demeanor often amused Tyler, but today it was making him impatient.

"You have something for me, Frost?" Tyler refilled his water glass from a carafe Marla had set out for the meeting and guzzled it down.

Keeping his eye on Tyler, Collin sat up and leaned forward. The drumming of his fingers caused the snap on his leather cuff to tip-tap along the smooth wood edge of the conference table.

"I'll tell you what I've got so far, but this is the mere outer layer. I assure you, there are gonna be deeper peels in this here onion."

It always took Tyler a few extra seconds to digest the gruff man's language. He wished Collin would just use clichés like "tip of the iceberg" the way everyone else did. Over the years, though, he had learned that behind the menacing facade, Collin was a compassionate man who thought of himself as a poet. Regardless of how he said it, however, he had Tyler's attention.

"Here's how it starts. There's no Suzanne Neuman that fits the age or description you gave me."

"I won't say I'm shocked. Her story smelled. She was pretty shifty too; so was the way she got spooked and ran out of here." He noticed Collin gnawing on the inside of his cheek. "But I'll reserve judgment, since it's obvious there's more."

"Ah," Collin said, "the man's taken the first bite of the smelly, bulbous plant."

"Get on with it, Frost."

"There was a Suzanne Neuman, lived in Docker, a small town a Frisbee throw from Worcester. Obit shows she died, September 28, 2009. She was seventy-nine. No children. Predeceased by a younger brother."

Tyler had questions but knew he had to let Frost control the flow of information.

"Here's where it gets intriguing," Collin said. "The Suzanne Neuman from Docker, Massachusetts, was a foster parent for the state. Took in countless kids over the years. But, in early 1992, for reasons I have yet to confirm, her home was listed as temporarily unavailable. Never took another foster again. But in September of '92, one Anne Neuman was registered as a freshman at Docker High. Wanna guess what her home address was?"

"Neuman's. What's the connection between them?"

"That's the trail I'm sniffing out, boss. Could be I found her but need to knock some nails into the wood before I get yer hopes up. I'll be tying up some loose ends for Lindeman's embezzlement trial. Then I'll head back to Docker to see what I can get from the neighbors, school, hospital, and whatnot. That copacetic with you?"

"Of course." Tyler reached into his jacket pocket and flicked the photo's corner back and forth with his thumb. "In your search for

Neuman, have you come across any item or address that might relate to the letters 'L.B.'?"

"If you have another angle to consider, I'm all ears."

Tyler pulled out the baby photo and slid it across the table for Collin to view. "I received this anonymously the day Neuman, the living version, came to my office. I don't know why."

"That so?" The investigator peered at the wallet-size photo as though committing it to memory. He flipped it to the other side and did the same. "Judging by the paper quality and the colors, I'd say it dates back a few, and it wasn't taken with a digital camera. Educated guess is early nineties."

"I may be grasping at nothing." Tyler tapped his phone and turned it so Frost could see the screen. "Although it was texted to me too."

"Every speck of dust has significance."

Tyler couldn't explain the discomfort he felt while Frost inspected the image he held. He reached across the table and took it back without acknowledging the inquisitive look he received.

"Forward it to me then," Frost said.

"Anything on the caller or who might be watching my house?"

"Still gotta couple yarns to knit there. On it, though. Never been an obstacle I haven't hurdled."

"I appreciate the extra time you're putting into this for me." Tyler shook Frost's hand.

"Don't mind one bit. You've always been good to me, boss man."

In his office that afternoon, Tyler walked laps around his desk, ignoring the sandwich Marla left for him. He'd never felt less like himself. And the conversation he'd had with his father six days ago had been a constant on his mind. While it had been freeing to talk about it finally and have his dad be as accepting as he was, his father's final advice had left a new hitch he had avoided—telling Billie.

Marla placed a fresh stack of work on the corner of his desk. "I confirmed the court reporter for tomorrow's deposition."

He looked from Marla to the numerous boxes of documents stacked against his bookcase. The daughter of an elderly client had discovered that her brother, who held power of attorney over their mother, was writing checks to himself from their mother's account. Tyler had completely forgotten. Prachett and Huck were losing faith in him. He needed this win.

"Let's get a couple of paralegals to assist," he told Marla. "And let them know to expect a late night."

TWENTY-EIGHT
Billie

Billie completed her progress report from the Renatis' home visit on her computer. Thinking of the glow radiating from the couple nine days earlier, she released a puff of breath and tapped her cheek twice. *Strength, courage, heart.* Then she called Dr. Fischman to schedule an IVF consultation but was put through to the nurse practitioner.

"I know you're anxious," Neila said. "Try not to put so much pressure on yourself. You just started the meds. It's important to monitor and track your ovulation before we initiate any discussion about IVF. That will give us essential information to determine viable next steps."

How could she not put pressure on herself, especially when Tyler was shutting himself off much of the time? She tried not to look at the fresh vase of flowers he'd sent.

"How about if I call you Wednesday with the results of the new labs we ran last week?" Neila asked.

Moments later, she received a call from Gianna, who hadn't been in contact since signing the adoption papers.

"Is she okay?" It was a whisper, but Billie understood.

"Yes." She answered in a soft, nurturing way. "She's very healthy, thanks to you. You did a good job following the doctor's instructions."

"And the parents?"

"They're taking excellent care of her. Now it's time to take care of you. We can talk more about ways to do that if you'd like to schedule an appointment."

"I can't come. My parents won't give me money for the bus, and I'm not allowed to go anywhere alone. I have to stay in the house when they're at work. They think I'll get pregnant again, but I won't. I didn't even do anything."

Gianna sounded upset and angry. At least the girl was expressing some emotion.

"Can you tell me what happened?"

"I don't know . . ." She sniffled. "I have to go. My mother just came home."

The line went dead, leaving Billie full of the anxiety she'd absorbed from her client. Gianna hadn't scheduled another session, and Billie suspected with sadness that the call would be their last.

A week later, Billie stared at the vibrant Georgia O'Keeffe flower prints she'd hung in her office. Neila had promised to call her with results of the battery of tests, blood work, and an internal ultrasound they'd run. The phone startled her when it blared. Tapping her cheek twice, she reached for the receiver.

"*Where is she?*"

The angry baritone voice confused Billie.

"Who is this?"

"Where is my daughter? Gianna!"

"Emilio?" Pulling a blank pad of paper toward her, Billie grabbed a pen. "What's happening?"

"She's missing," he said. "A woman from DCF showed up asking all kinds of questions, saying me and my wife are bad parents, like it's our fault our daughter had a baby. Was it you? Did you call the state on us, lady? What lies did you tell them?"

"Emilio, you said Gianna is missing?"

"The woman insisted on speaking to her, threatened to call the cops if I stopped her. But when I went to Gianna's room, she was gone. Popped the window screen out and split. Just tell me where she is. Is she safe?"

"I'm sorry, I can't . . ." Billie faltered, caught in an ethical quagmire. Gianna was her client, not Emilio. Client confidentiality was fiercely important to her. It was unclear, at that moment, if a parent superseded the rule when the client was a minor.

"Yes, you can, and you will!"

Billie's eardrum buzzed with each word.

"I will come down there and make you tell me! And if you're the one who accused me of hurting her, you're gonna pay."

Billie imagined the large man storming into her office and grabbing her. Would she maintain her composure or faint? She released her death grip on the arm of her chair.

"It's obvious you're concerned for your daughter. As am I." Billie kept her voice low and steady. "The truth is, I don't know where Gianna is."

"Liar!"

"Why would I lie?"

There was a painful, elongated silence. Then Emilio's washed-out, defeated voice replied, "Because she said so."

"What did she say?"

"Since she met you, she's been saying you were going to take her away from us. You were going to take her to a safe house."

"Emilio, we don't have places like that."

"You're telling the truth? You don't know where she is?"

"I really don't know. Let's give her a few hours to come home on her own, before DCF files a police report. I'll touch base with you again this evening. All right?"

A few deep breaths did not slow the blood coursing through her veins. She pulled the phone closer, intending to alert her supervisor, but dialed Tyler instead.

"Hey, babe," he said. "What's going on?"

Billie explained the situation with the Palomino and her father.

"If you're in any kind of danger . . ."

"I think it's okay now. I just wanted to hear your voice." She exhaled. "Somehow I put the fire out. I've never been threatened like that before."

"I never thought I'd have to worry about your safety with you doing adoption work."

"Me either. The peculiar thing is, I can empathize with the guy. I mean, he's a colossal ass, but he cares about his kid. He was lashing out because of fear. There are healthier ways to handle it, but I can understand a father going berserk if he thought his daughter was taken from him." Billie realized her hands were shaking. "I'm still rattled by the confrontation, that's all."

She was eager for Tyler to say something pacifying. He had a talent for doing that. His silence made her antsy.

"Aren't you going to say anything?" She waited a few more long seconds for his response.

"Tyler?"

"Ty?"

Impatient with his newfound indifference toward her, Billie hung up. She had to notify Jay anyway.

* *

Because of fall midterms, Billie hadn't seen Madison and Steve since their initial appointment two weeks ago. Their unwavering resolve to place the baby impressed her, and she found their shared respect and concern for one another inspiring.

Steve interrupted Billie as she discussed the different types of adoptions. "You keep saying, 'prospective parent,' what does that mean?"

"In adoption, it refers to the person or couple selected as the potential adoptive parents." She recalled the client she'd nicknamed "Mr. Toughnuts," who'd taken issue with the term. To an assistant DA, "prospective parent" meant someone claiming to be a child's mother or father, and he wanted to be clear he and his wife would be the legitimate parents.

"Have you considered the attributes of the ideal parents you'd hope for?" Billie asked when it seemed Madison and Steve understood their options.

Once they got past the typical answers (loving, caring, and happy), they described specific characteristics.

"They should be educated, with college degrees," Steve said.

"He should have a good profession so the mother can stay home. No nannies or day care," Madison chimed in. "The whole point is for the baby to have available parents."

"Can you describe what you consider good professions?"

"Investment bankers, maybe," Steve answered, "or lawyers."

"Or doctors," Madison said. "Anyone with a medical background."

"What about nurses or dentists?" Billie thought about some of her approved couples.

"Yes," Steve said.

"What about nonmedical helping careers like psychologists or social workers?" Billie held her breath.

"Sure, I think people in helping careers would be compassionate," Madison said.

"If they make enough money, then yeah," Steve added. "I grew up with a dog. I'd like the baby to have a dog."

Walker, Billie thought. It was what she and Tyler were going to call the puppy they'd get one day, named after Antoine Walker, Tyler's all-time favorite Celtics player.

"I'd like them to have brown hair," Madison added. "So the baby will fit in. Or red, in case he or she gets my real hair color." She grew pensive. "My parents are blonde," she mumbled. "Growing up, people always made comments like, 'Where did she come from?' or 'How'd ya end up with a ginger?' It was always obvious that I was different, though my parents never made me feel like an odd duck."

"I didn't know that," Steve said. "It must have been upsetting."

"One of the worst times," Madison said to no one in particular, "was at one of my dad's company picnics. The food line was taking forever. It was super hot, and the smoke from the barbeques was blowing on me. My dad's boss was in line in front of me. He kept turning and looking at me, and I remember thinking his plump cheeks were the color of a medium-rare burger and how funny his face would look between a bun. Then he looked over my head at my mother, grinned, and said for the hundredth time: 'Where'd this kid come from? The mailman an Irishman, huh?' His belly jiggled like Jell-O when he laughed."

"What a jerk," Steve said.

"I remember putting my plate on the side of the buffet and walking away to the swings. I heard my mother call out my name, but it was my father who followed me. He stood behind my swing, giving me the slightest shoves, so I felt I was floating in the breeze rather than taking off to another planet."

Billie saw Madison turn her nose a little toward the ceiling, her eyes closed as though she could still feel the wind.

"There was always someone pointing out my differences. Not just the hair color, but the shape of my face, the way I walked, and especially my smile. It would never have mattered if people didn't keep pointing it out. They were my parents, my family. So what if I stuck out like a sore thumb? My parents didn't care. They loved me. I'd known they'd adopted me since I could talk. At first, I didn't know what it meant and told everyone the same way a child would blurt out they have to pee. As I grew and asked more questions, I absorbed it better. It was something I knew and understood. A characteristic like a dark mole on the side of someone's face. It was a part of who I was."

"Who did I look like?" Madison continued. "Where are they now? Why didn't they want me? These were things I'd think about when I was ten and couldn't sleep. I'd stare at the shadows on the ceiling from the streetlights and trees. Sometimes, after a particularly tough day like the company picnic, my father would come in, open the window to my room, and help me step out onto the roof. We'd lie there looking at the stars. He'd pull out some chocolate, and we'd share it without ever saying anything. My parents did everything to make me feel included and special. I love them all the more for it."

"It sounds like you have quite a sensitive and accepting family," Billie said. "Did you ever do a search for your birth parents?"

"No," Madison replied. "I thought about it a few years ago, but my mother freaked. She was scared I'd reject her if I had a relationship with my birth mother. Of course, that would never happen. She's my mother. Knowing my biological parents would never change how I feel about her. So I gave up on searching; I couldn't do it to her. Maybe one day my mom will feel differently."

"Knowing her mom," Steve said, "I think she was probably more worried Madison would get hurt if she found them and they weren't good people."

"What about your family, Steve?" Billie asked. "How have they been knowing you've come here?"

"My parents are trying their best to be supportive. I mean, I appreciate their efforts, but their religious beliefs are making this extra difficult. Madison's parents have embraced us and the situation. They've been so kind to me, and I'm very grateful for them," he said. "And, one day, I'm going to pay them back for all the doctors' bills they're covering."

Madison and Steve continued listing physical features, amenities the house and yard should have, and some less tangible items. Billie was certain they were unaware they'd described themselves and the homes they'd grown up in. It was fairly common amongst the birth parents she'd worked with. When they'd had good parenting, they wished for what they had for the baby; when they came from imperfect circumstances, they requested the opposite.

At the end of the session, Steve said, "Madison and I decided we don't want to know the new family."

"I think we'll handle it better with a clean break," Madison said. "But we want to select the couple ourselves. You said we could, right?"

"Yes, we can review potential adoptive couples when we meet next."

After they left, Billie went over the list of traits they wanted. She and Tyler had the education, the means, and the lovely house and yard Madison and Steve imagined, plus a bedroom next to the master, just waiting for its transformation to a nursery. She looked at Tyler's photo on her desk, and then, after making tick marks next to each matching item, she opened her home study template and created a new file.

TWENTY-NINE
Anne

With daylight savings ending the week before, Anne still felt insulted to find darkness when she exited work. The spotlights on Rudy's signage cast a dim ocher-colored shadow around the doorway. As she stepped outside, a man leaning on the building's stucco wall, a cigarette dangling from his lips, startled her. His hands rested in his pants pockets. The way he looked at her sent bile into her throat.

"I'm looking for Laura Bennett."

"Never heard of her."

"I was thinking maybe you have. She's the daughter of Curtis Bennett. Ring a bell?"

Thunderous drumming filled Anne's ears while a painful current of electricity zapped her brain and organs.

"Did he . . . Did Curtis send you? What does he want with her?" She felt like a four-year-old trying to talk underwater.

"Don't know nothing about that, ma'am."

"No."

"No?"

"*No!*" Anne was astonished by the sharpness in her voice. "I want nothing to do with that *prick*!"

"Sorry, lady, not part of my job."

Then the man walked off into the dusk, leaving her heart pounding and the world whirling around her.

"Hey, you okay?" Rudy asked as he emerged from the building.

"I can't breathe."

Rudy guided her inside to his air-conditioned office and let her sit in his chair.

"Should I call an ambulance?"

"Not yet. I just want to sit here."

Once she cooled off and calmed down enough, Rudy agreed to take her home. She was too shaken to fend off the hand he placed on her thigh throughout the ride. Anne rushed from his car, getting herself inside before he could catch up. Then she shut and bolted the door to keep him out.

How Curtis even hired a private investigator, or how that goon had found her, was beyond her comprehension. But now, convinced he knew where she was, she was sure he could find the baby too.

Rudy hadn't questioned her the next day when she called and said she wouldn't be in. The idea that she'd scared the annoying little gnat into caring was snort-out-loud funny. It wasn't in his nature, though. His worry would be workers' comp claims, yet he was courteous enough to have a couple of installers drop off her car.

Later that morning, just before ten, Anne walked the few blocks from where she'd parked and stood motionless, once again in front of the Burkhead Family Service office building. Her fists clenched with the late fall chill creeping along her skin.

"Get it together," she mumbled.

She counted how long she could hold her breath, then tried to breathe out at an even longer count. Stanley had taught her this method of meditative relaxation to help her sleep. Pills worked better, but she found it was a useful technique when her anxiety was raging, like now. *Eighteen, nineteen, twenty.* She exhaled.

More composed, Anne poised herself to go into the agency. *Mama would tell you to chin up and go in*, she thought. "One foot in front of the other," she'd say. Her feet felt heavy as she hauled herself along the sidewalk. She faced the brick facade, willing herself not to turn around when a man nodded at her and held open the door.

With trembling limbs, she stood in front of the receptionist's desk in the lobby. She felt inside her pocketbook and stroked the object that had lingered in her bag through nine days of indecision and hesitation.

"I have an appointment with Paige Rellman," she said meekly.

Anne hadn't had the nerve to schedule with Billie. Back in August, when she'd sat in Tyler's office, pure adrenaline had fueled her. Being brave had been necessary for their love coming back together. But her loathing for his wife cloaked her with uncertainty and claustrophobia. Anne didn't yet trust herself not to hurt the woman who'd taken her rightful place.

"Third floor." The receptionist indicated the elevators with a head tilt.

"How can I help you today?" Paige asked when they'd settled in her office.

There was a clanging in Anne's head that made it difficult to answer. She hadn't spoken of this to anyone besides her mother and Mama Sue. Not even Stanley the shrink. Clutching her pocketbook until it pressed into her belly, she cleared her throat.

"I had a baby. A long time ago. I gave her up."

Anne feared Paige would look at her all judgy, so she glanced up and got lost in the abstract designs in the black-dotted ceiling tiles.

After a moment, she shifted to the Birkenstocks Paige had strapped over her socked feet.

"Was the adoption through this agency?"

The softness in Paige's words disarmed Anne enough that she could muddle on.

"I think so. My mother and I lived with a woman who was a foster parent and knew a social worker here. I met her once in the beginning, then she showed up at the hospital the day after my baby was born, and that was that."

"Were you given any information about the baby or her adoptive parents?"

"Nothing." Anne squirmed and shifted the bag in her lap. Then she looked at Paige. "Is it true the kid can search for me if there's permission in their record?" It was something she'd picked up on in the Hallmark movie she'd watched in October.

"Yes," Paige said. "In the past, everything was sealed. It was next to impossible for adoptees and birth parents to connect as adults. Now, if an adoptee is searching for their birth parents, we will only release information if we have consent. We wouldn't want to divulge identifying information if a birth parent didn't want contact. The assumption is, if there isn't documentation of consent, the birth parents want to maintain their anonymity."

It seemed to Anne that Paige liked to hear the sound of her own voice, but she caught the part where, if her child wanted to find her, she had to say it was okay.

"No one ever gave me that choice. I want to do it. How do I consent?"

Paige pulled something from a tiered organizer on her desk. Next to it was an unlit turkey-shaped candle and a few mini seasonal gourds.

"I'll need you to fill out this form with whatever information you have so I can find your file." Paige handed her a pen and a clipboard with a two-sided questionnaire.

She filled out her full legal name, her current address, and the address where she lived when the baby was born. It asked for the baby's birth date. Anne knew it by heart. Every year on July 14, she called in sick and lay in bed until it passed.

"It asks for the birth father's information," Anne said.

"Put whatever you know. Was there a name on the child's birth certificate?"

"I don't know. I never saw one. But there couldn't have been. I wouldn't have been able to give a name if they'd asked."

"You can leave that section blank if you need to."

Anne handed the form back and watched Paige skim through the information.

"It needs your signature here." She gave back the form and pointed to the line. "That's all it takes. If the child requests information, we can give it to her. And we know how to reach you if she requests contact. I don't want to mislead you, though. Recent law allows for the consent in the record to be valid, but many twenty-year-old adoptees, or older, don't yet know they have the right to it."

Anne wasn't listening to the long-winded gibberish. She was contemplating how she'd ditch Paige and begin her search for Tyler's wife.

"Of course, now there are social networking sites and registries to connect birth families and children, but again, you'd probably find most birth parents are unaware. It's something my colleague Belinda and I are working to improve." Paige handed Anne some pamphlets. "These explain the advances we're making in supporting birth mothers' rights, as well as some local support groups that might interest you."

Anne stuffed the pamphlets in her bag. "I almost forgot! Can I leave a card for her? For my daughter?" It was the first time she had ever allowed herself to say that word out loud. *Daughter.* She had a daughter.

"I'll make sure this gets into the case file." She stood to lead the way out. "I'm glad you came in today. Please reach out to me if you have any other questions."

A few feet down the hall, an office door with a nameplate that said "Belinda Campbell, MSW, LCSW" opened wide enough for Anne to see the pretty, happy woman with the glossy brown hair she'd followed countless times. Belinda Campbell was the one who went home with Tyler at night. Anne's face became fiery hot, and she felt like she was going to explode. She stumbled down the hallway, trying to get to the elevator before she was recognized. Billie walked toward her with the young couple who'd been in her office. The guy was short with light brown hair and wore the classic chinos and loafers getup. His arm was wrapped protectively around the shoulders of a girl with melancholy blue eyes. Anne turned her back and pretended to adjust her shoe.

"See you next time," Billie said when the elevator opened.

Anne squeezed into the back corner so the couple had to stand in front of her and block Billie's view. The girl put her arm around the guy, and as she did, Anne thought she saw the thing she'd been looking for on every child's arm, everywhere she went for the past twenty years. Inches above the wrist—a heart-shaped birthmark.

She wiped her clammy hands along her hips. *You've been wrong before*, she reminded herself. The shock and fear on the little girls' faces when she'd grabbed their thin arms. The many questioning looks of mothers and nannies who saw her scrutinizing their daughters at random parks and playgrounds. Anne shivered. If she'd never looked. If she'd never seen the infant when her mother dressed her in that teensy pink sweater. If she'd just closed her eyes, she might've been okay.

The pressure in her head was so great her vision blurred as they exited to the lobby. With tremendous effort, she jerked her hand forward toward the girl's wrist, causing the contents of the purse she'd forgotten to latch to spill. She dove after the drugstore lipstick that rolled by the couple's feet as they headed outside.

In a trancelike state, Anne kept the periwinkle dress in sight once she was out of the Burkhead building. She had to get closer, to be sure it was what she'd hoped, and not some sort of tattoo. Her pace slowed while the girl stopped to put a jacket on. When the couple turned right at the end of the block, Anne stood at the corner and watched the guy hold open the door of a small gray four-door car. The girl protected her round baby belly as she dipped down into her seat. Then the guy got in on the other side. Anne's feet smacked on the sidewalk as she ran toward the car. Before it pulled away, she saw a gold Woodson College decal on the rear window and a bumper sticker on the fender that said "I ♥ Engineering."

The November breeze outside her vehicle was too soft to cool her down, and the AC in the old can of bolts was shot. Anne pressed her back into the driver's seat. There was no recall of getting into her car or having moved it onto the street in front of Burkhead. She had dreamlike visions of waiting on the corner in the stale automobile, watching Billie walk to the parking garage. A car passed and she could clearly see Billie guiding the steering wheel as it went by. Turning hard to the left, Anne made a U-turn and sped away.

Hours later, when she woke on her apartment floor, she was lying in a pool of gritty ash. "No, no, no," she wailed as she clutched Mama

Sue's urn to her bosom. "Don't leave me. I'll fix it, Mama." She hastily scooped fistfuls back into the urn. "I'll fix everything."

The next day, her eyes still red and swollen and her heart aching, Anne roamed the Woodson College campus, determined to get a better look at that birthmark. Mama would want her to be sure. The ivy-covered dark brick buildings formed a rectangle around a grassy quad. It was easy to follow the path past each academic structure, all marked with a copper plaque showing the building name and the course of study. The library, with its long and wide steps, was the only unique structure. Mama Sue used to say they set libraries that way "to entice people to come in and get swallowed up by history or literature." Anne walked further and located Engineering, the tallest building in the farthest corner, and sat on the landscaping wall in front.

Chilled from hovering in the late afternoon prewinter breeze, Anne's teeth clattered. She'd only focused on the girl when she'd tailed them to their car yesterday. What if she wouldn't recognize the kid again? A group of students emerged from the building, chattering away. She smashed her cigarette against the stones she sat on and flicked it into the grass behind her. The door to the building opened again. A student walked out alone, a little stooped from the weight of the backpack slung over one shoulder. Without question, she'd seen him before.

The guy turned onto a smaller path next to the building leading away from the quad. The walkway ended at Roland Dining Hall, a nondescript white building. No one questioned if she belonged as she followed him into the marbled rotunda, but then the guy showed his ID to the attendant before he passed into the cafeteria. Anne thought about ways to get inside while she stood in line at a small coffee stand in the corridor. From that vantage point, she could see the guy at a table with the pregnant girl. Sipping on her small coffee cup, Anne sat on a windowsill and waited.

She couldn't believe her luck when the girl went to the restroom. Anne went into the stall next to her, rolling the toilet paper for effect, and flushing right after the girl did. When she heard the sink water flowing, she eased out of the door. The girl was wearing short sleeves on a November day, and Anne remembered the constant overheated feeling during her own pregnancy twenty years before. While the girl was rinsing soap from her hands, Anne hovered just behind her arm. The girl jumped, and water splashed when Anne's fingers skimmed the red heart.

Blindsided, Anne reeled backward into the paper towel dispenser. The girl's reaction was too abrupt for Anne to have felt more than a tickle on her fingertips, or to see any of herself in the girl's features. But it was enough to feel the force of the fright and revulsion. Unable to overcome the pull she felt toward the girl, she stepped closer, reaching out, desperate to hold her, to tell her it was okay.

"Forgive me," were the only words Anne uttered before the girl, *her girl*, rushed out of the bathroom.

THIRTY
Tyler

The weather was on the pleasant side, with no hint of the usual rain or snow that came with November's seasonal indecisiveness. Tyler pressed his forehead against the office window's cool glass, wishing he could be anywhere else. His gaze drifted down to the street twenty stories below, leaving him with the uneasy feeling someone was watching him.

"Jesus." He clutched his chest when he noticed Marla standing beside him. "You scared me. What happened to knocking?"

"You mean the loud rapping sound I made with my knuckles?" She ushered him out of the office toward the conference room.

Tyler took a chicken Caesar wrap and a bottle of water from the buffet table and then selected a seat positioned furthest from Huck, Prachett, and Lindeman. His mind filled with the details and gaps from Frost's report as he peeled his lunch open. The acidic burn in his stomach rose with the certainty someone was laying the groundwork to blackmail him. Hard as he tried, though, he couldn't think of anything past or present anyone could hold over his head. And if they did attempt to squeeze him, it wouldn't be someone who'd done their homework—he had little assets for the taking.

When the conference room quieted down, Tyler attempted to

pay attention. The meeting began with Prachett reviewing recent achievements and giving kudos to the attorneys who'd earned them. He didn't expect to hear his name on the roster, even with the big case he'd won and the new client referrals it had brought in. With his head being everywhere but at work recently, even he'd agree he didn't deserve any acknowledgment or the partnership he'd fought so hard for. But he was having a hard time reconciling the knowledge that he was going to disappoint Billie yet again.

Tyler bit into his wrap and watched disinterested associates play Words with Friends with each other on their phones. He could tell who was playing against whom because after they entered their move, they'd look up at their opponent, who'd pick up his or her phone, try to suppress their reaction, and then type. But all phones were put away and Tyler rolled his unfinished lunch back into the paper as Huck cleared his throat and stood at the head of the table.

"It is with great pleasure," Huck said, "that today I can announce this year's partner class. With their expertise and talents, these three dedicated hard workers have shown themselves to be superb leaders and exceptional advocates of our firm. We have every confidence their valued contributions will continue to deliver exciting opportunities for us all." Huck introduced the first two new partners. Both were women. One of them was the quick-to-rise associate who occupied the office next door to Tyler.

"And our third esteemed new partner," Huck said, "Tyler Scott."

Tyler was stunned but controlled his emotions as his colleagues applauded him. He acknowledged the partners with a respectful nod. When the meeting broke, he approached the partners to express his gratitude for their confidence in him, though he had no idea how he was going to live up to it. With the medical bills stacking up and probable extortion lurking over his shoulder, he had to find a way.

"Proud of you, young man," Lindeman said, before patting Tyler on the back.

"Private discussions about equity will occur between Thanksgiving and New Year's," Prachett added quietly before their handshake.

But it was Huck who gripped Tyler's hand tightly and pulled him into an uncomfortable hug. "Don't eff this up," he whispered.

THIRTY-ONE
Billie

"I'm going out to grab lunch," Billie said as she passed the reception desk. "Want anything?"

"I'm all set," Rita replied. "Hey, Billie?" Rita's normally jovial face turned pensive. "Do you recognize that woman out there? I keep seeing her walking around, but she's back too far for me to get a good look."

"That's bizarre." Billie pushed the door open. "I don't see anyone, but I'll keep an eye out."

Billie turned at every footstep she heard and checked if the people across the street were looking at her before she went into the mini-mart. She almost squeezed the coffee out of the to-go cup when the person in line behind her got too close.

Outside, she laughed at how idiotic she was being but still needed a minute. She sat on a public bench by the sidewalk, which was cold to the touch. The scrawny trees the city planted near the curbs were leafless, and their bare limbs bobbed with the wind. Billie took out her cell and pressed the speed dial for Tyler to return a call she'd missed.

"We did it, Bills!" His excitement was unmistakable.

"Wahoo! What did we do?"

"We made partner! They announced it at the meeting a few minutes ago. It won't be official until January, after it's all signed and sealed."

"So, you're a partner-in-waiting, like royalty," she quipped.

"Funny lady."

"Seriously, though, Ty, you've devoted every bit of yourself to make this happen. This is the best news." She was already imagining the fertility treatments they'd be able to afford now, the crib and rocking chair she'd buy. "And I have the perfect way for us to celebrate! It's a 'Have To' night."

Tyler made a throaty engine purring noise. "Ready, willing, and able! At your service. What time should we rendezvous?"

The "Have To" nights had turned out to be a surprise perk of tracking her ovulation. With an irrepressible grin, Billie hung up the phone.

Except for the difficulty of getting in and out of her chair, Madison seemed to handle her eighth month of pregnancy well. The fabric of the maroon dress she wore today stretched around her swelling body. She'd stopped dyeing her hair, and her roots were now a natural paprika color. Her cheeks had become extra rosy, which made the blue of her eyes pop even more. Billie always had a hard time looking away from Madison's eyes. There was something comfortable and familiar about them. It was like that tip-of-the-tongue sensation: she'd search, and the answer would come close to the forefront, and then Madison would look away, or someone would speak and break the spell.

Unlike their first two meetings, today Madison and Steve were a tad edgy. It was to be expected, given the day's agenda. With each session, Steve had become quieter, almost as if he was letting Madison take the lead. He knew what she needed and didn't hesitate to support it. His semi-invisibility provided her the safety to discuss difficult topics, but Billie remained concerned about how the experience was going to affect their relationship. So far, they were still supportive and united in their decisions.

Billie reached for the bio packets of couples they were to review. As with all their cases, she and Paige had scoured through the files of completed and approved home studies to find couples on their waiting list who closely fit Madison and Steve's parameters. Billie envied whichever couple they might choose. While she and Paige compiled the mix, she'd struggled with the temptation to slip the profile she'd created of her and Tyler into the contenders. Even now, as she held the matching couples' pages before them, she had to bite her lip to stop herself from propositioning Madison and Steve to let her and her husband adopt their baby.

"Do you feel ready to look at the couple choices?" she asked.

Madison twisted the tip of her ear with determination before she nodded.

"These are the profiles of the prospective couples who match your criteria." Billie offered a notebook to Madison. There were no photographs or identifying information in the book. The pages were a synopsis of each couple's home study, including descriptions of the couple's basics, like their educations, occupations, health, and ages. It gave a brief account of their upbringings and relationships with their own families and explained how they envisioned raising a child. Finally, there was a summary of the social worker's impressions of the couple. It was usually a sentence like: "This is a warm, caring couple who would be excellent parents to any child."

Madison and Steve pushed their chairs together to peruse the book. There was some finger-pointing at characteristics they liked, some nodding, and some elbowing as they turned the pages.

The book included a few couples for whom Billie had conducted the home study. She watched Madison and Steve devote their attention to descriptions, curious if they'd react to the Toughnuts' profile. After breaking through their defensive walls, their interviews went more smoothly. She'd found much to admire about the art gallery director and the assistant DA, who had a deep affection for one another. Since the wife planned to stay at home full-time when a baby came, Billie had added in their approved home study.

In the end, Madison and Steve gravitated to a couple who attended church each week like Steve's parents. The husband was an architectural engineer and the wife an occupational therapist. Billie knew the couple. They were the epitome of how she would've pictured Madison and Steve in ten years if they hadn't experienced this chasm. But she didn't believe they were the right family for this baby, and, she told herself—it was in her client's best interest to know.

"Er." Billie stopped for a second. She was getting overheated. "This may be a little unorthodox, but . . ." It was almost like she was having an out-of-body experience, seeing herself drive off a cliff, unable to stop. "I may have another couple you might be interested in." *What the hell are you doing?*

"Why aren't they in the book?" Steve asked. "What's the catch?"

"Their home study isn't finalized yet, but I'm confident it will be before your due date."

"No," Madison said. "I'm weary from all of this. We've made our choice. They're a good, solid couple. The one you're talking about isn't a sure thing. I don't want to think about it anymore. I need to go home."

Billie walked the couple out, then went and locked herself inside her office. Pacing frantically from corner to corner, she kept pounding her palm into her forehead. "Stupid, stupid, stupid!" She hit herself harder between each word. "What have you done? What if someone finds out?" The terrifying thoughts rammed at her like shots from a gun. "I'll be fired for sure. Oh, God, Tyler will never speak to me again." Pivoting when she reached the window, she stomped back to the other side. "They didn't even look at our profile, made such a mistake, not even giving us a chance."

Billie's fists clenched, then loosened. *If they didn't see the profile, then nothing happened.* "I need to get my shit together." She got her stuff to go home. *And I need to remove myself from this case.* She thought about taking some time down on the Cape. Maybe she'd be able to go horseback riding, which would be the best medicine for her right now. She and Tyler both needed a refresh. The question was, could she get him to agree to go without explaining why? She reasoned that they could extend the celebration for his promotion, and he'd likely agree if she suggested his parents' place at Lake Sunapee instead of Cape Cod.

When she brought it up to Tyler that night, he opted out. Within minutes of informing him he was in the partner class, they had unloaded an excess amount of work on him.

"I think Huck is testing me to confirm they made the right choice. I'll probably be in the office swimming in a box of papers," he said. "You should go on your own."

With so much mind clutter she needed to sort through, she decided that being by herself was the best idea.

Billie couldn't take the next day off without notice, but leaving at the end of the day meant dealing with Friday night rush hour. So she left early Saturday and planned to stay until Monday morning and drive directly to work.

The Top of the Hub restaurant, fifty-two floors up at the top of the Prudential, with its low lights and panoramic view, cinched the romantic ambiance. Billie and Tyler sat at a coveted table for two by the window overlooking the Boston skyline.

"I was afraid you might cancel when your meeting went late," he said.

"Nope. Another few minutes and I would've locked them all in the conference room and run here. I'm not on call either, so I'm all yours tonight."

"Sounds like a perfect birthday. I wish I'd been able to come to New Hampshire with you over the weekend. I missed you."

"I missed you too." It was partially true. The weekend alone had been rejuvenating. With the "Have To" night only two days before, she'd ruled out riding but walked to the stables a mile down the road. She'd fed the horses hay and sugar cubes and helped brush down one of their mares. She'd taken solitary walks around the lake, removing her shoes and socks to wiggle her toes in the frigid water. At night she'd get comfortable on the floor, lean against the coffee table, and watch the orange-tipped flames in the fireplace. This morning she'd taken a kayak from the shed and paddled out to watch the sunrise. Alone on the tranquil lake as the vibrant sun touched the silhouetted mountains and tickled the water with sparkles, she was filled with light.

Sometime over the weekend, Billie recognized how lucky she'd been that her attempt to force her home study on Madison and Steve hadn't gone further. She concluded the better approach to avoid scaring them off was to have an adoption attorney she worked well with contact the couple. Which meant she'd need to find a way to get Jay to sign off on a home study for them. With Tyler's career soaring, the costs wouldn't be an issue. She looked lovingly at her handsome husband across the restaurant table, certain he would be happy once everything worked out.

"As I feared, I was at the office nonstop," Tyler said. "Which, by the way, you would have known if you'd called me."

"You could have called me too, you know."

"Well, you look beautiful and refreshed. It must have been a great weekend."

"I could have told you about it if you'd come home from the office before midnight last night."

The server situated an elegant stainless-steel wine stand next to the table. Its mirrored finish reflected the shimmering city lights in the distance. He popped a champagne cork with finesse, then poured them each a glass. The ice crunched as he nestled the bottle into the bucket.

"Your appetizers will be out shortly," he said.

"Happy birthday, Partner." She lifted her glass and held it out.

"Soon-to-be." Tyler clinked his glass with Billie's above the middle of their table and took a few sips.

Alcohol wasn't advised while she was taking the ovulation meds, so she only wet her lips enough to taste. Then a peculiar silence befell them. Tyler fiddled with the bread basket as though the slices of sourdough bread held some philosophical meaning. Billie ran her finger around the flute's smooth glass base, wondering what they used to talk about.

"Hard to believe I'm thirty-four." Tyler placed his knife and fork neatly on his now finished entrée plate. "I'm an old man now."

Billie looked out over the Charles River, thinking of Madison and the baby she would birth in a few weeks. The baby she wanted too much.

"Hey, I'm just kidding around."

Billie felt his fingers press on her own.

"Look at me, Bills."

He looked sad, which made her feel even worse. She didn't want to ruin his birthday.

"It's going to happen," he said. "We're not too old."

Before she could answer, the waiter placed a white chocolate crème brûlée accented with a sparkling candle and two spoons on the table.

"Happy birthday," Billie said before she and Tyler got swept up in the rich custard.

When they left the restaurant, Billie looked at the sky. The pretty stars she'd admired from the restaurant window were now hazed over by the city lights, and honking horns and dirty sidewalks replaced the romantic atmosphere. The temperature had dropped since they arrived, and she regretted the lightweight coat she'd worn. Tyler held her snugly to him when she shivered. He unlocked the car, but instead of opening the door, he pressed her against it. His kiss tasted like their dessert's sugary cream. Her woes evaporated with his passion.

"Take me home," she whispered.

Their lust and giddiness reminded Billie of when they'd been dating. Speeding, and a lack of traffic, got them to the house fast. Tyler slammed the brakes before he completed the turn into the driveway, and they fell silent. A Mylar birthday balloon anchored to their mailbox swayed in the air like it was waving at them.

"Is that from you?" Tyler asked.

"Uh-uh."

"I bet it was Ashley."

"What if it's not?" Billie sputtered. "What if it's . . ." She paused. "What if it's the stalker?"

Tyler reached into the back and removed his racquetball racquet from his bag.

"Are you nuts? That's not going to protect us from anything," Billie said.

"Stay in the car."

"No, we should go next door and call the police. Don't go out there on your own."

But he did. Billie pressed the door lock as soon as he got out.

"Please, please, please," she whispered. An array of worst-case scenes filled her mind: someone in the shrubs jumping him, someone smashing the car window, someone inside the house, Tyler hurt . . . or worse. She leaned to the driver's side, placing her hand over the steering wheel, ready to blast the horn if she saw one little out-of-place movement.

"All clear," Tyler said when he came back. "No windows or doors open, no broken locks."

With some trepidation, Billie stepped into the house. Tyler was right. Nothing visible was amiss. But she made her usual rounds, checking all the inside locks on the windows and doors and making sure the shades remained closed. This time, though, she shoved a mop against the patio door, pushed the vacuum in front of the garage door, and pressed a trash can against the front door. She set out booby traps by placing a six-pack of soda, an iron, empty hangers—whatever she could find—below each window. Upstairs, she inspected the guest bathroom. The shower curtain was still open the way she kept it, to be sure no one could hide behind it. Tyler didn't tell her she was being ridiculous or try to stop her. In fact, she caught sight of him examining the closets.

"Maybe we should call the police," Billie said.

"And report what? Someone left a birthday balloon on my mailbox?"

"Well, we have to do something. There have been other creepy things. Aren't you freaked out at all?"

"I don't like it, I'll admit," he said. "But the police can't investigate based on nerves. I'll check in with Collin Frost in the morning and see what he can find."

For the rest of the night, Billie and Tyler lay side by side in bed, unable to rekindle the birthday romance they'd felt earlier.

THIRTY-TWO
Anne

Oily puddles lingered on the road after another intense storm. The hazy, damp air clung to Anne as she paid the gas attendant with one of her last ten-dollar bills. Cash was becoming a problem. The Gnat had left tons of voicemails. At first, they were filled with concern, telling her to take as much time as she needed to get well. Then he got pushy about when she was coming back. She hadn't returned any of the calls. Now he was refusing to mail her final paycheck, saying she'd have to come in and clean out her desk if she wanted it. But she had no time for that.

Anne parked in front of a modest suburban home. It was the kind of place in which she wished she could raise a family. The car with the Woodson bumper sticker was in the driveway. She didn't know her daughter's name yet, but she and her boyfriend had come to this place for Thanksgiving and had stayed for a week. The girl's belly was very swollen, and when they went for morning walks around the block, she waddled like a penguin. Anne pulled a stale strawberry Pop-Tart from its foil wrapper and munched on it while waiting for their post-breakfast excursion. They were early risers but hadn't come out at their usual time. She worried she'd somehow missed them. It was after one. She was lighting one of her last cigarettes when the front door opened.

Something was off. The girl was moving more slowly than usual, and the boyfriend led her to his car. Meanwhile, the overhead garage door opened, and the older couple who lived there got in their sedan. Anne joined the caravan as they rolled down the street.

Pretending to read a magazine she'd found on a chair, Anne kept a watchful eye over St. Monica's ER waiting room.

"Weston?" a far-off voice called out, and the group of interest hastened into the depths of the facility.

People in the waiting room were chatty. They wanted to share stories of their wounds or the accidents their loved ones had been in. It was as though, by virtue of being in this war zone together, they all shared some religious bond. Anne pressed her nails into the meaty part of her palm. Then the woman next to her, who'd cut her hand while preparing lasagna, asked, "What ya here for?"

"My daughter's pregnant." The strange words twirled out of Anne's mouth.

"Congrats!" The woman got excited. "She must be up on the seventh floor, right? That's where I delivered my kids. They're five and three now." The woman continued gabbing when Anne moved away in search of the elevator.

The maternity ward had a hateful, bright, perky ambiance. It lacked any subtle spots for Anne to observe yet blend in.

"You looking for labor and delivery, hon, or the nursery?" the nurse behind the desk asked.

Scared she'd need ID, Anne pretended to hunt through her bag. The woman barely looked away from her computer screen as she pointed to the floor. "The purple tile line is nursery, tangerine for labor and delivery."

Anne looked around, noticing for the first time how small and scarcely staffed the hospital seemed. She followed the tangerine line and walked around the corridor. As she approached the family waiting room, she saw the older couple from the house, the ones she should have been grateful for but detested. *It should be me and Tyler sitting together in this waiting room*, she thought as a wave of jealousy washed over her. She kept walking and found a room with a file on the door marked Weston. Nurses and doctor types were moving in and out, and the girl's pains and curse words were coming at elongated intervals.

Anne clutched her abdomen, remembering those sounds and the monstrous shredding and squeezing of her insides. And then they'd drugged her and robbed her of the memory of her baby's first moment of life. Twenty years of rage threatened to unravel. She struggled to stay calm and not draw attention to herself. Her insignificance to the focused staff permitted her to listen in—the girl's name was Madison, she wasn't dilated enough, it was going to be a long day. When they told Madison to walk around, Anne hustled back to the elevators and explored the purple line.

"Aren't they beautiful?" a woman standing next to her in front of the nursery window asked. "People just love coming here," she continued. "We all stand and ogle the babies like they're puppies in a window. How can you not feel good looking at that? I'm a surgical resident up on nine. I come here on my breaks for the warm fuzzies. Everyone comes here—staff, patients, families of patients. These little miracles make the real world evaporate."

THIRTY-THREE
Tyler

"Hey, big shot," Moe said. He stood a couple of feet from where Tyler was getting out of his car in the fitness and racquetball club parking lot.

"What's up, father of my godson?"

"Don't lock your door yet," Moe said. He held up a bakery box by the string. "Ashley made some whoopie pies for your belated birthday."

"She's awesome." Tyler placed the box on the back seat floor. "Does this mean she's forgiven Billie and me for canceling dinner last weekend?"

"Nope, she's still disappointed. She had a whole thing planned to fuse your birthday with your big news."

"I'm in for it on my thirty-fifth next year, aren't I?"

"Already in the works," Moe said.

Tyler laughed as they walked into the gym.

After their match, Tyler and Moe sat at a high-top with their drinks from the juice bar. Tyler felt older and bulkier than the toned-to-perfection group passing by on their way into a Zumba class.

"Have you had your promotion meeting with the firm yet?" Moe asked.

"It's scheduled in early December. I should have a solid offer by Christmas."

"Well, I hope you get a decent compensation package."

"To be determined. It all depends how the partnership does at year end."

"What will you do if it's too low?"

Tyler considered the question while Moe took too big a drink from his smoothie and swiped the back of his hand across his mouth.

"I'm not sure. My reputation's good, and I've made enough decent contacts to look elsewhere. But I hope I won't have to."

"Sounds like a ton of pressure," Moe said. "How's it affecting you and Billie?"

"How do you mean?"

"I'm asking if you guys are okay?"

"Sure," Tyler said.

"I can't imagine having all that—trying to get pregnant and having to kowtow to your bosses—going on all at once. Ashley and I are just worried about you guys, you know?"

"Well, it's all good. I've always worked hard, and Billie's always been amazing about it. And I promise there are no issues in the 'trying' department." Tyler winked at his friend.

"Just checking you're not carrying too heavy a load. You want to be careful to protect those little swimmers, you know."

Tyler shook his head at Moe's juvenile remark, but they both grinned. When they were together, they always seemed to regress to their childhood mentality.

Moe finished his drink and tossed the cup in a nearby trash can. "I still got it," he said as it landed in the target. Then he looked at Tyler with an adultlike seriousness. "It's all worth it to you, isn't it? Stretching yourself out of bounds for your career and Billie?"

"I wouldn't do it otherwise."

"Wouldn't you, though? Let me ask you something. If you had to choose one, partner or parent, which would it be?"

"That's a terrible question." Tyler tried to rein in the aggressiveness in his voice. "Why would you ever ask anyone that?"

"Because I've known you forever. I've seen you with Nicholas. You're like an old grandpa who loves his grandkids, delights in hyping them up and plying them with sugar, and then gleefully goes home, knowing it'll be the parents' problem to handle, not yours. So, I have to wonder, are you really serious about having a kid? Is being a father really what you want?"

Tyler felt naked, and his mind went blank for a second. In all the years since they'd met, he had never credited Moe with a shred of emotional insight. Yet he'd nailed Tyler's conflict without ever having exchanged a single word about it.

"I suppose that's a fair description of what I've been like. It worked well for me for a long time—a salve, perhaps, for what I couldn't control. But lately, I don't see things the same way so much. Like, maybe there are more rewards than failures, which make the risks worth it. So, my friend, the truth about being a father? Yes, it's what I want." As he thought about it, he grew more sure of himself and a wave of optimism welled inside him.

Tyler received a text as they left the gym. He'd stopped replying to them after he'd slipped up the one time in October. It had been over a month, yet the messages kept coming a few times a day. They always said the same irritating things, so he'd tried to convince himself there wasn't any harmful intent behind them.

Moe stopped on the sidewalk in front of Tyler's car, with his back to the sun. Tyler shifted his position to open his eyes fully.

He watched a landscape truck that had its bucket lifted to the roof, installing Christmas decorations.

"You up for a challenge?" Moe asked.

"You just mutilated me on the court. What more does your sadistic mind want from me?"

"I have an idea that could help make things up to Ashley and give you and Billie a taste of parenthood."

"I'm going to regret this, but tell me anyway."

"Ashley wants to visit her great-aunt on Saturday, but we can't bring a toddler to a nursing home. It would just be for the day. I think it would be a great test run for you and Billie."

"You could just ask us to babysit, skip all the angles."

"Where's the fun in that?"

"We'll do it on one condition," Tyler said.

"Name it." Moe sounded like he thought he'd already won.

"We get to take Nicholas to the Boston Children's Museum."

"You beast. You know Ashley won't deal with missing her son's first experience there."

Tyler laughed at his friend. "It was your bargain. Are we in or out?"

"Give me back those whoopie pies," Moe joked.

"Not a chance. Let me know when to pick up our little ward," Tyler said. Then, as Moe walked away, he yelled, "Hey, while we have him, we can change his name to Ward, right?"

Tyler hoped Billie would be excited. She seemed to view everything from a "what I don't have" perspective as the months went on and pregnancy seemed further out of reach. He found it draining. He'd specifically asked about the children's museum for her because she lit up whenever they walked around the wharf.

"You volunteered us for what?" Billie asked when he called her.

"It'll be great. You've always wanted a reason to go inside the museum and play."

"Yeah, with our kid."

"C'mon, sweetie. You love the giant Hood Milk Bottle there."

"You don't understand how hard it is for me to be around places like that right now. It's wall-to-wall idyllic families and the perfect Ashley-like mommies I can't be."

"I get it. I do. But it's been a while since we've had any fun," Tyler said. "We could use a crazy day, and Nicholas is an easy child."

"I know. Can I think about it?"

"You're asking if Ashley can wait to solidify her plans?"

"Strong argument." Billie breathed out heavily. "Fine. I give in. I'll do it for you."

"I'll let them know."

"If we survive until the end of the day," she said, sounding less uptight, "and if Ashley approves of Nicholas's condition when we return him, you're buying me burgers from the takeout place near them. The one with the good steak fries."

"Done," Tyler said. "Love you, Bills."

"You too. See you tonight."

THIRTY-FOUR
Billie

Billie waited until the adoption unit's weekly staff meeting broke up. As usual, Jay remained seated while he and the secretary discussed action items raised in the discussions.

"This needs your signature." She placed the last page of her home study in front of him.

The adoption attorney she'd spoken with after she returned from the lake ten days ago assured her he'd orchestrate the connection between her and the designated couple. There was one caveat. He'd only move forward once he had a current, approved home study.

As soon as Jay scrawled his name on the line, she pulled the paper from him and headed for the door.

"Wait a second," he said.

Billie's throat tightened as she turned back.

"Stop by later, will you? There are some updates for the manual I'd like you to work on."

"Sure. Sure. No problem." Her mouth was so dry her top lip stuck to her teeth as she spoke.

Once out of the meeting room, Billie hustled down the hall. She walked straight into the secretary's office, placed the home study signature page in the top opening on the shredder, and watched her dreams crosscut into the bin.

Billie's intercom was ringing when she returned from the secretary's office.

"Steve Quinn's on the line," Rita said. "It's the second time he's called."

Billie heard a lot of background noise when she answered.

"Hey, um, Madison wanted me to update you," Steve said. "We're at St. Monica's Hospital."

"Is everything okay?"

"She's in labor."

"But she's only thirty-seven weeks." There'd been no sign during their recent session that Madison was this close. Her belly hadn't even dropped the way most of her clients' did when the baby positioned itself to enter the world. Though nearly full-term, being three weeks early still posed risks of preterm complications. "Is she doing all right? Are you?"

"So far, everyone's doing fine. Her water broke earlier, but the labor is slow. The doctor knows our plans, and he had the social worker come to talk to us. I gave her your name and number. She said, assuming no complications, she'll contact you when the baby is born."

The only thing Billie could do was go into prep mode. She placed two folders in front of her, Madison's file and the file of the potential adoptive couple Madison and Steve had selected. They'd only be contacted if, indeed, the baby was relinquished. Then she printed the packet of required legal documents.

As a hospital without deep resources, St. Monica's was a small, poorly run operation. Their policy was to send healthy mothers home two days after delivery. They wouldn't keep a baby in the hospital unless it was medically warranted. So Billie would be responsible for transferring the newborn, who temporarily belonged to no one, from the hospital to a foster home until he or she was relinquished to the adoption agency.

When there was little left to do on the case except wait, Billie put all her energy into making sure she didn't grab her coat and go see Madison in person.

Ashley handed Billie a CD after she buckled Nicholas into the car seat. "They're his favorite songs. Make sure you have this on while you drive." And then, when Billie got in her seat, Ashley pushed a heavy backpack on her lap. "Your survival kit," she said. When Ashley had said goodbye to Nicholas the eighteenth time, Moe pulled her away from the car.

"I don't know who has more misgivings about this adventure, Ashley or you. Get in the spirit of it, Bills." Tyler turned up the stereo when they drove off, and Nicholas quacked along to the "Five Little Ducks" song.

Billie sang along, holding her fingers to show how many ducks had come back and gesturing to the "Eyes, Nose, Mouth, Ears" song, but the spirit Tyler thought she should have wasn't there.

At the museum, Tyler's energy and bewilderment matched that of Nicholas. When they came to the "Bubbles" room, the toddler handled the slippery floor like a pro, while Tyler moved around like a drunkard. In the "Raceway," he lifted Nicholas high so the boy could place a golf ball on a ramp, and then he put his godson under his arm like a football and ran to beat the ball to the bottom. Billie heard Tyler laughing in a way she hadn't realized had been missing for a very long time.

But, feeling distant, she didn't interact with them. Her heart was fixated on Madison and Steve's newborn. The infant that wouldn't be hers. All she felt was the pain and emptiness of losing another baby.

"Auntie B," Nicholas said, closing his soft little hand around her finger, "you do san-box with me?"

"Sure, kiddo," she said. "Sandbox it is."

"You want a ride, bud?" Tyler picked up Nicholas when it was time to leave, and the boy dropped his head on Tyler's shoulder. "Sign of a successful outing." He put his free arm around Billie as they walked. "We're pretty good at this parenting thing."

Billie looked up at her husband. "What?"

"I can't wait for us to do it full-time, no matter how we get there."

For months, she'd had the impression she was alone in the fertility fight. To know she'd been wrong, and they both wanted to be parents, lifted her. Then it hit her—she'd literally shredded their last best chance to make it happen.

Madison and Steve arrived early for their appointment on Monday. Framed by raw red inner rims, Madison's eyes were glassy. The gray puffiness underneath revealed her grief and exhaustion.

Between updates from the hospital social worker and Steve, Billie was aware labor had lasted over fifteen hours after they admitted Madison. Her heart twisted, imagining how weak her client must have been. The good news was that the baby, a girl, was expected to be fine. As a precaution, they'd kept the baby until her bilirubin and other essential functions and tests were clear. They'd released Madison after a quick two days, but Baby Girl Quinn remained hospitalized, stable but under continued observation.

Madison and Steve trudged down the hall to Billie's office,

keeping several inches between them. Their silence was leaden with pain. Resolved to stick with their plan, they'd come to review the relinquishment documents.

"I'm sorry." Madison's words spluttered between sorrowful gasps.

"Take your time," Billie said. "We won't begin until you're ready."

Steve looked away from Madison. Billie saw him swipe a tear fleck with a quick flick of his hand.

"It was horrible," Madison said. There was a hint of rage in the glare now fixed on Billie. "It took so long."

"A nurse hooked an IV with Pitocin to induce the labor sometime later at night," Steve explained. "I could only tell it was night because the hall lights were dim and it was quieter."

Billie noticed Madison was pulling her ears again. Visualizing the two of them in such an ordeal tore her apart. She knew they had tried their best to be stoic. She hoped if she was giving birth to Tyler's baby one day, they'd be as brave and clearheaded as this young pair.

"It wasn't that much longer when the nurse let your parents come in," Steve said. "I remember looking at the window and seeing the moon. It was close to full."

"What about your parents, Steve?" Billie asked.

"I called them every couple of hours. They cared, but my mother still thinks we're making a mistake, so they couldn't handle being there. To tell the truth, it was easier for everyone that way."

"My mother was the complete opposite," Madison said. "She was making a huge fuss and doing too much to make me comfortable. It's the way she's always been when I've been sick and she's worried. It was crazy annoying, and I didn't want to say something cruel, so I made her and my father go back to the waiting room. But then the baby came, with her perfect cries, perfect fingers and toes. I held her close to my chest, and, in that moment, she was my baby. For that moment, I was her mother."

Tears cascaded down Madison's cheeks. Billie and Steve waited. Then her soft moan crescendoed into an agonizing wail. Her fists clenched and raised toward her shoulder. Her neck and face turned the purply red of raw steak, and her eyelids squeezed so tight her eyeballs seemed to disappear into their sockets.

"Women brag about how painful and difficult childbirth is, but it all vanishes the second they get to hold their child." Madison's gasps turned to hiccups between sobs. "But you know what? I won't get that. I don't get to have the joy that makes you forget what you went through. All I will ever have are empty arms and the memory of the pain."

A tear escaped from the corner of Billie's eye. Steve, pale and broken, didn't bother to brush his away this time. Neither could speak, for there were no words that would ever be sufficient enough to console Madison.

Madison and Steve decided to schedule the document signing after the baby's discharge. They needed to feel confident the baby was all right.

THIRTY-FIVE
Anne

"Another pot?" The waitress looked as lethargic as Anne felt. Time had become irrelevant, though she was aware it was well after midnight when she'd stepped into the IHOP near the hospital. Anne sat in a shredded vinyl booth with her fourth pot of never-ending coffee. She'd been hanging out at the restaurant each night since the baby was born, spending most of the last three daytimes at the nursery window. She'd blended in well since the first night when she'd taken a pair of scrubs from the laundry bin in the nurses' locker room during a shift change and easily swiped an exhausted nurse's ID from her purse. Still, Anne was careful to roam other wards when families came for a view, often using the time to take quick birdbaths in restrooms.

The baby, born slightly early and jaundiced, stayed after Madison's discharge two days ago. Anne watched over the scrumptious baby whose cart was now marked "Baby Girl Quinn," removing herself when Madison and Steve (she'd finally heard someone say his name) came for their visit today. She wanted to talk to Madison, but after their encounter at Woodson, her daughter was frightened of her own mother.

“Maybe something to eat?” the waitress asked. After all the hours of serving nothing but coffee to Anne, she seemed uninterested.

“Nah, thanks,” Anne said. The morning light had edged its way over the sky. In a few hours, they would evaluate the baby for possible discharge tomorrow morning. Idle time in the hospital had taught her plenty, like doctors didn’t start rounds until after eight, they’d run blood work and other labs, and results would take a few hours. Adding this knowledge together, Anne planned to be there in the afternoon when the doctors made their recommendation. She had to make sure her daughter and grandbaby were going to be okay. But first, there was somewhere she needed to be.

THIRTY-SIX
Tyler

The recent case that had consumed Tyler had finally come to a close. As he walked out of the courtroom, his client gave him a pat on the back and a vigorous handshake. He loved the feeling of a good win.

Tyler stood outside the courthouse doors, breathing in the crisp end-of-fall air. He was eager to see Billie and tell her about it. She'd been more than patient with his devotion to the case. He also knew he'd been testy and standoffish around her since he received the baby photo. It was undeniable that she worried he was reacting to the infertility and blaming her. He owed her an apology. His smile returned as he decided tonight would be a "Don't Have To" night. He headed in the direction of the bakery to get a box of Billie's favorite marzipan cookies. As he rounded the corner, he smashed into someone coming the other way.

"I'm so sorry." The woman crouched down to pick up the briefcase he didn't even know he'd dropped.

"Are you hurt?" he asked.

"No. I'm fine. I wasn't watching where I was going at all."

He grasped the handles when she held out his case, but she didn't let go that easily. A strange feeling stopped him from moving past her.

"Have we met?" She looked at him for an uncomfortable moment, her eyes wide and unblinking. "Ms. Neuman?"

"That's not my name."

Tyler shook his head. Up close, this woman was a tad more put together. Her brown hair, though messy, was clean. Her makeup, which wasn't as thick, left a masklike line around the frame of her face. And, come to think of it, she wasn't wearing glasses. But the vagrant essence resembled the Neuman who'd come to his office last August. Tyler wasn't sure what he was thinking when he'd called out to her, except the inclination to find the culprit tormenting him and Billie was becoming impossible to control.

"I'm sorry. I must have confused you with someone else."

"No. You didn't." Her voice was small and far away.

"What?"

"I told you my name is Suzanne Neuman, but it's not."

Tyler was trying to understand what she was saying. Why was he still standing there? It was clear this woman and her previous bag-lady presence was some kind of wacko. Yet he didn't feel in danger.

"Tyler, I'm Laura Bennett."

He heard her say it, but the words weren't computing. "Laura Bennett?"

"You've forgotten who I am, haven't you!"

His intellect seized. *Laura Bennett. L.B.* He'd sat in his own office, a desk length away, and not realized it was her. But she'd known who he was. Tyler shivered as goose bumps covered his skin.

"From middle school, Laura Bennett?" All his experienced tricks to stay cool under pressure were failing him. But if his fear was the reaction she was hoping for, he wouldn't give in. "Well, I'll be damned." In the back of his head, he knew to run, to get away, and fast. But she had an agenda, and the need to get his questions answered overcame his sensibilities. "There's a café across the street. Why don't we go catch up there?"

Filled with uncertainty, the two sat and eyed each other, neither daring to speak.

The waitress, chomping a wad of gum, worked hard to produce an order from them. Laura asked for a BLT and fries. Tyler asked only for a cup of coffee. The tension between them held until the waitress placed Laura's triple-decker in front of her. The wolflike ferocity with which she ate her sandwich was astonishing.

"What happened to you?" Tyler asked.

He'd meant the question as "Where did you disappear to?" but in all honesty, a part of him was asking how she'd become a bedraggled caricature. She looked significantly more than her thirty-three years.

"I had a baby," she said in a low, clear voice. She lifted her eyes to meet his.

"How nice for you. A boy or girl?"

"When I went away. In eighth grade. I wasn't sick, not the way everyone thought." Laura's lips quivered with the emotion she was holding back.

"What are you talking about?"

"I was pregnant."

So it was true. All those terrible rumors about her were true. The gossip about her father abusing her like those other girls, true too. Worse, Bennett had gotten his own child pregnant. Tyler's throat spasmed in revulsion. He attempted to mask the gags with a fit of coughing, thinking she'd endured enough humiliation.

"We"—she hesitated, then her face lit up—"*we* had a baby. You and me. A girl."

A buzzing surged inside his head. His mouth was as gritty as beach sand. He remembered bringing homework to Laura when she got sick a few weeks after his bar mitzvah. He walked into her house as he always did, and she was watching some black-and-white movie.

"You don't look sick," he'd observed.

"I was this morning. I've been fine since," she said. "Actually, I'm hungry. I'm gonna get some Cheez Doodles. Want some?" She'd stood up and bounced into the kitchen area. She was licking the tips of her orange-stained fingers when she came back and passed him the bag.

"What's the matter?" he'd asked when Laura groaned. Her cheeks were chalky and her forehead pocked with sweat. Instead of answering, she dashed to the bathroom. Tyler squeezed his eyes when he heard her retch.

Laura had stayed out of school so long their classmates thought she had mono. "Ooh, the *kiss*-ing disease," his friend John drawled. He'd stood up from the lunch table, miming making out for emphasis.

The table full of jocks in their matching navy sports jackets with white lettering elbowed each other and slapped the table.

"Please don't smooch me too." Moe shielded himself as the guys laughed.

"He hasn't been kissing anyone but me." Angela Finelli put her food tray on the table and squeezed in next to Tyler.

From what Laura was saying to him now, she was already pregnant by then.

It didn't make sense to him, though. Mr. Bennett was the one, not Tyler, a thirteen-year-old who had no idea what he was doing. He let another few moments pass while he attempted to sort through his thoughts.

"Why?" Tyler tried to speak, but the words got stuck in his throat. "Why now? If it was mine, why didn't you tell me back then?"

"Not *if*, Tyler."

"Okay. It was poor word choice. I believe you," he lied.

"My father found out. He threatened to kill my mom. I was afraid he'd hurt you and the baby too." Laura's voice cracked as she spoke. "My mother told the school that I went to my aunt's for medical treatment, but I was with her boss's sister."

"Your father went to jail two decades ago. The child would be . . . nineteen? Twenty?" He was so muddled he wasn't sure of the math. "Why are you telling me now?" He was questioning himself, questioning if he believed her.

"I've always wanted to tell you. But when they arrested him, you'd already gone on to college. I did try once, though. The day they sentenced my father, I left a letter in your parents' mailbox. I figured we were safe with him locked up. But you never wrote to me or called me. Why?"

Laura whimpered before he could think of anything to say.

"Why?" she repeated, this time more forcefully, and raspberry rage flushed into her cheeks and forehead. "I guess you'd just forgotten about me. Stopped caring. You were living your good ole fancy life without me!"

"Laura, if I'd gotten a letter from you, I would have contacted you. I worried when you'd disappeared. If I'd seen a letter, if I knew there was a baby, I would have been there. I never got anything from you."

Oh, shit! He thought about the unstamped envelope his mother once found in their mail and left for him in the foyer box. His name had been handwritten in cursive, with happy-faced stars drawn on the corners. Those dumb smiling stars—the same doodles she'd always made on her homework. Tyler remembered seeing the letter fall behind the foyer table when he'd run to the kitchen the day his mother set fire to the oven.

Uneasy at how this emotional stranger he'd once known might react, he kept the fact that he'd lost the sealed letter to himself. His eyebrow twitched as he looked across the café table at her. "You still haven't explained why you're here now."

"He was getting out. My father. Early release." Laura began nibbling on her fingertips.

Memories of Mr. Bennett flooded Tyler. He kneaded his throat where the man's hands had squeezed it. Then he thought of reading about Bennett's arrest and the sickening realization that the scumbag had probably molested Laura. But what she was saying made little sense. Collin Frost had confirmed her father was behind bars a short time when he died.

"I mean, I thought he was getting out. He didn't, wasn't." Laura's words faded as she pressed her hands against her face. Her fingers dragged over her cheeks until her eyes were on him again. He thought she seemed detached, like someone had blown out the light inside her.

"I'm still scared of what he might do to you," Laura said.

Tyler clutched the table in front of him. "What happened to the baby?"

"I gave her up," Laura whispered. She reached across the table and placed her hand on top of his. "It should have been us," she continued. "We should have grown up, gotten married, and had a baby. We would have been a perfect family."

The glazed, far-off look that came across Laura's eyes when she spoke was disquieting. Tyler slipped his hand out from beneath hers. He reached in his pocket and withdrew the now familiar photo, which fit so well in his palm. The one that Billie had slid across the table from him, and, off guard, he'd told an implausible lie about. He concentrated on the image. That face. The coloring. Hypnotized by the baby's likeness to Laura, he searched the details with painstaking focus. And then the one element that had eluded him came into focus—a wisp of light red hair peeking out from under the hat. He'd forgotten to swallow, and the rough dryness in his throat burned.

"Is this . . ."

Tyler looked up when Laura's chair scraped the floor. She appeared horror-stricken before she hurried to the café door.

"Don't go." He threw some bills on the table, but when he got outside, Laura was a blur at the end of the block. He looked after her for a while, then gravitated to a bar across the street.

"Tequila shot. No lime." He slipped onto the barstool and dropped his face into his palms.

"Keep 'em coming." His instructions seemed muted as he reached to grip the little glass between his fingers.

Tyler recounted the first revolting wave of comprehension many years ago of the pain Mr. Bennett must have caused Laura. Was it days or weeks after she disappeared when he'd walked out of the gym from JV basketball practice, and Mr. Bennett jumped him? He once again swept his fingers along the smooth skin on his throat, a subconscious reaction to the memory.

After two shots, the shock of the entire interlude was numbing. Aside from the letter that he never got a chance to read, she hadn't given him a say in any of it. He had no idea what he would have wanted, if he'd have been on board with an abortion or supported adoption, or if he and his parents would've raised the child. It made no difference; she'd taken away his right to decide the type of parenting his child would or wouldn't have, without him even knowing he had to choose.

Between the third and fourth shot, he tortured himself with thoughts of how he could ever tell Billie. The concept of what it would do to his wife strangled him. How could he tell her he might already have fathered a child when they'd been struggling to get pregnant? What words wouldn't crush her when he let her know that he'd gotten someone pregnant, just not her? Tyler couldn't bear the agony he predicted she'd feel . . . couldn't tolerate being the one to make her feel that way.

Logical comfort came with the fifth shot. There was no proof the baby was his. Laura's father was a sexual deviant, after all. Maybe she thought she could extort something from him. He'd certainly seen enough cases for that to be a valid possibility. *I'll demand an effing paternity test.* Tyler lost count after the sixth shot.

After the bartender called him a cab, he paid his tab and, when he went to put his credit card back in his wallet, he pulled out a business card. He pressed it onto the bar and thumped his finger on it.

"Can you dial this for me?" Tyler asked.

He wobbled a bit as he leaned over the bar counter and pressed the phone receiver to his ear. At the beep, he left a mangled voicemail for Collin Frost. A couple of minutes later, the bartender folded him into a taxi headed to the home address on the license Tyler waved in the air.

THIRTY-SEVEN
Laura

Laura was proud of herself and the way she'd confessed to Tyler about going to his office and leaving the baby picture. She knew she'd sounded calm when she bumped into him on purpose yesterday. She'd even stayed cool walking with him to the café. The extraordinary elation she experienced being with him felt electric inside her. Her lungs felt like they'd explode. Yet she'd kept her composure and handled herself like an adult, right up until he pulled out the photo. He'd known it was special and kept it with him! It aroused a mix of excitement and anger, which confused her. The intense turmoil and painful, searing light behind her eyes made her do what she did best: run.

It all threw her off-balance. Why did she freak out when Tyler seemed to figure out the truth? She'd waited a lifetime for him to know, so why did she panic? Mama Sue often told her, "Sometimes the thing we want most is the thing we most fear."

She'd texted him a couple of times last night to tell him how much she regretted bailing like that. No matter how often she checked her phone, there'd been no response. The frustration swelled until she called his secretary, claiming to be Suzanne Neuman again.

* *

Laura arrived at the hospital before the baby was due to be released. She stayed in the cafeteria while Madison and Steve spent time with their baby. She tore through a couple of bags of chips from a vending machine before the compulsion to watch became too fierce. Laura returned to the seventh floor but couldn't find them. She'd observed enough to know the discharge process took longer than that. Her steps sped up toward the nursery while sharp, piercing sensations rolled along her skin. With her hands pressed against the nursery window, she scanned the bassinets from the back row to the front. An unfamiliar feeling of ecstasy soared through her when she saw the baby. Awake and content, the infant looked beautiful with her tiny nose and her itty-bitty hand resting on her full cheek. A blanket covered only her feet, so Laura got an eyeful of the baby's soft pink going-home outfit.

Two nurses came out of the nursery toward Laura. One looked young and the other had on Elmo scrubs. The older one said, "Let me know when the adoption agency comes for the Quinn baby."

Singeing heat stung Laura's skin before a veil of numbness consumed her. The baby seemed smaller and far away, the same way things looked through the wrong end of a telescope. She grabbed the emptiness in front of her, trying to hold on to the baby. And then there was nothing.

THIRTY-EIGHT
Tyler

Tyler cursed himself for walking into the bar around the block from his office yesterday afternoon. He never drank like that. He was half certain that at some point, he'd tried to get a server to dance with him while he sang, "Sexy and I Know It." If anyone recognized him or posted videos of his behavior, he'd lose both the promised partnership and his marriage.

Fielding the cotton mouth, bed spins, and construction site pounding, Tyler staggered out of bed. It wasn't like Billie to leave without waking him, but the house was quiet. He rubbed the stubble on his face, wishing he could remember what he said to her when he came home last night. Or even how or when he'd made it home. When he got himself to a semi-functioning place, he called Marla.

"I need you to reschedule the ten-thirty meeting. I won't be in this morning."

"No problem." She ran through some messages, then added, "FYI, that Suzanne Neuman person called twice. She's been asking when she can see you but wouldn't set an appointment."

His aching head felt like a freight train had crashed into it.

"Okay. Let me know if she calls again."

He put on his running pants and layered a couple of T-shirts for warmth. Before he went out, he made one more phone call. “Hey, I need a favor.”

After a long run he hoped would sweat the alcohol out of his system, Tyler showered and then took a cab to The Kettle, a greasy spoon near the highway. Collin Frost was waiting for him in a back booth with two mugs of freshly brewed coffee on the table.

“So, what’s the word, Frost?” Tyler asked.

“The neighbors had no problem recalling Neuman taking in a kid and her mother in the early nineties. Neighbors were used to Neuman’s fosters, but she’d never had an adult before. The mother’s name was Kathleen. The kid kept to herself the first year, and eventually it was obvious she was pregnant. A contact at the hospital confirmed it. The baby, a girl, was born July 14, 1992, discharged to a representative of Burkhead Family Services.”

Tyler’s head jerked. “Burkhead? Are you shitting me?”

“I don’t much like coincidences.”

A painful hammering pounded against Tyler’s temples. He popped two Tylenol, flushing them with a glass of orange juice. The sweet citrus revived him enough to wonder: *If I were my own attorney, what would I need to know?*

“Who’s the father on the birth certificate?”

“None listed,” Collin answered. “Chatter says Anne Neuman was not well-liked in high school or after. Described as weird and creepy. Went through a bunch of jobs before leaving the area. I tracked her to a town ’bout forty minutes from here. Lives in a rental, alone. Confirmed the pseudonym. Her true name is Laura Bennett. Your L.B., as one might conclude. Works at a plumbing company. Employees say she hasn’t been showing up. I staked out her place. She went in for a few hours, then left again. I tailed her beat-up car to Woodson's campus. She seemed distinctly interested in a couple of kids there. The female appears to be very pregnant."

Tyler shuddered as chills rinsed over him. "Has she done anything that indicates she's dangerous?"

"Nothing so far, boss."

"And the child? Any leads?"

"Working on it. Gonna start with Burkhead."

Although Frost seemed at ease, Tyler could feel the man scrutinizing him.

"You didn't flinch when I revealed the Neuman-Bennett connection," Frost said. "Whatever it is you're holding in your satchel . . . spill."

"She confessed to me yesterday. And she says . . . She claims I'm the father of the baby."

"Well, now you getting Tonka-Trucked last night makes sense. Is what she's saying possible?"

"I suppose. But doesn't it seem more likely it's some kind of extortion attempt?"

"Leave your woes with me. Best way to find out is with whatever Burkhead can give us. Are you ready to bring Billie in on this? She could be a big help with getting the info we need."

"Let me think on it," Tyler said. "I'll give you a call later. I owe you."

"You do indeed, boss."

The two men patted each other's backs as they departed. Tyler walked toward a blue sedan idling by the diner entrance and climbed into the passenger seat.

"Thanks for the ride," he said.

"Sure," Moe said. "Man, you look rough."

"Appreciate it."

"Assuming it's why your car stayed in the city overnight? Billie must be thrilled."

"Have a little mercy and drive."

"We're detouring to my house first. You can take the car from there. Ashley's going off to some who-knows-what, so I'm hanging with Nicholas this morning. I'll take the train downtown later and get the car after work."

Tyler pushed the button to lower the passenger-side window. The frigid air felt nourishing.

Moe used the driver's-side controls to close the window. "You're not only letting all the heat out of the car," he said, "but the wind is blowing your lady-killer hair all over the place."

Tyler pressed to lower the window again, but it wouldn't go.

"Ha! Child locks, sucker."

Tyler grunted, leaned back in the seat, and closed his eyes as Moe navigated the poorly plowed suburban streets. "Do you remember the kid who disappeared from town with her mother years ago?" He looked over at Moe.

"Why bring her up?"

"She contacted me."

"No kidding. So, the old man didn't kill and bury them in the backyard? What does she want?"

"Not sure." There was too much at risk to say more.

"CeCe once told me the craziest story about that girl and John DeAngelo."

"I need details. And aspirin. Where's Ashley's first aid kit?"

"Glove box."

Tyler found the bottle and swallowed another two tablets down. "So, tell."

"Remember when your dad gave us the Scotch at your bar mitzvah?"

"Sure. Why would it matter?"

"Because he kept slipping shots to me and John during the party. Pretty much did me in. I sort of remember walking around the building. Staggering would probably be more accurate. Apparently, CeCe came looking for me but found them instead."

"Them who?"

"That girl, Laura. And John. They were having sex in one of the religious school classrooms."

"You get that I'm severely hungover and my brain is not processing well. So you'll understand when I say this as softly as I possibly can—how the fuck is this the first time I'm hearing this?" But Tyler's brain wasn't so fogged up that he couldn't see he hadn't told his best friends everything either.

"John never said anything." Moe gave a little shrug. "I figured it wasn't true." He parked on the street by his house and opened the door. "She's all yours." He swept his hand in the air over the dashboard. "Be kind to her." He got out and held the driver's door.

"Christ, no, don't slam it."

Moe laughed as Tyler struggled to slide over from the passenger seat.

"Hey," Tyler called out the window as it lowered. "When was the last time you heard from John?"

"Not since he kicked off his big California campaign for Congress. You?"

"Same."

"Maybe he's avoiding us because we know he's not the rule following do-gooder his PR team is painting. I mean, we've all got skeletons best left in the closet, right?" Moe winked, tapped on the side of the door, and walked off.

Weakened and nauseous from the thoughts and reactions banging inside his head, Tyler moaned. He leaned his forehead on the steering wheel to relieve some pressure and wondered how many other eighth-grade friends had used Laura for sex. Although, if he was being fair to himself, she had seduced him, not the other way around, but still, it was unforgiveable. And what about Moe's skeleton comment? Could it have had some pointed meaning? What if he'd known about the tumbleweed of lies Tyler kept about Laura back then? Or was Moe hinting at his own current crises and Laura's claims? What exactly did Moe know, and how?

Suddenly, Tyler was full of suspicion about his best friends, whom he didn't know everything about, apparently. They'd all been dumb prepubescents who knew nothing of consequences. He and John both had something to lose if found to be the father of Laura's baby. Both were redheads. But only one was a public figure with a team who'd do anything to change the narrative.

Tyler could, should contact Collin Frost. But time was running out, and he feared it would be too late before Frost got back to him. He took out his phone and texted the number he now knew belonged to Laura: Meet me tomorrow for an early lunch at Triste Cucina.

THIRTY-NINE
Billie

Billie took a sip of the jumbo coffee and set it back into the cup holder. It was her second so far. She needed the caffeine boost for the drive to St. Monica's. Tyler's boozy snoring had kept her up most of the night, and she was pissed.

"Come on, let me in." Billie honked at the car to her left, which wouldn't make room for her to switch lanes. Her thoughts stayed on Tyler's moods and behavior, which had been increasingly unpredictable since they'd started trying to have a baby. He'd been deep in a trial, but that excuse could only explain so much. The infertility had to be a factor. He would brush her off or become obnoxious and irritable if she attempted to help him open up. A couple of times, he shouted at her to "stop social-workering" him. So she'd been trying to give him time and space until he was ready to explain. But last night he came home soused around nine thirty. He'd banged and pressed the front doorbell until she let him in the house.

"Twick or tweet," he said.

His clothes were a mess, stained, and his shirt partially untucked. He was tripping over air as he entered the foyer and then giggled at himself. His goofy expression reminded Billie of a boy trying to get past his parents when he'd missed curfew and reeked of pot.

"Why are you coming in the front?"

Before she could get the door shut, bright headlight beams lit up the driveway. A car reversed into the street and sped away. On a hunch, she peeked into the garage.

"Who brought you home, Tyler? Where's your car?"

"Let's dance." He took her arm and twirled her, then himself. With a groan, he splayed out on the floor.

"I dun feels sho goo . . ." The rest came out even more garbled. But it was obvious from the greenish hues coloring his face that he wasn't going to last much longer.

"Okay, big boy, let's get you upstairs."

Billie pushed his back upright, then went in front of him and tugged his arms until he rose with her.

"That's it . . . Come with me." She continued to coax him up the stairs.

It was rare for Tyler to be so far gone that he couldn't maintain a coherent conversation. He'd never been much of a partier. This morning she'd left early for work without waking him, hoping he'd sleep off the booze and whatever was eating at him.

Thanks to Boston's notorious traffic, the trek from the agency to St. Monica's Hospital took her an hour and fifteen minutes. It was close to Madison's parents' house, where she'd stayed as the due date drew nearer, and where she was now while she recuperated.

Billie waited at the reception desk for Sabrina Lu, the social worker and liaison between the hospital and adoption agency. With the jaundice subsiding, the baby was strong and ready to be transported to foster care. Billie bounced on her heels, heady from too much caffeine and the eagerness to meet Madison's baby girl. Would the infant look like the baby she'd been dreaming about each night—the recurrent dream where Madison rings her doorbell and hands the baby to her, and then, as she kisses the baby's head, she hears her mother say, "She's not yours to keep."

Sabrina rushed down the hall with a haphazard stack of papers and folders overflowing in her arms. Billie was well aware of how overburdened with cases hospital social workers were, especially with an understaffed facility like St. Monica's. Sabrina sifted through her mess and pulled out some stapled pages. She took a pencil from behind her ear and swiped at the long black strands that fell over her smudged glasses.

"Okay, here we are." Sabrina scratched a few notes on the forms, then stood on her toes to lean over the counter. She gave instructions to the receptionist and took a fresh wad of papers to add to her arms. "Let's go up to the nursery. We can talk on the way."

They followed a scuffed magenta line to an elevator bank and waited for it to descend to the lobby.

"Those kids were special," Sabrina said. "I tried to give them as much of my time as I could. I know this is a tough thing to go through. But they impressed me. They behaved nicely, emotions were appropriate to the situation, and they relied on each other in a healthy way. Nice couple." She stopped talking as they crushed themselves into the crowded elevator but resumed as they stepped out on the seventh floor. "They came every day to see the baby, you know."

Billie did know. Madison and Steve couldn't bear the thought of the baby being alone in the hospital. And so they had come each day to visit and make sure she felt loved.

"They were here earlier this morning, sad but sweet. They dressed the baby in a pretty sweater and hat and swaddled her in a soft pink blanket before saying goodbye."

Billie was aware of this too. Madison had sent her mother and

Steve on a reconnaissance mission in the attic to find the clothes she had worn when the Westons brought her home. Madison had explained that she wanted to hand them down to her baby—wanted her to have something from her birth family. Steve's mother had surprised them with the blanket she'd knitted. When Madison called Billie this morning, she'd mentioned the ensemble.

"We're ready," Madison had said during the call. Her voice was soft, and Billie could feel her sorrow. "We've said goodbye."

Sabrina's sneakers squeaked and Billie's heels tapped as they walked to the north wing of the maternity floor. They were now following a purple-lined path toward the nursery. When they got there, a stout head nurse dressed in Elmo scrubs was shouting and gesticulating to a younger, somewhat stupefied nurse.

"*Now!*" the Elmo nurse shouted.

When the panicked nurse turned and sprinted, Sabrina cleared her throat. She once again rifled through her hodgepodge of papers and shoved one in Nurse Elmo's direction.

"We're here for Baby Girl Quinn," Sabrina said.

Nurse Elmo turned a startling shade of ash. "You should come with me."

Billie assumed they were following Nurse Elmo into the nursery. Most hospital staff let her wait there while they organized the baby's discharge papers and supplies. Even though the hospital social workers always called the unit to let them know to prepare the baby in advance, they never did. To Billie, it was one of the bonuses of the job because she got to coddle the newborn in a room full of babies while the staff took care of the red tape. Of course, this time would be much better. Despite knowing she was too attached to this particular baby, her heart still pushed her in a different direction. The closer they came to the nursery, the harder it was to tamp down the itch to speed everything up so she could feel this special baby in her arms already.

When they walked past the nursery to a staff-only elevator bank, Billie thought it was odd the baby would be on another floor, but some places had unusual policies when it came to adoptive situations. Light from the ceiling threw shadows across Sabrina's face. She clutched her files, warily glancing between Billie and the nurse. Billie went on alert. *Did someone report me for pushing Madison and Steve to relinquish the baby? But I didn't, did I?* She felt like she might suffocate in the confined elevator.

"Where are we . . ." The elevator doors rumbled open and drowned out Billie's question. Nurse Elmo began a hasty pace down the hall, forcing Sabrina and Billie to hustle to keep up with her. She came to a stop before a tall door. With a brief, purposeful rap, she entered an airy conference room with a windowed back wall that framed an unremarkable view. Hospital executives and a St. Monica's in-house legal representative ringed the table. The last introduction was Chief Dolby, head of St. Monica's security.

"What is this about?" Sabrina found the words before Billie.

"Take a seat," the lawyer said. "It seems we have an, er, situation."

"I think there's been some misunderstanding." Billie remained standing as she spoke. "I'm not staff and don't belong in this meeting. If someone could please direct me back to the nursery, I'll . . ."

"Have a seat, Ms. Campbell. This concerns you as well."

Struck that the lawyer knew her name, Billie was unaware she'd obeyed. *Oh God, the baby is sicker than they thought or . . .* Perspiration kissed her neck and beaded between her thighs where it pooled into the seat of her slacks. *No. Please don't say she's dead.*

"Approximately thirty minutes ago, it was discovered that Baby Girl Quinn is missing from the nursery."

A sensation of losing gravity, as if she were diving toward the floor, threw Billie off-balance as she heard the words that the baby was missing.

"*Missing*? How is that even possible? How do you misplace an infant? Why are we sitting here?" Billie got to her feet again. "We need to lock down the hospital, search every room, every floor."

Sabrina looked like she'd turned to stone in the chair as she clung to her files. With ghoulish timing, a symphony of phones pealed with an Amber Alert.

"I assure you," Chief Dolby said, "my staff is checking every nook of the hospital, and we are reviewing our security tapes. We have notified local police, and they are on their way."

Billie had visions of the baby lying in the hospital's sterile bassinet, cold, crying, and alone. She dug her fingers into her thighs.

"However, it is our belief," Dolby said, "that the baby has been removed from the premises."

In that instant, Billie understood what the phrase "blood runs cold" meant.

"I have personally interviewed the staff on duty this morning," Dolby said. "What we can piece together, at this time, is that earlier this morning, after Ms. Lu called the nursery ward to let them know you were on your way to pick up Baby Girl Quinn, a new intern did the discharge exam. It appears, not long after, a nurse using your name arrived at the nursery to transport the baby. The intern didn't know protocol was to contact Ms. Lu in social services."

"Staff is being dealt with internally, and I assure you, our policies and procedures will be updated as well," the lawyer added.

"Your liability and the potential legal consequences are of no concern to me at this moment. There is a helpless infant that you released to a . . . we don't know how deranged stranger." Billie found it impossible to control the rage and terror within her. "The only thing that matters is that baby girl's safety."

"If it were me, I'd let my agency know what's going on ASAP," Sabrina whispered.

"Is there a phone? I need to notify my supervisor." Billie shook her head, remembering her cell.

Uniformed police detectives in gray or blue blazers and hospital administration moved like bumper cars around the conference room. Billie tried to stay out of the way. Tempted to search for the baby, she eyed the chrome door pull on the faux wood-grain door, but Jay and their executive director had given stern instructions not to leave. Using her social work powers of observation kept her as sane as possible. She located herself close enough to the hub to hear the private exchanges. When she spotted a pair whispering by the coffee table, she edged her way over. She gagged when she poured a cup and its decay-like stench reached her. Billie hovered near the catty duo, St. Monica's board members, who blamed their chairperson for refusing to modernize hospital security because of budgeting. A feverish heat spread in her cheeks as she chucked the cup in a garbage can and went on to another conspiratorial group. She deviated from her surveillance post every so often to call Tyler. So far, he hadn't answered. The need for his voice to help anchor her was overwhelming. *Strength, courage, heart.* She called both his numbers at more frequent intervals. There was no reason he wouldn't be there. His court case had ended yesterday.

"Dammit, Tyler! Where are you?"

Desperate for his comfort and guidance, Billie continued alternating calls between his cell, office, and the house. Then she realized her stupidity and called his firm's main office number.

"He said he was coming in late today," Marla said. "I'd hoped he'd be here a couple of hours ago, but I haven't heard from him yet."

"Ms. Campbell?" The deep voice came from behind her.

Her breath caught with anticipation when she saw Security Chief Dolby flanked on either side by two police officers.

"Can you come with us for a moment? We have some questions."

Billie tried to make eye contact with Sabrina, hoping for validation, but Sabrina was looking at the ceiling like she could find the answers to the universe there.

Chief Dolby walked with an air of authority as he led her out of the conference room. The officers followed behind.

"Have you found her?" Billie asked.

"We can talk in my office."

Small black-and-white TV screens filled the space the hospital chief called an office, each one showing a variety of hazy angles of the hospital. Billie could make out a bank of elevators on one monitor, a nurse's desk on another. Dolby asked her to sit.

"You said you left your house at six thirty this morning. Is that correct?"

"Yes."

"Can anyone verify that?"

"Verify? What? What is happening here?"

"Ms. Campbell, can anyone confirm where you were at ten fifteen this morning?" the chief repeated.

This morning around ten fifteen, she was driving on the turnpike, alone—*strength, courage, strength, courage*. The words reverberated within her.

"I don't understand why you're asking me this. If something has happened to the baby, please, you have to let me know."

"Perhaps you should see this." Chief Dolby nodded to a technician sitting by one of the monitors. The technician pushed a switch, and the screen changed to a digitized video with a time stamp on the upper right corner. Billie narrowed her eyelids to make out the content. The back of a woman in blush-pink scrubs, whose hair was the same length as hers, stepped into a hallway. You couldn't see her face, but she most definitely had a baby in her arms and was being guided out of the nursery.

"What the hell?" Billie whispered.

"You see. The time stamp says ten fifteen, the same time the newborn went missing. And you can also see, as we all can, that is you who is carrying the baby."

"It's not me, I swear. I don't know who that is . . . What is happening?"

"Excuse me a moment." Dolby rose to confer with a third officer who'd knocked on the door.

In the brief moments when he had his back turned, Billie hid her phone under the counter and shot another text to Tyler. Then one officer took Dolby's place and continued to pummel her with questions about her whereabouts, her marriage, her state of mind, until she couldn't take it anymore.

"Wait," she begged. "Just stop for a minute." She pressed her hand against the air between them.

Dolby moved behind the officer, looking like a tiger who knew he was about to snare his prey.

"Can we be logical for a second? I mean, think about it, it's not even plausible for me to have taken the baby at ten fifteen and then come back here at ten forty-five asking for her."

"People return to the scene of the crime all the time," the officer said. Billie didn't like the way his eyes narrowed when he spoke to her.

"Somebody would actually do that in a situation like this?"

"There are sick people in this world, Ms. Campbell." Dolby's lip curled into a sinister sneer.

"What would I even have done with the baby in thirty minutes?"

"Seems to be what we're attempting to determine, isn't it?" The officer was shifty—the kind of cop who'd go for the jugular and not let up until he got what he wanted.

"You really believe I would take a newborn and leave her helpless somewhere?" It was more Billie trying to comprehend it than a question.

After they ran the video the ninth time, she wedged herself between Dolby and the monitor, looking so closely she could have licked the screen. She pointed at the woman, whose back angled toward the camera. "See, that woman is rounder in shape, and I think shorter."

"Nah, it's you." The officer glared at her. "Why don't you just admit it, Ms. Campbell?" He posed his bulky six-foot frame over her in a powerful and intimidating stance. "Perhaps we should continue this at the station."

"What are you talking about? Am I being charged with something?" Billie looked from one person to another. "Do I need my lawyer?"

Do they know? All Billie could think of was a certain folder on her computer. She'd been clever to shred the signed copy of the fake home study she'd written for herself and Tyler, but she never thought to delete the original drafts. And with her proficient note-taking skills, they could find the logs she'd kept from her calls with the adoption attorney she'd hired to contact Madison and Steve. A fresh wave of perspiration took hold along with a gripping sense that the world was toppling in on her.

A startling, heavy knock on the door made Billie flinch. The third officer returned, this time with the intern she recognized from the maternity floor. The young girl looked far more despondent now as her eyes nervously flitted across each face in the room—until they settled on Billie.

Chief Dolby and the officers seemed displeased when the intern shook her head.

"No, it wasn't her," the intern said.

After a quick call to the interrogating officer's superior, Billie was told she was still a person of interest, but they weren't going to charge her yet.

"This isn't over," the officer said. He pinched her elbow as he walked her back to the main room. If he meant to be menacing, he'd succeeded. Billie speed-dialed Tyler's cell again, her breath coming in short, rapid gusts, then clicked end call. She took a fist of ice from the soda cooler and held it to her neck.

Billie made another call to her supervisor to report the video.

"The police are going to have to speak to the birth parents and their families," Jay said.

"Oh, God." It was an unbearable factor she had suppressed. When they first informed her of the disappearance, she'd hoped that Madison had changed her mind and come back for the baby. But the hospital execs shot the theory down. For one, the nurse on duty had met Madison, Steve, and their families, so none of them were suspects. Two, there was no motive since Madison was still legally the infant's mother, and the baby could be discharged to her care.

"Has someone notified them yet?" Billie asked.

"No. But as their liaison to Burkhead, you should be there when they talk to Madison and Steve."

Everything in Billie's core wanted to crumble. She didn't feel capable of handling such an encounter. Those kids were already dealing with tremendous grief, and now she was going to slice them in half. She wasn't up to the task of breaking their hearts any deeper.

Billie expected everyone would project their anger onto her. But she understood her responsibility; she was a professional. She had no choice.

As she approached her car, she paused to watch the sun, which had begun its shift toward the western horizon. She fumbled to start the ignition. Unable to control the tremors in her fingers, Billie gripped the wheel as tight as possible. Everything felt shaky, and her neck muscles twinged.

"Fuck you, Tyler!" she screamed. Sobs superseded the anger. "Help me."

A shadow crept over her window, and her heart stopped at the hard knock that quickly followed. She recognized the man waiting by her car door as one of the plainclothes detectives who'd been inside the hospital. To Billie, he was just a gray blob: gray complexion, gray hair, gray eyebrows, gray stubble, gray tweed blazer.

"Detective Sam Walton." He stuck his hand through the window after she rolled it down.

She folded her arms across her chest and threw him a discerning glance.

"All right. I get it." He chuckled amicably. "They put you through it up there," he said, and thumbed in the hospital's direction.

"Is there something you want from me?" Billie asked.

"I'd like to give you a ride to the house. I'm heading there anyway, and it hardly seems like a good idea for you to walk into the fire alone."

"You're watching out for me? Hard to believe. Do I have a choice here?"

Detective Walton shrugged like an innocent child. "The family lives just a short drive away. I'll bring you back to your car afterward. On my word."

* *

Billie was grateful Walton drove an unmarked car, and she could sit in the passenger seat rather than in the back, behind a criminal's cage. Nevertheless, she felt like a villain. The conversation with Madison, Steve, and their parents was going to be more horrendous than was imaginable.

Billie pulled a honey-menthol throat lozenge from her bag. She kept it resting on her tongue, hoping the vapors would clear her sinuses and help slow her breathing.

When Walton eased the car into a toll lane and opened the window, Billie welcomed the blustery air. She listened to the low-pitched sound from the cars zipping through the E-Z Pass lanes, frustrated the police car didn't have a pass. As their car crept forward, she smelled oily fumes and felt the jacked-up bass from a stereo nearby. She tried to find patience in the rhythmic sound of tossed coins swirling in the baskets and down the pipes echoing from the vehicles ahead. As he accelerated on the other side of the toll, Walton closed the window, which left a stark silence.

Walton pulled to the curb of a residential street and shut off the engine a few minutes later. The news she was about to deliver to Madison and Steve weighed even more on her.

"With the work you do, I'm sure you've had to deliver bad news before." He turned his head and waited for Billie to nod. "Do it all the time in my line of work. Been twenty-five years and I've never gotten used to it." He looked at her the way her grandfather did when she was little and had a bad day. "It's going to be difficult," the detective said, "but I've got you covered." Walton got out of the squad car and stretched his back. Then he gestured Billie toward the brutal but unavoidable conversation.

The first assault came as they entered the Westons' living room and found the hospital representatives already settled into the furniture. Steve was huddling in a corner, stewing in silence. Madison was pacing by a bay window, savagely twisting her ear. By their gaunt faces and the red welts around Madison's and Steve's eyes, it was obvious the team had already revealed the crisis. The hospital attorney was quick to defend their presence.

"As the legal parents of Baby Girl Quinn, it's our obligation to inform them of the emergency."

Madison, tortured and full of hormones, lunged toward Billie with palpable anger.

"We trusted you! You were supposed to take care of her. How could you let this happen?" she shrieked. The veins in her forehead bulged. The gorgeous blue light in her eyes had faded to a dusky blue powder.

Madison's mother rushed to her side, and her daughter collapsed into her outstretched arms.

Billie didn't stop Madison or her parents from berating her. It was what they needed, and she was positive she would've done the same.

Detective Walton's key chain jangled as he pulled it out of his pocket to unlock his car. "I know it doesn't feel like it," he said, "but you handled yourself pretty well in there."

"I guess."

"Tell me something. Why do you think Steve's parents weren't here?"

"They live a little ways out, so maybe they're on their way. From what I understand, they haven't been too involved."

"How's that?"

"Steve's mom is fervently against the plan for adoption." Billie reached for the passenger door handle and gulped. She got into Walton's car and studied his pensive expression. "You don't think she was the one who took the baby, do you?"

"Everyone's a suspect until they're not."

Billie felt the undercurrent of accusation in his tone. She clipped the seat belt together, feeling every knot and kink in her shoulders. He'd already started the car, and she wanted to get as far away as she could. Walton waited to speak until they were back on the highway.

"You been in adoption a long while?" he asked.

"Since grad school. Only job I've ever had."

"Must be tough work, especially for someone who's infertile."

If Billie had been in the driver's seat, she would have slammed the brakes and fishtailed into the median. And yet she felt like she had.

"It . . . I . . . What are you suggesting?"

"I guess I'm just wondering how far would someone go to be a mother?"

Billie's ears buzzed from the shock coursing through her after Walton's supposedly innocent question. When they got to the hospital lot, she got into her car with trembling hands and started the engine. He followed her back downtown, and every time she dared to glance in her rearview mirror during the long, insufferable drive, he seemed to look right back at her.

The agency lobby was chaotic with police who wrote on flip pads while questioning miscellaneous people Billie couldn't identify. Then she caught sight of Rita flicking her head toward the executive's door behind her big desk.

Billie's heels clipped Morse code as she sped through the lobby. She looked eagerly at Rita.

"Nothing. I'm sorry," Rita said. "No updates on the baby, and no calls from Tyler."

Paige, their supervisor, and the agency's legal team were already in Executive Director Swanson's office when Billie stepped in.

"Has there been any news? Do they know who did this?" The mournful expressions around her were answer enough.

"Have a seat," Director Swanson said. "We're trying to gather more information to assist in the investigation. Is it possible," she asked, "for one of your clients to have done this?"

"Anything's possible," Billie replied. "I can't think of anyone we've worked with who looks similar to me. Certainly none with any connection to this baby. I don't know. It's hard to think."

A knock at the office door brought Sam Walton and a fresh wave of doom.

"Our conversations with agency staff have been fruitful," he said. "It seems that on several occasions, people observed a woman, average height, thick glasses, messy brown hair . . . Someone used the word 'shabby.' The woman in question seemed nervous and not likely a client since they only saw her outside the premises." He referred to his notes. "One of the home health aides, named Rosa, gave a similar description. Said one time she thought the woman was following a couple of college-age kids—the female had dark hair, bangs, and looked pregnant."

Billie tried to concentrate through the static whirring in her head as he continued. There was a rustling in the room as discomfort and confusion generated a renewed sense of alarm.

Paige gave Billie a side-eye and mouthed, "Tell him."

"Something in particular on your mind there?" Walton asked.

"I think someone's been watching my house," Billie stammered. "There were cigarette stubs by the curb, footprints a couple of times.

And now . . ." She could hear the hysterics rising in her voice. The colors of the room distorted and swirled like the spin art toy she'd had as a child. Paige pressed a warm hand on her back. "My husband hasn't answered my calls. I don't know where he is."

"I'll get a patrol car to your address right away."

FORTY
Tyler

Tyler's foot slipped from the brake as another Amber Alert pierced his hangover. He pushed his sunglasses back up his nose after the Lexus's abrupt halt. The quick flash of light made his eyes ache. The persistent sound continued from his cell. Watching the taillights in the gridlock ahead, he fished inside his briefcase to silence the noise.

Drivers leaned on their horns. Red and blue flashing police lights flickered in the rearview mirror. Tyler watched an ambulance fly along the Massachusetts Turnpike's icy, narrow edge, followed by a tow truck with yellow-orange flashers. Whatever was going on ahead, he and the other snow-dusted vehicles were going to be stalled for a long while.

The jazz on the radio he'd put on to subdue his growing frustration was interrupted by an announcer's grave voice delivering the headline: "An unknown female abducted an infant from St. Monica's Hospital earlier this morning. Police are asking anyone with information to contact authorities."

Tyler hoped his wife didn't get stuck in a lockdown. He knew one of Billie's clients was at the hospital located somewhere near Westborough. She'd worked with plenty of birth mothers in the past, but this particular case had consumed her. Billie had even mentioned wistful daydreams of adopting the woman's baby herself. He feared the pressures of dealing with their own infertility was getting to her.

After he parked Moe's car near his own reserved space, Tyler moved listlessly to his office building.

"Good to see you, Mr. Scott," the building security guard said.

Tyler responded with a feeble smile, the voice barely registering. His focus was on the burden he felt, knowing Billie would find a way to take the kidnapping chaos personally. She'd sermonized often enough about the ways stress disrupts ovulation. Something about the hormones getting screwed up, misfiring, and preventing conception. Again. But with Billie's emotions all over the place, she'd flip about some baby going missing.

Marla gave him a sharp and disparaging look when he stopped in front of her desk. Her role went well beyond support staff, but her judgmental frown had a rare edge.

"What? Can't a man take some time off? It happens."

"Not with you, it doesn't. I won't ask, and I don't want to know."

"Marla! Where's your mind at?"

"It's with your wife." Her barbed glare darkened as she pushed some case files toward him. "She's been calling all day, and I don't like the way she sounds. There's some kind of emergency at work."

He dug in his briefcase for his cell, still powered off from when the Amber Alert blasted. He fumbled to turn it on as he sped into his office. It took forever for the screen to light up, but it blew up with countless news alerts about the kidnapping when it did. Then came a rapid succession of calls and text notification bubbles. He'd missed twenty-three calls and voicemails from Billie. She'd sent him fifty-two texts. The last message lingered on his home screen: WTF? Where r u? Cop questioning me. Suspect. Tyler tried to read it out loud to be sure he understood, but he was panting too hard, his tongue heavy. *Jesus, Billie, what have you done?* With shaking fingers, he kept hitting the wrong call back button. When he finally got it right, her voicemail was full. Adrenaline careened through him.

"Marla!"

"What's up?" She was already standing by the door.

"Call Donald Aster."

"The criminal defense attorney?"

"Yeah. Have him on standby. I'll contact him when I know what's going on."

"What *is* going on?"

"I'll be in touch as soon as I have an answer for you."

Tyler ran to the elevator. When his phone vibrated, he felt both nervous and relieved to hear from Billie. But the text bubble showed an unknown number: I need to see you now.

He dabbed his sweaty neck. How had the controlled routine of his life disintegrated? But he already knew the answer. He reached into his overcoat pocket and pulled out the photo that had triggered the landslide.

"Suzanne Neuman," he said under his breath. The sound of the false name Laura used back in August filled him with angst. He slipped the photo back into his pocket and stepped into the elevator, silently seething as it stopped for passengers and slowed them down. Droplets of sweat landed on his cell phone screen as he rushed into the crowded lobby and dialed Billie's office number.

FORTY-ONE
Billie

Billie dragged her heavy legs through the lobby and then to her office to retrieve the additional files the executive director requested. She was growing more incoherent; half of what was said to her evaporated seconds later. Sobs burst out when she approached her desk and saw the disarray left by whoever had rifled through her things. It was only a matter of time before the police came back with a search warrant. Her long bout of tears had left her eyes swollen and stinging. She found Halls lozenges in her desk drawer and popped one into her mouth. Trembling inside, Billie turned on her computer to search for and delete any evidence implicating her in the infant's kidnapping. She almost passed out when the intercom buzzed.

"It's him," Rita said.

"I called your cell, but your voicemail is full," Tyler said. "What's going on? Why are they questioning you? Why would you be a suspect?"

"Where have you been?" she wailed. "I needed you!"

"What's happened, Billie? Are you hurt?"

"I went to pick up the baby, and she was gone."

"I can tell you're scared, but it's hard to understand you. It sounded like you said the baby was gone. The kidnapped baby on the news isn't your client's preemie, is it?"

"Gone! As in . . . someone took her! A woman. She pretended to be me!"

"This doesn't make sense. Who would do that? Why?"

"The police are investigating, the hospital, the agency . . . It's just . . . mayhem."

"I've already left the office and am getting the car. I'll be to you in fifteen."

"No, you can't. I mean, I want that more than anything, but you have to go home. The detectives are waiting there for you. They think the person who's been watching our house is related to this."

"Jesus! I'm on my way. I'll call you from there."

FORTY-TWO
Laura

Laura parked in the shady corner spot on the least occupied level at the downtown garage, changed her clothes, and stuffed the scrubs under her seat. She used the newspapers and old T-shirts that littered her car to cover the slightly open windows. "Mommy will be back before you wake up," she whispered.

"The usual?" the hot dog vendor asked. He slid his hands along his grease-stained apron and threw a bun on the grill.

The recognition made Laura feel like a welcome part of the crowd.

"Little late for you today, eh?" the vendor said, handing her the food.

She took the hot dog, ketchup only, and can of soda to her favorite bench behind the cart. It was covered with a light dusting of snow she brushed off. She'd been coming to the spot for months, but she wouldn't need to anymore, because today was the day she was getting her happy ever after. Her excitement must have been visible because, for the first time, passersby smiled in her direction.

This morning, Tyler had finally texted her and invited her to lunch at a nice restaurant. A date! The idea made her giddy. Laura's thoughts went straight to her new outfits she could wear and the way she'd style her hair. But the reservation at Triste Cucina was supposed to be tomorrow, not today. She texted him back to say she needed to see him now.

Tyler was running with his phone against his ear when she saw him come out of the building across the street. She checked her cell; he wasn't calling her.

"I don't get it," she said aloud. "My text was clear." Knowing he wouldn't see her, she jumped up, kicking over the soda she'd placed by her feet, and ran to the curb.

"Tyler!" She waved both her arms with force. It was impossible for him to hear her above the city traffic. She lost sight of him when a recycling truck pulled in front of her, its exhaust asphyxiating. When the truck backed up, its beeping grew louder as it rumbled past her. The sound mimicked the high-pitched hospital monitors long ago, right before they'd anesthetized her young body. Laura pressed a hand over her accelerating heartbeat. *Look at me and squeeze my hand.* Her throat tightened. *Keep your eyes on me—that's it, breathe.* "Mama?" *You're doing great, pumkins. Okay, count backward with me, from a hundred . . . ninety-nine . . . ninety-eight.* The noxious, high-pitched sound faded. A smelly truck in reverse, that's all it took to send her back twenty years to a hospital only fifty miles away.

Her phone timer jolted her. The half hour she'd allotted herself had ended. With little time to spare, she grabbed her purse from the bench, almost tripping over someone's Shih Tzu.

"Curb your damn dog," she cursed as she continued running the two blocks to the self-park garage. When she exited the littered stairwell onto the vacant floor, Laura checked to be sure her car was undisturbed. The exquisite cargo in the old Rudy's Plumbing box on the back seat floor seemed unscathed, although a tad overheated.

"He should have looked for me harder." Her words floated toward the windshield as she drove. "But he'll come, I know he will. Don't you worry. He wants us to be together."

She flipped a finger at the truck driver looking down at her from his cab. "What are you looking at?"

She took a deep breath. "It's going to be okay." She reminded herself to stay calm. "We're all going to be crazy happy."

Laura merged onto Route 93 North without a destination or a plan. She kept driving, keeping the windows low enough to circulate air in the car, but high enough for the wind not to overwhelm her. The sky was a soft powder blue, and the sun glinted off the tall glass buildings. This time of year, boats and crew teams practicing in their long, thin boats no longer dotted the Charles River. The rippling water, devoid of life, had a calming effect. When the cityscape was on the cusp of suburbia, she saw a motel sign off the highway. The place looked run-down enough to allow the privacy she required.

With the baby in her arms, Laura tossed a FastBurger's bag onto the bed, locked the motel room door, and pulled the shades. She kept the baby snuggled close, listening to the soft purring of the infant's breath as she leaned against the bed pillows. For the first time in her life, she felt whole.

FORTY-THREE
Tyler

Tyler was halfway between the city and their home when his insides began churning. The world wasn't making any sense and was clouding his head. His car swerved, inciting an angry horn that blasted past him. He pulled onto the shoulder and pressed the hazard button. The car rocked as each vehicle whizzed past. Tyler took out the photo and balanced it on the steering wheel, creating a focal point for concentrating. He needed to sort this out logically, as if his life were a legal case, but it seemed too disjointed. He attempted to make it less abstract. Fact: Someone was watching his house. Fact: A baby was missing. Query: Why did the police think they were related? And then there was the other bomb that was exploding, the one that had emerged from his past. Fact: Laura was back in his life. Fact: She'd lied about who she was. Possible fact: Laura had a baby. Possible fact: The baby was his. Query: Could he believe anything she said?

Tyler pressed his palms against his eyes. He was sorry for what Laura experienced when they were kids, for what she'd been through. Even if her story wasn't true, she was definitely messed up by whatever had happened. At the café yesterday, her unnatural, haunted look gave him the impression she thought he had feelings for her, as though she didn't realize they'd barely known each other, or that decades had passed. He could tell she had a warped grip on reality. Adding her oddities and comments to everything else Collin reported, it was more than possible Laura could be the one lurking around their property. He straightened himself in the seat, turned the hazard light off and his blinker on, and pressed the gas pedal until he was traveling well above the posted speed limit.

Emergency vehicles cluttered his street, forcing him to park down the block. A uniformed officer corralled him as he scrambled toward his lawn.

"I live here." Tyler's breaths turned into winter clouds. "It's my house."

"ID."

Placing it in the officer's open hand, he felt much older than the picture on his license, taken only two years before. The officer radioed his credentials to empty air. In the endless wait for the broken static voice to reply, he watched the police crisscrossing his property like ants searching for food. Some of them were fingerprinting the windows. Drifting clouds blocked the sun, and as the wind picked up, Tyler thought there was a scent of danger.

The radio voice spit out something unintelligible, permitting him to enter his own home. He sprinted to the front door, where a detective was spewing commands from the portico.

"Have you found anything?" Tyler asked. "Is my wife safe? Do you know why this is happening?"

"Mr. Scott, we're all anxious for answers. My guys are still gathering information. Now that you're here, we'd like to have a look inside too. After that, you and I can have a sit-down."

The suggestion felt ominous. Did they find something? Had they somehow gotten into his texts? The lawyer in him tried to cloak his distress.

“Is there somewhere out of the way you can wait?” the detective asked.

Tyler fumed at being pushed aside. This was his life. He’d never been good at being helpless, but he was sensible. He had to let them do their job.

“Is my study okay?”

“That’ll do. Appreciate your cooperation.”

FORTY-FOUR
Billie

Billie inhaled the silence and safety of her small office. It lasted for a mere second before the terror overtook her again. Every hour that passed meant one less hour the baby might be found alive. She was so out of it she couldn't remember who mentioned the morbid statistics, yet the warning played over and over as the minutes ticked on.

She dialed Tyler, hoping the police at the house had found some answers. It seemed insane that all of this was somehow connected to her personally. That someone had been watching her and took one of her babies. It made no sense. Why would someone want to do this to her?

"The cops collected some cigarette butts and anything else not washed away by the rain. They're going to keep a patrol car out front," Tyler said. "Are you doing all right? What's happening there?"

"It's going to be a late night. With the baby in jeopardy, no one plans on leaving."

Billie's supervisor tried several times to get her to go home, arguing, "You're no good to anyone if you don't take care of yourself." It was a social worker's creed, but she wouldn't budge. The executives and legal reps, and now members of the board, were having constant round-robins behind closed doors. The cops were reinterviewing every member of Madison's and Steve's families, hospital employees, and Burkhead staff. There was nothing to do but wait. For the last few hours, she'd been sitting in her desk chair, staring out the window.

The intercom buzzed. Her arm felt heavy as she reached over and pressed the speakerphone button.

"I'm in the file room," Paige said. "You need to see this."

Billie stood in the doorway of the unused storage closet that her department had converted to house old records. Paige was pacing and hyperventilating.

"What's going on?"

"I had a birth mother who gave a child up for adoption twenty years ago. She left permission to contact and this letter." Paige displayed an envelope above her shoulder.

"Why does this matter right now?"

"I was keeping myself busy doing some filing, and she came to mind. It took me a while to locate her record, but I found her case number in the index and pulled it. Look."

Paige pulled Billie's shirt until they were shoulder to shoulder. A file compiled of subsequent records lay on the open cabinet drawer, which served as a temporary desktop.

Billie scanned the first file: Laura Bennett: Birth mother. Then she looked at the tab on the adjunct folder attached to it: Baby Bennett D.O.B. July 14, 1992. And a third folder: Sally and Milton Weston: Adoptive parents.

Still in a fog, the meaning eluded Billie until Paige pulled out the finalized adoption decree from the baby's folder. It was the first official document that legalized the baby's new adoptive name: Madison Weston.

"Holy shit!" Billie said. "Can I see the letter?"

"Hey, that's confidential!" Paige yelled when she slit the envelope.

Billie unfolded the letter. The writing looked like grade school handwriting, but before she read it, she felt something else in the envelope and shook it out. A photo dropped onto the file drawer, and a deep guttural sound escaped from the base of her throat.

"Billie! What is it?"

Billie could no longer feel Paige's shoulder pressing against hers. She was only aware of a cold tingle moving along her scalp. "I've seen this photo before," she whispered.

Paige picked it up. "How is that possible?"

"Bring the file downstairs to the director and call Detective Walton! Tell them about it." She yanked the photo away from Paige.

"Hey! Leave the picture!"

But Billie was already halfway down the hall. After grabbing her coat and bag, she barreled down the stairs instead of waiting for the elevator. Outside, she tried to hold the phone steady as she hustled to the parking garage. Tyler answered on the first ring.

"What's going on? Did they find the baby? Is it okay?"

"Who is she?" Billie could barely hear her own devastated voice.

"What are you talking about?"

"The photo I found in your suit pocket. What the fuck is going on? No more lies. If you know something, Tyler, you need to tell me."

"You're right. There are some unimaginable things you need to know," he said. "I'll explain everything when you get home."

Billie wasn't sure how to prepare herself to hear the worst things possible: he didn't love her anymore, he'd had an affair, he was leaving her. Though her chest was on fire and her breaths were strained, she'd somehow kept moving up the cement stairs and made it to the ninth floor. "I'll be there in thir . . ." The phone slipped from her hand. "You!"

FORTY-FIVE
Tyler

"Billie? Billie?" Tyler kept repeating her name after she'd yelled. He heard a clattering sound like she'd dropped the phone before it went dead. Praying she'd call back, he used the house phone to call the number of the detective who'd questioned him earlier.

"She's in trouble. My wife. Something's happened to her." He could feel his words jumbling as he tried to explain. "Please hurry." He felt more frantic with each question the detective asked him.

"The patrol officers stationed outside will stay in the house with you until Detective Walton arrives."

Tyler nearly banged into the wall when he heard the doorbell and rushed to the foyer. For the past fifteen minutes, the officers seemed unaffected sitting at the kitchen table while he'd paced feverishly between them and the front door. He let Detective Walton in, and they went to the living room to talk. Tyler sat stiffly on the couch, and the detective pulled a side chair close to him.

"One of our units found Billie's car in the parking garage," Walton said. "The front and back doors were open."

"Bil . . . Billie?"

"No sign of her."

Tyler heard a groan and realized it came from him.

"Her cell was on the ground. This was near it." Walton tapped his cell phone screen and turned it for Tyler to see. "Mean anything to you?"

"Yes," he said faintly. He dropped his head into his hands. "I need to show you something." Detective Walton followed him into the study.

Tyler rifled through the compartments in his briefcase, then snatched his jacket from the back of his chair. After fishing in his pocket, he raised a duplicate photo before him. Panic and confusion choked him as he gasped and made small high-pitched noises. For a second, he worried he was having a seizure.

Detective Walton's forehead creased, and his brows knit together when Tyler passed it to him.

"I'm not sure what's going on, exactly, or how all of our lives have collided," Tyler said.

"How 'bout we start at the beginning," Walton said.

"A woman came to my office back in August. It turned out she was someone I knew in eighth grade." He cleared his throat. "She said she had a baby when she was thirteen." He pointed to the photo. "This baby. And . . ." Tyler didn't think he'd ever stammered and sweat the way he was. "And she put the baby up for adoption. And . . ."

"And? Go on."

"She claims the baby was mine. Collin Frost, my firm's investigator, did some digging for me and, while I still don't trust the woman's story, it's plausible."

Walton let out a long whistle like a missile dropping. "And you say you've seen her? Can you describe her?"

"Disheveled, skittish, a bit heavyset."

"Would you say average height, unkempt, with messy brown hair?"

"How do you know that?"

"Tell me something. In your opinion, do you think she's deranged, like capable of stealing and harming a child?"

"I want to say no, but I don't really know her anymore. She did seem unstable. What are you getting at?"

Detective Walton flipped the photo onto the desk and thumped it with his finger. "What we have learned, Tyler, is this photo is of one of Billie's clients when she was a baby. She is also the birth mother whose baby was wearing this exact outfit when she was stolen this morning."

"Oh my God." It hurt to breathe, and Tyler didn't know where to look. "Wait. Wait. So, this photo." He lifted it off the table and waved it in the air. "This baby is the baby she placed for adoption? When I was thirteen? The baby's twenty? And this baby . . . my baby," he couldn't grasp that part yet, "this baby in the photo, just had her baby abducted?"

"Seems like."

"Jesus. Do you think this woman took both Billie and the baby? She's not going to hurt them, right?"

"She have a name?"

"Laura. Laura Bennett. Also goes by Anne Neuman."

"How did she contact you?" Detective Walton asked.

"The first time was at my office, like I said. But she texts—from a blocked number."

"When did you hear from her last?"

"This morning. I messaged to set up a lunch for tomorrow. She replied, wanting to meet right then, but with everything going on,

I didn't pay attention. This is all my fault. If I'd texted back, Billie would be home safe right now."

"I'll need to borrow your cell to go through the texts."

"Frost can help too," Tyler said. "He knows her background and where she lives."

"You've filled in some important blanks and verified what we already suspected. There's a squad at her address, and we already issued an APB."

"You'll find Billie. Won't you?"

The police and FBI wasted no time setting themselves up in the house in case some communication or ransom call came through. Uniformed officers with weapons strapped to their hips congregated in the kitchen. Billie would've hated seeing guns in her home. Sergeants, lieutenants, captains were all a blur swarming their living and family rooms. Walkie talkies squawked, constant chatter hummed, and endless used coffee cups and pizza boxes decorated every flat surface. Tyler attempted to tune out the nervousness to focus on Billie's rescue, but nothing could quell his anxiety.

FORTY-SIX
Laura

"She'll stop crying if you change her diaper," Billie said.

"Shut your trap. I know how to take care of my baby. You just stay in that chair." If she kept holding the baby, the woman would do anything she said.

Laura could tell Billie was deliciously terrified when she first got in the car. But for most of the ride up to New Hampshire she kept talking like they were friends and asking questions very much like stupid Stanley would have. The woman was trying to trick her to keep Tyler to herself. Laura made sure not to turn her back while she opened kitchen cabinets and drawers in the Scotts' vacation home. "This will do." She lifted a roll of duct tape, placed the baby on the couch, and secured Billie's wrists to the arms of the chair.

At five in the morning, Laura turned the lights on in the family room and took pleasure in watching Billie flinch and blink. She didn't look so perfectly pretty after sleeping tied to the chair. Laura laid the baby on the couch as she'd done a few hours before and went to the kitchen.

"Do you think she'll be safer if you put her on a blanket on the floor?" Billie asked.

"Stop talking." Laura lifted a shiny, clean carving knife, and as she got closer, Billie paled and pressed back so hard she almost tipped the chair. The knife easily slit the tape around her wrists. "Stand up." Laura pulled Billie's arms behind her back and retaped them together. "Let's go."

"Don't leave the baby there," Billie said. "Let me help, please."

"I'm her mother. I can take care of her myself."

"You did have a baby, Laura."

"How do you know my name?"

"Because you had a little girl, just like this one. She looked a lot like this baby, I'm sure, even wore this same outfit. But this isn't her."

"She is. She's mine and Tyler's." Laura could feel her anger rising as the woman tried to confuse her. "You need to be quiet once and for all." She tore another strip of tape, placed it over Billie's mouth, and pulled her into the backyard. The bitter cold embraced them in the strange and quiet stillness of the dawn hour. With the black winter sky blinding her, Laura gripped Billie's arm tightly as they trod through the deep snow to the boat shed.

The weekend Billie came here alone, she'd unknowingly shown Laura the fake rock where they hid the key. She hadn't expected to travel so far when she followed Billie that morning. She'd slept in her car and snuck into the lake house for food and warmth whenever Billie went out. Laura roamed each room, daydreaming about Tyler. She also swiped cash from Billie's wallet, which came in handy when she almost ran out of gas on the drive home.

"Sit." She pushed Billie on the floor and rolled more tape around her ankles. "I won't let you take Tyler and my baby away from me."

The woman's muted sounds of protest annoyed her, and those damn tears could loosen the tape around her mouth. Didn't matter. No one was around this lake this far into December. Billie could scream as loud as she wanted.

Back inside the house, Laura scooped up the baby and changed her diaper as best she could.

"We've taken care of the problem, haven't we?" She kissed the baby's feet. "Nothing can stop us from being with Daddy now. Isn't that right?" She lifted the baby and went to the kitchen to make a sugar-water mixture, which she soaked up with a cloth for the baby to suckle on. She'd learned to tend to some baby animals this way in vet school.

Still cradling the contented baby to her, Laura went into a bedroom and got comfortable on the large bed. She was humming when she took the Scotts' phone off the nightstand and dialed her mother.

"Are you okay? You haven't been answering or responding to my messages. Are you home?" her mother asked. "I've been worried. And then your boss called me. I guess he got my number from your emergency contact sheet. He said you've been fired? What's happening, Laura? Are you sick?"

"No, Ma, everything is just as it should be."

"Your voice is funny. What's going on?"

"I wish Mama Sue were here. She'd be so happy."

"I miss her too."

"Maybe we'll see her soon."

"Are you sure you're all right? You sound—I don't know, you don't sound like yourself."

"I've never been better. Everything's the way it was always supposed to be."

"I'll call you and check on you later, okay?"

"All right," Laura said.

"You'll answer the phone, right?"

"Ma?"

"Yes, honey?"

"She's so pretty, isn't she?"

"Who, Laura?"

"Thank you for making her sweater. Tyler's going to love it too."

She was careful to place the phone back on the night table, so it didn't clunk and wake her baby. It wasn't long before she dozed off.

Laura woke when the baby, still secure on her chest, wriggled. The little sweetheart had been quiet through the deepest void of the night.

"You smell so good, baby, yes you do!"

She fed the baby with the last bottle of formula from the hospital and burped her by gently patting her back. She held the warm, gurgling baby close to her bosom, with the soft head nuzzled under her chin where it had always belonged. Laura changed the baby before their drive back to Boston. There were barely enough diapers to get through the rest of the day, but she'd be with Tyler by then anyway, so she wasn't worried. She'd texted him last night to make sure he'd show up for their date today. For once, he'd replied right away. Knowing they would take care of the baby together filled her with peace. She tucked the baby into the car seat she'd taken from Billie's SUV and kissed the baby's head.

"We're going to see your daddy for lunch," she said. "Then we're going to come back and live in this wonderful place together."

FORTY-SEVEN
Tyler

Detective Walton, Collin Frost, Tyler, and a slew of others he was too bleary to identify squished around the dining table. They'd been plotting and planning the sting operation throughout the night and considered every possible what-if scenario. The baby's safety was the number one priority. Billie's case seemed secondary. Their best theory was if they found one, they'd find the other. They were gambling with his wife's life, and it didn't sit well with Tyler, but it was the only hope he had to hold on to. He whispered Billie's mantra, "Strength, courage, heart," willing his words to reach her.

Hints of daylight made their way through the dining room windows. Soon they'd be leaving for Triste Cucina, where it would all take place. The house grew eerily silent when one agent raised her hand and snapped her fingers. The woman was talking on the phone, and Tyler felt the surge of anticipation as everyone waited for either the greatest or the worst news possible.

"We've got something," the agent said. "Officials spoke with Bennett's mother in Arizona. She received a call from her daughter and gave us the number from caller ID. It traces to a landline in New Hampshire. Local officials are on their way now. The name on the account comes up as Douglas Scott."

Tyler's skin went to ice as his heart seemed to stop pumping. He stood unsteadily, but when he reached for the back of the dining chair for support, it wobbled, causing him to lose his balance and fall backward. He had no idea who pulled him up, but he felt more coherent once he began reciting details about his family's house in Sunapee.

Someone brought in a cache of what looked like toys. The lead agent sorted through the kits.

"Dunning," he called out. "Let's get this wire set up on Mr. Scott."

Tyler tried to set aside his debilitating fears and focus on Billie and the baby's safety. He was fully aware of the dangers he'd volunteered for and couldn't fail them.

Walton and Dunning taped the wire beneath his shirt.

"Let's get a test going. Speak naturally," Walton instructed.

"This better work," Tyler said.

"We'll be able to hear everything. And our teams will be well-placed and ready as soon as you give the word."

"Got it," Tyler said.

Walton put a firm hand on his shoulder. "You can do this."

With well-choreographed grace, the law enforcement teams moved out of the house, and their motorcade headed downtown to Tyler's lunch date.

They'd been on the road for ten minutes when one agent in the front seat turned around. "No sign of Bennett or the baby. But they may have found Billie."

"Is she ali . . ." Tyler couldn't say it. His imagination went wild with agonizing scenarios of the horrible things she could have endured.

"No word yet. I'm sorry."

The restaurant felt ghostly without the typical oil and spice aroma that usually filled the place when Tyler went there. He thought about all the times he'd come with Billie, and the way she always savored the hot garlic bread when the server brought it to their table. He yearned for her to be standing next to him with her soft hand safe in his.

Over the two hours it took to prep the restaurant for their imminent operation, as agents disguised themselves as waitstaff and diners, Tyler was told, "We'll let you know," whenever he asked for updates about Billie. It could only mean the answer was grim. He felt like lead as someone rechecked his wire and instructed him on the script he needed to follow.

"Okay, people, we've got eyes on her vehicle," another FBI agent said. "T minus five. Let's do this."

FORTY-EIGHT
Laura

The Triste Cucina waiter seated Laura at the reserved table. She cradled the baby and waited for Tyler to join them.

She could tell from the tilt of his head and his shining eyes that it pleased him to see her. He smiled the same beautiful smile he'd always shared with her. She wanted to grab him around the neck and squeeze him but stayed in the chair to keep the baby safe. Instead, she reached for his hand and pulled him closer.

"Come meet our daughter."

"She's beautiful," Tyler said.

Laura could feel a rapturous light emanate from her. She held the infant while he inspected the baby's fingers and toes. The baby closed her miniscule fingers around his while making sweet suckling sounds with her teensy mouth.

"It looks like you've been taking wonderful care of her."

That delighted Laura into a bout of giggles.

"She's such a good baby, even slept most of the night."

Tyler pulled a chair next to her, and she leaned into his side. She angled the baby so he could see her. Laura felt his warm breath as he reached in front of her chest to stroke the baby's face. Her breasts tingled as his arm lingered, barely touching her.

"We're going to have a wonderful life, aren't we?" Her eyes clung to Tyler's.

"May I hold her?" His gaze swaddled her like a cozy blanket.

He reached his hands around the tiny bundle, and releasing the baby to him felt like the most natural thing in the world. The baby was sucking on her lips and mewing in his arms. The sleeve of her crocheted sweater had scrunched in his fingers. Laura focused her gaze on the translucent pink skin of the baby's forearm. She blinked and shook her head, then took a huge breath and squinted.

"It's not there," she murmured, "there's no birthmark." She grabbed the edge of the table to stop swaying.

"It's a go!" Tyler said.

Uniformed cops spilled into the restaurant and formed a wall around them. Tyler handed the baby to one of them, who quickly took her away.

"Give her to me!" Laura screamed. Someone squeezed her arm and lifted her out of her seat. Their grip tightened as she protested.

"You did a beautiful thing for our baby, Laura. You made sure she had a family who raised her and loved her the way she needed. You did good."

"Please, Tyler," she moaned. "Stop talking! I need our baby. And we can all be together."

"Our child, our daughter, is grown up now. Her name is Madison."

"I don't understand," she wailed. "I want my baby. They took our baby! Don't let them do that again, Tyler, don't, you can't. I can be her mother. I can take care of her."

"She's not ours." He set his hands on his hips and blew out a long breath. "But she is our grandchild."

"I'm sorry, so sorry," she whispered. She looked at Tyler, the adult, whose boyish cheeks had been replaced with a man's stubble and aged creases. The walls that had confined years of pain shattered as tears soaked her face.

"Where is Billie?" he asked.

Picturing the woman in the old, dark shed, Laura could almost feel the frigid air seeping through her bones.

"Please tell me."

She heard the agony in his voice and wanted to comfort him. She struggled to free her hands but stopped when she saw the anger in his eyes. Her heart pounded fiercely as a deep, ugly red seeped into his neck and face.

"What did you do to her?" Tyler lunged at her.

She shrank back against the officer holding her.

A policeman grabbed his elbow and spun him around. "That's enough, Mr. Scott. We've accomplished what we could here."

The man guarding Laura pulled her arms behind her until her shoulders pinched. He snapped a tight set of handcuffs onto her wrists. "Let's go."

Sobbing, she didn't resist when the hands gripping her pulled her outside the restaurant. Swirling red and blue lights reflected off the glass windows on the buildings behind them. The cop tightened his hold on her and turned her away as a woman rushed closer.

"I have to see her. She needs me." The woman's anxious plea matched the desperation in her eyes.

From the group of police behind her, Laura heard a deep authoritative voice say, "Let her go." Then, without warning, the hold on her loosened and Laura fell into her mother's arms. She could hear her mother's shushing, and the cyclical motion of the gentle hands on her back calmed her as they used to when she was a toddler.

"I'm so sorry." She kept her forehead resting on her mother's shoulder but wouldn't look up.

“Can you tell me how this happened?” her mother asked.

“I don’t know.” Her head gyrated against her mother. “I found her, Mommy, I found her.”

“Who, honey?”

“My baby. Only she wasn’t a baby anymore. And she went to the hospital, and I had to make sure she was okay.”

“Then what?”

“And I went to look in the nursery window, and then things got weird. My baby was there, all content and calm, in the pink sweater you made for her and the hat with Mama Sue’s flower. She’s beautiful, you know? And she smiled at me. And then . . .”

As Laura became agitated, the officer pressed his fingers deep into her skin.

“They were coming for the baby.” She finally looked up at her mother. “I wanted Mama Sue to tell me what to do, but I couldn’t find her. There was no time. I couldn’t let them take my baby. Not again.”

Her mom brushed her wet cheeks and then placed her palms against them. “It’s going to be okay. I’m here now,” she said. “You’re going to be okay. But honey, I need to know—did you hurt Tyler’s wife?”

FORTY-NINE
Billie

When they found her, Billie was cold and weak but stubbornly insisted on being taken to Tyler without a hospital evaluation. Now she stood within the semicircle of emergency vehicles surrounding the restaurant's facade. Watching Kathleen keep Laura steady elicited a raw craving for her own mother. But her attention was on the commotion stirring at the door. Someone grasped her forearm to stop her, but she freed herself and ran to the building when Tyler emerged.

He took her in his arms and lifted her off the ground. "Christ, I was so scared." He squeezed her tight. "You're really okay?" He carefully examined the bruises on her wrists and gingerly stroked the mark on her face left from the tape.

"I will be. What about you?"

"Am now." He put her down and held her out so he could see her. "You're filthy and smelly," he said, kissing her cheeks, her forehead, and her eyelids, "and I've never been happier to see you. I love you so much."

"I love you too," Billie said. Her voice trembled as she clutched his shirt and whispered, "How is the baby?"

"She's all right. Listen, before we go over there." Tyler scuffed his shoe on the pavement. "You should know, Laura thinks the baby is mine."

"She said as much."

"Well, not the baby, her mother. I thought my old friend John DeAngelo might've been the one, but he swears he was never with Laura. We're both going to do paternity tests, but it's pretty obvious I'm her father."

Billie put a finger to his lips. "It can wait."

"I should have told you." He let out a heavy sigh and shook his head. "I understand if you're upset with me."

"Ty, can we go see the baby?"

A uniformed officer waiting close by guided them to the ambulance where the baby was being examined. Tyler was permitted to hold her, and he stroked and cooed to the baby snug in his arm. "She's perfect," he whispered.

The only word Billie could find to describe his expression was wondrous. She wrapped an arm around his waist and gazed at the infant. They'd been through a lot together.

"She's an angel. Aren't you, sweetie pie?" Billie's voice had turned to that silly goochy-goo pitch people are reduced to when they're overwhelmed by cuteness. She could only smile when Tyler chuckled and kissed the top of her head before the paramedic took the baby back.

An unmarked sedan pulled into the mob of vehicles. Before the car came to a full stop, Madison, Steve, and the Westons jumped out and rushed to the rear of the ambulance. Even though she knew the police had already briefed them on all the details, Billie took Tyler's hand and withdrew as fast as she could. At the far end of the lot, Kathleen was talking calmly to Laura as she helped her daughter duck into the back seat of a squad car. A piece of Billie felt for Laura, who'd spent her life grieving for a child she wasn't able to parent. She looked over at Madison, the daughter whose life Laura had forever impacted by her long-ago choice. She ached to shield the young woman from any further heartbreak.

Walton was speaking with Madison and Steve, who exchanged a glance before Steve nodded and took Madison's place hovering over the baby and the paramedic. Madison seemed transfixed by the police car that was about to roll away and didn't notice when she walked past Billie. She hesitated, then managed the last step to the rear of the black-and-white. Kathleen, who was about to get in on the other side, eyed her over the roof. The half-open passenger window next to Laura allowed Madison to peer inside. Time seemed to stop for Billie, as did all the noise in the area. It was impossible to predict what Madison was going to do to Laura. Billie heard the officer's heavy boots moving in.

Madison reached into the window as Laura reached out and caressed the beautiful heart-shaped birthmark above her wrist. They remained hand in hand for a moment, taking in each other's essence, mirrored facial features, and coloring. When Madison released Laura's hand, she looked up, gave a half nod to Kathleen, and stepped back. Within seconds, the squad car drove off. The only movement came from a rental car accelerating behind them, driven by Grant, who'd flown in on the red-eye from Phoenix with Kathleen.

Madison stood unattended in the emptiness left behind by the squad car. Billie couldn't thwart the instinct to protect the young woman she'd become so fond of, even if her presence was unwanted. She approached Madison's side, intending to be silently supportive.

"Detective Walton told me what happened to you," Madison said. "I'm sorry. And I'm also sorry for the horrid things I said to you."

"You were scared and angry," Billie said. "I'm not sure I would have handled it as well as you if the situation were reversed. You're a mature and extraordinary young woman. Come," she implored, taking Madison's arm, "there's someone you should meet."

Billie steered Madison to a man who was watching their every move.

"This is Tyler, my husband."

Madison's eyes grew wide and moved quickly between Tyler and Billie. Her unasked question hung loudly in the air.

"This is your father," Billie said.

It felt lengthier than the actual few seconds before Tyler cleared his throat and tentatively hugged Madison. The more Billie watched their embrace, the more she saw the similarities; Tyler was patting his daughter's back with the same long fingers she had. Madison wasn't as tall, but they both had the same long legs. They both had reddish hair (though his had faded to a cinnamon brown), styled with a sweep across their foreheads. The resemblances were heartwarming.

When Madison stepped back, tears covered her face. Billie couldn't recall having ever seen Tyler cry before or struggle for words the way he was doing now. Their sobs combined with simultaneous laughs as they observed each other.

"Forgive me. I didn't know. I never knew." Tyler reached out and touched Madison's face as if he was trying to see her with his fingertips. "I never knew," he repeated. "All this time, I was a father. No one told me. I would've been there."

"You were there for me today," Madison said.

The two reached for each other again. Billie stayed to the side and let them have their moment. Her throat was dry, and she experienced a sense of bittersweetness she'd never had before. She felt her love and respect for Tyler deepening. At the same time, she felt more connected to Madison. She wasn't sure yet how she felt about her husband having a grown child, but if that were the case, Madison was the best choice. Although it wasn't clear to Billie if or how she'd fit in now.

As her husband and his daughter stood together, she became aware that the crowd of curious onlookers had thinned, and any unneeded emergency personnel had dispersed. She noticed Collin Frost emerge from a nearby stoop, hop onto his motorcycle, and ride off. Then Tyler pulled her to include her in the embrace with Madison. She was part of them too. When the huddle broke up, and they saw the blubbery mess they all were, the three laughed at each other.

"Hey," Madison said. "If my father is your husband, does that make us related?"

"I couldn't wish for anything nicer," Billie replied.

With the baby enfolded in his arm, Steve seemed uncertain as he neared their group.

"They think she's fine," he said, "maybe a bit dehydrated. They want to take her to the hospital for observation. I agreed on the condition that we're allowed to stay with her at all times."

"That was smart," Tyler said.

"Steve," Madison said, "this is my birth father."

It was typical for Steve to evaluate in his head before he spoke. So Billie let out a hardy laugh when he responded, "Whoa, you have her eyes!"

Madison took the baby from Steve in a way that Billie thought showed natural ease.

"Come meet my parents," Madison said.

Tyler and Billie followed the couple toward the ambulance, where they introduced Tyler to the Westons. The glee on her husband's face as he kept looking from Madison to the baby filled Billie's heart.

* *

Feeling overwhelmed since her life turned sideways two weeks ago, Billie took solace in the guest room, where she felt closest to her mom. She looked at the bridal bouquet artwork and remembered her mother's loving expression when she'd given them the frame. She wished her mom was by her side now and longed for a dollop of her mother's wise advice. There was no one else to whom Billie could openly admit how much it hurt to know her husband had a child, even if he'd never been her father. It confirmed, once again, that it was her fault they didn't have their own and made her angrier at her own body.

"I thought I'd find you up here," Tyler said.

"I'm taking respite from the world. How are you holding up?" She plumped a throw pillow. "A lot got dumped on you too."

"My mind is pretty much blown. Not sure how to come to terms with it all yet. I mean, to be the reason for a baby being in danger." Tyler scratched the stubble on his chin. "How are you feeling about it, though, Bills?"

"The social worker in me says it's not like it's been a secret you kept from me. It's something that happened when you were thirteen. But as your wife, it's like, oh my God, I really don't know how to digest it. It's going to take me a while to figure out how I feel. Same as you." She sighed deeply.

"I need to tell you something." Tyler sat on the guest bed. "Will you sit with me?" He patted the peach-and-mint comforter.

Billie sat cross-legged, facing him. Whatever else he had left to unload, she was determined to watch him say it.

"I've been talking with John. He still swears he never had sex with Laura—not even drunk sex, and his paternity test confirms it."

"I see," Billie said. "Well, it's what we kind of expected."

"She's not mine either."

Billie was having trouble processing what he was saying. She couldn't tell if he was upset, hurt, disappointed, or relieved. Nor was she sure how she felt.

"I got a call with my results before I came upstairs. The test shows I'm not her father. However, there are strong overlapping familial DNA segments between us."

"Which means what?"

"We're cousins."

Billie shook her head. "I don't follow."

"CeCe made a mistake when she said she saw John having sex with Laura at my bar mitzvah. She and Moe both assumed it was John because he was the only other redhead at our school. But I realized there was a third boy our age there too. A cousin who looked a lot like me. Bills, Madison is Charlie's girl."

Five Months Later

CHAPTER FIFTY
Billie

The remnants of the rice cereal and bananas looked like finger painting as the washcloth smeared it across the high chair tray. Marilee had gleefully spit the mixture from her mouth when she'd had enough. Billie had already wiped the gooey mess from the delicious baby's face and hands, and now Marilee lifted her arms to be picked up. Billie eagerly obliged. There was nothing as fulfilling as having those chubby arms cling to her neck and inhaling the blend of Johnson's baby shampoo, Dreft detergent, and the baby's delectable scent.

After a quick diaper change and a hearty game of peekaboo, Billie laid Marilee on an activity mat with sensory toys to pull and swat over her head. The five-month-old quickly twisted her body onto her belly and kicked her legs. Her cooing and babbling were better than any radio station.

"Hi, Billie!" Madison said. She threw her book bag on the floor by the front door and sprinted to the baby. "How's my starfish?" Marilee's arms and legs swam faster as her mother reached to pick her up and plied her face with kisses.

"How was your exam today?" Billie asked.

"I think I did okay. Final grades won't be back for at least a week." Madison passed Marilee back to Billie. "I'm going to run up and change, and then I'll help you set the table for tonight. And Steve should be home soon too."

Billie couldn't help but smile at how this nugget had changed her life. She nuzzled Marilee's neck and made silly sounds, anything to elicit the baby's addicting giggle. After they found Marilee safe and medically sound, Madison and Steve had brought her to the Westons' home. No one discussed it, but everyone seemed to understand that adoption was no longer a consideration.

Billie and Tyler had visited them after they got his paternity results. They ran another test using his uncle's DNA, which confirmed Charlie was Madison's biological father. Madison seemed a little disappointed it wasn't Tyler yet glad they were still blood relatives. Or maybe Billie was just projecting her own feelings about it all.

The families had spent time together, and over the Christmas holiday, Tyler and Madison had talked a great deal about Charlie and his family. The Westons had invited them for brunch on New Year's Day. During the football marathon, Madison stood up and blocked the living room television.

"Steve and I, and my parents, have talked this over, and . . ." She stopped and swatted her bangs, then pulled at her ear while everyone watched and waited. "And, if Tyler and Billie are okay with it, well, there's not much room here, and we figure that you guys live closer to Woodson, and we"—Madison wagged a finger between herself and Steve before side-glancing at Billie—"well, we'd really love your help raising the baby while we're in school."

Billie remembered the feeling of Tyler's hand in hers. How his fingers squeezed between her own before he asked, "What exactly are you proposing?"

Madison and Steve had moved into their home at the beginning of the next semester. It had toppled their world over in the most wondrous way. Billie was proud that Tyler and Madison had bonded, and she and Madison had developed a deep relationship that melded friendship, respect, and admiration. Over the past few months, Billie and Tyler had not only blended their family with the Westons and Tyler's parents, aunt, and uncle (the Quinns stayed on the outskirts), but they'd invited Kathleen and Grant into their lives as well.

Billie and Tyler always insisted Kathleen stay at their home whenever she traveled to Boston to visit the psychiatric residential facility where Laura served her sentence. Madison had been eager to get to know her grandmother and wanted her to be part of the baby's life. But her emotions were raw, and she refused to talk about her birth mother. On the one hand, she was angry at Laura for giving her up, for never telling Tyler's family about her, for taking Marilee.

On the other hand, she suffered gut-wrenching guilt for not having searched for her birth mother. "Do you think if I'd found and met her sooner, none of this would have happened?" she'd often asked. Madison was working on these feelings in therapy and, with plenty of family support, agreed to visit Laura with Kathleen.

After the first visit, Billie could see it had upset Madison. When they'd arrived, guards patted down both women. Then Madison explained how they'd thumbed through the lunches and snacks she and Kathleen had taken care to pack.

"They touched everything, even lifted the bread and lettuce," she had reported. "The guards confiscated soda because it had caffeine, took away plastic utensils because they could be weapons. Then we walked through metal detectors past the creepiest, dark, echoey wards. Right out of a scary movie."

"How was it seeing Laura?" Billie had asked. She and Kathleen exchanged a glance.

"She was sitting alone at a table in a tiny visitor's room. The floor was peeling, and the fluorescent light buzzed loudly overhead. At first, she wasn't paying attention, but then we started talking." The visits had gotten better after that, and each time Madison had come back with details of the commonalities she shared with her birth mother. At the moment, Billie could only recall a few: they both were left-handed, liked pistachio ice cream and hated onions, loved peppers on pizza, and the biggest one—both twisted their ears when nervous.

Marilee squirmed in her lap when Madison came downstairs. Billie was in awe of this remarkable adult-kid with the most accepting heart. She looked more like Laura, but the way Tyler described it, she had a lot of her father inside.

With Marilee in a baby bouncer, soothing herself into a nap, Madison and Billie covered the dining table and the folding tables that Steve and Tyler had lugged up from the basement last night. Counting herself and Tyler, Madison, Steve, the Westons, the Scotts, Charlie's parents, and Kathleen and Grant, the house would be full of adults fawning over Marilee for an end-of-school-year dinner. There was no shortage of excuses for get-togethers.

"What's wrong?" Madison asked. "Why are you crying?"

"I'm happy, that's all."

They chuckled at the unexpected emotion. Then Madison gave Billie a most satisfying hug.

* *

If they had been there, Billie's own parents would have fit well into the eclectic group that filled her dining room. She listened to the harmony of voices engaged in myriad conversations, relishing the clanging of silverware. She surveyed the gorgeous food stains on the tablecloth created from escaped pieces of dressing-soaked salad, fingerling potatoes that had rolled off plates leaving oily rosemary trails, and wine splatters from sloppy pours. Tyler caught her eye from the head of the table opposite her. When she responded with a slight nod, he placed his crumpled napkin on the table and came to her side. She held her breath.

Before Tyler could clink a glass, the boisterous din roared to a hush. Roberta rested against her husband's shoulder and squinted at her son and daughter-in-law. Billie averted contact with her all-knowing eye. Charlie's mother folded her napkin and placed it neatly on the table and then did the same with her husband's napkin. Milton Weston, a cheerful guy, smoothed sparse threads of gray hair that spawned from Brillo-like patches above his ears. Then he leaned his potbelly against the table to reach the wine. Milt was always up for a good toast, which Billie suspected he thought was coming. His wife, Sally, shimmied her rear end in the chair until she was facing Billie and Tyler and flicked crumbs from her lap to the floor. Billie peeked at Kathleen and Grant, who always seemed like newlyweds; she could tell Grant's hand was resting on Kathleen's thigh. Madison and Steve kept the portable baby monitor between them in case Marilee stirred. The young couple faced the head of the table, waiting like attentive students for the professor to begin his lecture.

"As I look around this table, I'm astounded and grateful for how specific moments in time have brought us all together," Tyler said. "How, in five short months, we have come to know and care for each other like we were always a part of each other's lives. Indeed, in a way, we were. Nevertheless, whatever road brought us together, Billie and I thank you for filling our home with love and family."

"Hear, hear!" Milt shouted. He sloshed some wine down and went for a refill.

Tyler's father, who would never let anyone drink alone, slid his glass across the table for Milton to fill.

"It is because you're our family," Billie started, "that we need to share this with you. Because it affects you all." She looked at Tyler and felt her courage dissolve. He took her in his arms, rubbed her back, and then lifted her chin, forcing her to look at him.

"I can't. I'm afraid," she said.

"I have you," Tyler said.

"Honey, we're all here for you, whatever it is," Roberta said.

"You all know that Tyler and I have struggled to start a family." Billie looked from face to encouraging face of the people who loved and supported her.

"Look at that flush on her cheeks!" Sally said.

"Classic sign," Kathleen added.

"You're pregnant!" Roberta shouted.

A smile snuck onto Billie's face until she saw Madison's serene expression. The room grew quiet while everyone watched the unspoken rally.

"Why?" Madison asked.

"Why what?" Billie answered.

"Why were you so nervous to say something? What's wrong?"

"We're only in the first trimester," Tyler said.

"There's a long way to go, a lot of hurdles and risks to overcome," Billie said. "I'll have to endure a bunch of tests and be extra careful."

"And she promises to rest and not overdo it," Tyler added.

"Yeah, right," someone said above a collective groan.

"It's really too early, even to say anything, but how could we not share it with all the people we love?" Billie said.

"We'll feel more secure when we make it to the second trimester," Tyler said.

"Right." It was only then Billie realized she was rubbing her abdomen. "You never know how things will turn out, but we're hopeful. And no matter what happens, we'll always have all of you and this crazy, unconventional, wonderful family we've become."

ACKNOWLEDGMENTS

Writing a novel is not as simple as telling a good story. It takes a lot of patience, dedication, a functioning delete button, and an abundance of learning. Becoming an author was only possible because of the kindness, friendship, and support of many:

I am eternally grateful to Laura Zinn Fromm for seeing something in a very inexperienced writer and nurturing her potential. My deepest appreciation to Rebecca Heyman, whose invitation to The Work Conference transformed me from a writer to an aspiring author. Praise for Taylor Larsen's encouragement and ability to weed weird verbiage/purple prose. Without her, this story would never have found its shape. Many thanks to Jenna Blum, Ellen A., and Salt and Sage's sensitivity reader, Nicole Hawken, for their kindness, enthusiasm, and insightful guidance. And I am forever indebted to the magnanimous Georgina Green, who immediately understood this story, the characters, and my writing voice. Because of that, this happened.

The sincerest thanks to the other too-many-to-name teachers, coaches, editors, workshop cohorts, critique partners, writing friends, and readers who helped make this novel shine. Special thanks to my good friend Jill Snyder, whose legal, medical, and artistic wisdom and moral support I often rely on, and who tolerates my twisted humor. And to all the people I have crossed paths with over my lifetime who withstood my lengthy, detailed-filled responses to your quick questions—no surprise I became a novelist!

My heartfelt appreciation to my beta readers Linda M. and Ashley S., whose grace and candor about their personal adoption journeys inspired me. Our powerful discussions exposed me to more contemporary perceptions of adoption, and the aim to shift focus onto the babies' earliest biopsychosocial experience. I haven't worked in the field for years, yet the fight for legislation to give a voice to adoptees, to do more to educate prospective adoptive parents, and to improve the rights and support of biological mothers continues.

I am incredibly thankful to Brooke Warner, Lauren Wise, Crystal Patriarche, Grace Fell, Leilani Fitzpatrick, Anne Durette, Krissa Lagos, Mimi Bark, Kiran Spees and all the staff at She Writes Press and BookSparks who assisted in this project.

Thanks to my mother, who took me on outings to Doubleday and the New York Public Library when I was a little girl. Those awe-inspiring spaces instilled a love and respect for reading, for the weight, the unique inky paper smell, and the sense of anticipation when cracking open the spine of a new book. And to my dad, I have felt you with me all along.

I am nothing if not for my children. They let me bounce plot ideas off them on a drive in San Francisco when it was a mere premise, helped me develop characters on two ten-hour plane rides, played "Does this dialogue sound real?" on weekend getaways, text-edited at midnight, and read draft after draft. They challenged me to make the book, and my writer self, flourish, and rooted for me, encouraged me, and believed in me without fail. There are not enough words to express my love for them.

I am forever creating in my head, finding a spark of inspiration in the least expected moments, often typing away and lost in a story for hours. Writing is a passion. To my family and friends, this book, my debut, is where I have been the past couple of years. For the many times I said, "Not yet," when you asked to read it—yet is now.

ABOUT THE AUTHOR

photo credit: Diana Kupershmit

Zelly Ruskin is a social worker who worked in adoption and foster care. She loves traveling, hiking with her (now adult) children, and, as a survivor, is passionate about and volunteers for brain aneurysm awareness. Zelly and her ridiculous doodle, Strudel, currently live in New York City.

For book club discussion questions and more information, visit the author's website at Zellyruskin.com.

Looking for your next great read?

We can help!

Visit www.shewritespress.com/next-read
or scan the QR code below for a list
of our recommended titles.